"I have a rer

"You don't need to use it.

Those lethal eyes of Leo's searched her face. They seemed to darken, smoldering with something she was afraid to define. Something that suddenly deprived her of oxygen. She was still much too close to him, but couldn't seem to move.

Carrying her hands to his mouth, he began to demonstrate that remedy, nibbling on her fingers, placing kisses in each of her palms.

Drawing her tightly against him, a growl low in his throat, Leo angled his mouth across hers. His kiss was deep, demanding.

Jennifer's senses rioted. Threatened to go out of control. And might have, if there hadn't been the sound of someone, making them aware they were no longer alone.

TO THE RESCUE

JEAN BARRETT

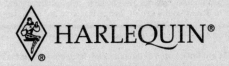

HARLEQUIN®

TORONTO • NEW YORK • LONDON
AMSTERDAM • PARIS • SYDNEY • HAMBURG
STOCKHOLM • ATHENS • TOKYO • MILAN • MADRID
PRAGUE • WARSAW • BUDAPEST • AUCKLAND

To Barb and Dick Norene, in appreciation for your support and friendship. You are the best.

ISBN-13: 978-0-373-22956-7
ISBN-10:   0-373-22956-9

TO THE RESCUE

ABOUT THE AUTHOR

If setting has anything to do with it, Jean Barrett claims she has no reason not to be inspired. She and her husband live on Wisconsin's scenic Door Peninsula in an antique-filled country cottage overlooking Lake Michigan. A teacher for many years, she left the classroom to write full-time. She is the author of a number of romance novels.

Books by Jean Barrett

HARLEQUIN INTRIGUE

*The Hawke Detective Agency

CAST OF CHARACTERS

Jennifer Rowan—She is desperate to prove herself innocent of murder, but can she survive the rugged P.I. who puts her heart and soul in jeopardy?

Leo McKenzie—He is determined to catch his brother's killer, but he hadn't counted on the irresistible allure of the woman who is his chief suspect.

Father Stephen—The abbot's monastery may not survive if the valuable Warley Madonna is not recovered.

Brother Timothy—Will his medical skills be enough to save the latest victim of a deranged killer?

Geoffrey—The young novice seems to be troubled about taking his final vows.

Patrick—He wants to join the order, but is it for the right reason?

Harry Ireland—The traveling salesman may not be what he seems.

Fiona and Alfred Brasher—What secret is the couple hiding?

Sybil and Roger Harding—She has a sharp tongue and a fondness for gin. He's a devout ex-monk who's worried about his wife.

Chapter One

Who is he? How did he find me?

Needing answers, Jennifer hugged the shadows at the top of the stairs, her heart registering anxiety with rapid beats as she listened to the conversation in the lobby below.

"You're sure you can't give me her room number?"

His voice was deep and mellow. That much Jennifer could tell, but nothing else about him. Although she had a limited view of the front desk and the young woman who stood on duty behind it, the man who had come in off the street wasn't in her line of sight. She would need to lean forward in order to glimpse him, but she feared even a slight movement would betray her presence.

The clerk, her thin face peppered with freckles beneath a cap of red hair, shook her head in regret. "Be worth my job if I was to go and tell you that, sir."

The woman had been far less careful when he'd approached the desk a moment ago with a confident "I'm here to see Jennifer Rowan. She is registered with you, right?"

He shouldn't have known that. Jennifer had told no one she planned to spend the night at this inn. But his bold assumption that she was here had won an admission from the clerk that,

yes, Jennifer was a guest at the King's Head. The clerk hadn't
bothered to ask him his name.

"Sure wouldn't want you to go and jeopardize your job—"
he paused, moving in close to the desk in order to read the
clerk's name tag "—Wendy."

Jennifer could see him now. Or at least enough of him to
understand why the desk clerk wore a willing smile as he
leaned toward her. From what Jennifer could tell at this angle,
he was good-looking in a rugged sort of way. That deep voice
was also persuasive, with a tone that was appealingly personal.

"But how about calling her room and letting her know someone
is here to see her. You could do that much, couldn't you, Wendy?"

"I wouldn't say no to that, sir. Not that I'd have to, being as
how Ms. Rowan isn't in her room. Went out a bit ago to buy
herself a London paper. Real disappointed, she was, when I told
her we only take the local paper here. Well, why would we need
anything else when we have the telly?"

But Jennifer hadn't been willing to wait for a TV newscast,
which wouldn't have provided her with enough details anyway.
Only a London paper would have a full account of Guy's
murder. She needed to know if there was any new development
in the case, whether she was at imminent risk of being arrested.

As far as the desk clerk knew, Jennifer *wasn't* in the inn. Wendy
had watched her go out the front door in search of a shop that
carried the London papers. What the young woman didn't realize
was that, once out on the street, Jennifer had feared she would be
soaked within seconds. A hard rain had begun to fall. Wendy
hadn't been at her post when Jennifer immediately returned to the
inn to fetch her umbrella. If the tea mug now at the clerk's elbow
was any indication, she must have been in the kitchen.

Umbrella in hand, Jennifer had been heading toward the
street again when the stranger below had asked for her by
name. Alarmed, she had shrunk back into the shadows where
the hallway emerged at the top of the stairs. But she couldn't

go on standing here. The dimness, presumably the result of a burned-out lightbulb in the fixture overhead, wasn't enough to conceal her if either of them happened to look up.

Frozen in place, Jennifer prayed he was satisfied by the clerk's explanation of her absence. That, whoever he was, he would leave the inn and go out on the street to look for her in the shops. But it didn't happen that way.

"You wouldn't have any objection if I waited here in the lobby for Ms. Rowan, would you, Wendy?" he asked the clerk.

"That's all right then, sir."

Trapped! What was she to do? He had already removed his coat, was running a strong hand through his wet hair. It was when he looked over his shoulder, probably to locate a comfortable chair in which to take up his vigil, that Jennifer seized the opportunity to make her escape from the stairway.

Backing slowly, silently away from the landing, hoping none of the old floorboards would announce her retreat with a sudden groan, she waited until the lobby was entirely swallowed from view before she turned and fled to her room.

Once inside, and with the door secured behind her, she went and sat on the edge of the four-poster. Only then did she realize she was trembling. It was imperative that she think rationally about her situation, come to some decision, and in order to do that, she had to calm herself.

The setting itself was certainly tranquil enough. An ancient inn, the stone-built King's Head featured wide hearths, leaded windows and low ceilings crossed by heavy oak beams. She gazed for a moment at one of those windows where the rain bubbled on the glass against a heavy, gray sky.

Though she managed to control her panic, her frustration was another matter. She had failed to learn the answers to the questions that continued to race through her mind.

He had asked for her by name. How was that possible when he was a stranger? Unless—

Had Guy's charwoman surfaced from her coma, told the police what she had witnessed? If so, then her information would be enough to make a strong case against Jennifer as Guy's killer. Was this man a detective who had somehow managed to track her here?

But if that was true, if he *was* official, then why hadn't he presented his ID to the desk clerk? Told her he was here on police business?

There was something else. Like Jennifer, he had an American accent. Puzzling, but she supposed he could be working with the London police. It wasn't unknown for American officers to be connected with English police departments.

In the end, there was only one certainty. Whoever this mystery man was, he was looking for her. That made him a potential danger to her. Because if he knew she was on the run, and why—

She had to leave. Had to get far away from him. *Now.*

Never mind her plan to spend the night here in the inn and then go on to Warley Castle in the morning. Forget the late hour, the threat of the weather and a lonely road across unfamiliar terrain.

Jennifer was desperate enough to risk all of these in order to reach her destination without further delay. If she stood any chance at all of vindicating herself, then it was urgent that she get the answers she was hoping for before it was too late.

She threw the few things she had unpacked earlier back into her suitcase. Since she had already paid for a night's lodging in the inn, there was no problem about running out on any bill she owed. But there was the concern of the man down in the lobby who guarded the front door.

She couldn't use that route to slip away from him. A service staircase then? Surely there had to be one in a place this size. It was time to find out.

Suitcase and umbrella in hand, her purse hanging by its long strap from her shoulder, Jennifer crossed the room, unlocked the door and eased it back. She checked the hallway in both directions. It was silent, empty. There were few guests in the inn at this time of year. She met no one as she hurried along the passage.

An unnumbered door drew her to the end of the corridor at the back of the inn. When she tried it, she found herself looking down into the poorly lit well of the service staircase she was seeking.

Descending swiftly through the gloom, she arrived in another passage at the bottom. There were several doors along its narrow length. The nearest one had to be the kitchen because she could hear behind it what had to be the sounds of dinner underway.

Praying no one would emerge from that area to challenge her, Jennifer headed toward the door at the end of the passage. The window in it, framing the gray daylight beyond, told her it was a back entrance.

It had to be a fire exit, readily opened from the inside, because she had no trouble with the door when she reached it and let herself out of the inn. Not until she exhaled in relief did she realize how much she had needed to release her tension.

She found herself in a service yard at the rear of the building. Rain was pelting down on the cobbles. The air was cold, evidence that the temperature had dropped since her arrival in Heathside.

Raising her umbrella, Jennifer crossed the yard and made her way to the car park where she had left the little English Ford she had rented back in London.

She was shivering by the time she stowed her suitcase in the vehicle and settled herself behind the wheel. Nerves more than the cold, she thought.

Once she was underway, with the heater issuing a welcome warmth, she was able to ease her worst fear. Not that she could relax when she had to deal with every American driver's problem of keeping to the left while negotiating narrow streets that hadn't been designed to accommodate modern traffic. This, in addition to finding a route through the old town in a steady rainfall, kept her occupied.

Jennifer didn't pay any attention to the dark-colored SUV that slid out of an alley as she passed, swinging into the street behind her. It was just one more vehicle in the congestion.

MERCIFULLY, the traffic thinned once she left the center of town. She didn't need to consult the map. She had already committed to memory the route she needed. There was a fork in the road after she crossed a bridge. She chose the posted left branch, climbing a long hill out of the river valley in which Heathside was nestled.

Jennifer caught her breath when she crested the rise. The immediate contrast between the town that had dropped out of sight behind her and the largely unoccupied expanse of moorland that stretched away in front of her was both sudden and startling.

She found herself clutching the wheel as the little Ford was shaken by the blasts of wind that, uninterrupted by any forest or settlement, blew with ferocity over the high, open moors.

It was early March, the days still short. But even with the afternoon light beginning to ebb, hastened by the mass of racing clouds overhead, Jennifer was able to appreciate the panorama of the treeless swells that rolled off to the horizon in every direction.

The Yorkshire moors were desolate affairs in any season, but in winter like this, with the turf and heather brown and barren, they were especially bleak. But there was also a raw beauty in this wild landscape. Jennifer could see it in the broken stone walls that framed the slopes, in the becks that tumbled through the folds between the hills, and in the tough grass where the occasional, rough-coated sheep browsed.

The road was a minor one, with few travelers. That didn't worry her. Not until the rain turned into sleet, making the already wet pavement treacherous beneath her wheels.

It was then that Jennifer remembered the weather report she

had heard on the car radio earlier today. A major storm was expected to blow in off the North Sea. With all that had happened back at the inn, she had forgotten about that forecast. But now, in all this remoteness, and with darkness approaching and the long road in front of her...

Turning on the radio, she tried to find a weather update. All she got was pop music.

She was so busy with the dial, while at the same time being careful how she drove, that she paid little attention to the vehicle behind her. There was no reason why another traveler shouldn't be out here. In fact, his headlights slicing through the gloom were a comfort. An assurance that, no matter how isolated the sodden terrain, she wasn't alone in this vastness.

Driven by the powerful wind, the sleet continued to sting the car, the wipers swishing across the glass working hard to keep the windshield clear. Just how bad was it going to get?

Jennifer worried about that as the winding road carried her across the endless tracts of vacant moorland. As the ice began to form on the road, she slowed her speed to avoid spinning into a ditch.

She couldn't say at what point she became concerned with the vehicle behind her. She had expected the driver to turn off on one of the side lanes at some point or that, growing impatient with her crawl, he would pass her. He did neither. And, though he kept a safe distance behind her, what had seemed a comfort began to feel like an unnerving pursuit.

Reckless or not, she tried several times to lose him by increasing her speed, but he wasn't to be shaken. That's when it struck her. He *was* deliberately following her.

Had he been there all along? As far back as Heathside?

The light was too poor to identify his make. She had an impression of something large and dark-colored, maybe an SUV. Had an SUV tailed her out of town? There was something sinister about the possibility.

"What do you want?" she muttered. "Who are you?"

But Jennifer could guess exactly who he was. The man back at the inn! If he'd grown tired of waiting for her in the lobby, or suspicious of her failure to return to the inn, and had gone out on the street to look for her and spotted her emerging from the car park…

It *had* to be him, which meant her flight from the inn had been for nothing. Unless…

The sleet had stopped falling. The stretch of road ahead of her looked free of any slick spots. Though it was probably useless of her to make the effort, Jennifer squeezed the pedal to the floor.

The little car leaped forward, charging down into a glen and up the slope beyond. The road curled around a bend where a terrace had been sliced out of the hillside to carry the route.

She glanced into her rearview mirror. His headlights were no longer behind her. Had it been that easy?

Slowing the car, Jennifer peered through her side window, checking the deep hollow below her. There was no sign of the SUV. He couldn't have just vanished.

Stopping the car, she backed up past a wall of gorse for a better view. That's when she saw the SUV. It had left the road and landed in a ditch with its nose angled down against an enormous boulder.

An accident. He'd had an accident!

The temptation to throw the gear into forward and race away into the gloom was very strong. But Jennifer couldn't bring herself to abandon him. What if he were injured, helpless?

Through the thickening twilight, she could just make out the door on the driver's side of the SUV. She sat there on the elevation with her engine idling, waiting for that door to open, hoping he would climb out. That he would be all right. But nothing stirred.

Damn.

She had no choice about it. She had to go down there and do whatever she could to help him.

With careful maneuvering, she turned the car and drove back down the incline into the sheltered glen. When she reached the scene, she took the precaution of easing the Ford around again until it faced the direction of her destination. If this was all just a ruse to lure her into a trap, she wanted to be able to make a fast departure.

But when Jennifer left her car and almost lost her footing on a patch of ice, she was inclined to believe that the accident itself had been no trick. Her own vehicle had traveled over it without her even being aware of its existence, but the SUV must have spun off the road when its wheels struck the ice. A lone sheep, whose form she could dimly distinguish at the side of the road, might have been responsible for that if the driver had slammed his foot on the brake in an effort to avoid a collision with the animal.

Equipping herself with a flashlight from the glove compartment, Jennifer made her way down into the ditch. She felt a wetness on her cheek as she approached. That's when she realized that flakes of snow were swirling through the air. This wasn't good.

Nor was the sight of the man slumped over the wheel when she managed to scrape the door open and lean into the SUV. There was no movement or sound from him. He was either unconscious or—

Don't think it.

Because, whether he was her enemy or not, she didn't want him to be dead. Although she knew next to nothing about checking for vital signs, she reached for his limp arm and felt for a pulse on the back of his wrist.

After a few seconds of nervous searching, she managed to locate a slow, steady beat beneath flesh that was reassuringly warm. Her relief that he was alive was only momentary. There was still the possibility that he was seriously injured.

If she could see his face—

He was a solid man. She had to shove the flashlight into a deep pocket of her coat in order to free her hand. She needed both of her hands gripping his hard shoulder to haul him off the wheel and back against the seat. Recovering the flashlight, she switched it on, focusing its glow on his face.

It was a strong face, the same one she had seen at the inn, but there was noticeable swelling on the forehead. Probably the result of his head striking the wheel.

The vehicle looked like an older model, maybe before air bags were in general use, which would explain why none had deployed. But his seat belt—

No, she realized after a quick glance, the belt wasn't buckled. Either he had foolishly neglected to wear it or had managed to unfasten it before he passed out.

Whatever the explanation, all that was important now was securing help for him, because he could have sustained injuries other than the bump on his forehead.

Backing out of the car, Jennifer swung her purse off her shoulder and fumbled inside it for her cell phone. When she tried it, the lighted display indicated no signal. Either the remoteness of the region or the weather must be responsible. It was snowing in earnest now.

Striving not to panic, Jennifer clambered out of the ditch and went to stand in the middle of the road. She looked in both directions, as though desperation alone could produce the gleam of headlights from an approaching car. But there was no other vehicle on the road. She was on her own.

The daylight was rapidly dying. And so might the man in the SUV if she didn't do something about him. But what? Drive back to Heathside and bring help? No, it was too far away now. It would be better to go on to Warley Castle for help.

But there was a problem connected with that. The snow was already accumulating on the road. By the time she reached the castle, it might be too deep to permit any effort to rescue him.

Besides, Jennifer knew she couldn't bring herself to leave him here. He needed immediate attention and shelter from a temperature that had become dangerously frigid. Her destination could provide both.

No choice about it then. She would have to take him with her. But how on earth was she to achieve that when he was unconscious? She couldn't carry him to her car. He was much too heavy for that.

What was her chance of rousing him just long enough to coax him to shift himself under his own power into her car? Maybe not good, but it was all she had.

Sliding back into the Ford at the side of the road, she spent a few precious minutes positioning it on the shoulder as close to the ditch as she dared and with its passenger door directly opposite the back end of the SUV. He'd have only steps to go. Providing, that is, he could exert enough energy to climb out of the ditch.

Making sure the passenger door was wide open and ready to receive him, Jennifer eased herself down the slope that had now grown slick with snow. She eagerly hoped he would be awake when she arrived back at the driver's side of the SUV. He wasn't.

Bending down to scoop up a handful of snow, she leaned into the vehicle and rubbed the stuff over his face, thinking its icy wetness might revive him. There was no reaction.

All right, if an application of snow wasn't going to work, then it was time to try something less gentle. Seizing his arm, she shook him vigorously, shouting into his face. "Come on, hear me, whoever you are, and open your eyes!"

To her joy, he groaned, but his eyes remained closed. She didn't know what else to do, except to get tough. With the palm of her hand, she began to slap him across his beard-roughened cheeks.

Success! He stirred at last, cursing angrily and batting at her hand. "You try that again," he growled, "and I'll—"

"I *will* slap you again if you don't listen to me. You have to come with me. I'm going to put you in my car and take you to a place where there will be someone to help you."

No reaction.

"Do you understand? You've had an accident. You need to get out of your car and into mine. It's only a few steps away. Can you manage that much if I help you?"

He mumbled something she didn't comprehend. He was obviously dazed, perhaps in a bad state of shock, but her urgency must have reached him on some level because he began to drag himself out of the car.

He was weaving when he finally came erect beside the SUV. "Hurts," he complained, pressing a hand against his chest.

Another concern, she thought. He must have injured more than just his head. There was no time to question it.

"We have to move. You can rest once you're inside my car."

"Yeah," he said gruffly. She wondered if he had any idea at all who was speaking to him.

The next few minutes were difficult ones. Not only as solid as stone, he was tall, easily six feet or more in height. Supporting that weight, with her arm flung around his waist and his own arm draped over her shoulder, was a challenge she undertook but never wanted to repeat. Somehow, stumbling and staggering, they fought their way out of the ditch with the snow driving into their faces at a furious pace.

Jennifer was winded by the time they reached the Ford. She was able to deposit him in the passenger seat where he immediately collapsed, lapsing back into unconsciousness.

Although she wanted nothing more than to get them away from this place as quickly as possible, she spared another moment to trudge back to the SUV. The engine must have stalled when he smashed into the boulder, but the key was still turned on in the ignition and the headlights burning. She switched off the lights, pocketed the key, then trained her flashlight into the back. There was a suitcase on the seat.

Taking the piece of luggage with her, she went back to the road where she shoved it into the trunk of her car next to her own suitcase. Once behind the wheel of the Ford again, she leaned over him to fasten his seat belt in place. He might be in no state to care, but she did.

"No more risks," she informed him.

She got no response.

THE SNOW AND THE WIND had been bad enough down in the glen. But once they were out on the high moors again, the conditions were fierce. The howling gale alone made the car, which trembled under its force, difficult to handle. The snow made it all the worse.

There were moments when Jennifer could barely see the road. And when she could see it, she was alarmed by the drifts that were building along the shoulders, spreading ridges onto the pavement itself.

She didn't dare let herself imagine what would happen if the road became impassable before she reached her objective, if the car was no longer able to plow through those growing white swells. All she could trust herself to do was to stubbornly pursue the route, even though it carried her straight into the teeth of the raging storm.

From time to time, Jennifer glanced at her silent passenger sprawled in the seat beside her. He hadn't stirred since they'd left the scene of the accident. His eyes remained closed, his body inert.

How bad was he? she wondered. And what good did it do to worry about him when she had done all she could by rescuing him from the crippled SUV? At least he was out of the cold now.

Since they were still wearing their coats, both of them were snug with the heater humming away, releasing a blessed warmth. But if they should become trapped out here, run out of gas and the heater quit on them—

What are you doing? Stop thinking about that. Just drive.

There was no other choice. But as the ribbon of road endlessly dipped and turned and rose again, Jennifer wondered if she had misjudged the distance. Or was it the blizzard that seemed to lengthen the miles?

They were in the very heart of the moors now, in its most isolated depths. It would be easy to miss the turning to Warley Castle now that it was dark and snowing so hard. She might already have passed it.

And then suddenly, unexpectedly, as she rounded a bend on the brow of a hill, the castle was there in front of her.

As if by a deliberate magic, the wind dropped at the same time the shroud of snow momentarily lifted. The clouds overhead briefly parted. Halting the car, Jennifer found herself looking across a valley at a steep-sided, craggy peak. The last faint light of day streamed down on the summit where, looking as though it had been carved out of the rock itself, the castle perched, like a great sailing ship in a turbulent sea.

No introduction to that medieval pile could have been more dramatic.

Sitting there, gazing at the structure, it seemed inconceivable to Jennifer that such a formidable fortress could contain anything so benevolent as a monastery. But that's exactly what the castle housed, and had for centuries.

Guy had told her how Warley had come to be occupied by the brothers, but she didn't want to remember the story now. The very thought of Guy awakened the shock of his death, and with it a rush of fear and anguish.

As though triggered by those dark emotions, the wind rose again while overhead the clouds closed the gap. With the pale light vanished, the castle became a mass of black stone, grim and forbidding.

The curtain of snow also descended again by the time Jennifer reached the turning on the floor of the valley. The little Ford valiantly climbed a twisting lane through banks of snow that threatened to soon block the way. With the engine straining, it seemed to take forever to crawl to the top of the rise where the castle loomed in front of them.

Made it, she thought thankfully as the car finally chugged through the portal of a massive gatehouse that once would have been barred by a lowered portcullis.

Swinging into the bailey, Jennifer brought the car to a stop and got out. The place was dim, with only a single lantern burning on one of the walls. But its light was sufficient enough to guide her to a heavy oak door. There was a chain suspended beside the door. She tugged on it, and from somewhere inside a bell clanged hollowly.

As she waited for a response, she looked over her shoulder where she had left her passenger in the car. There had been neither sound nor movement from him since they had left the glen.

Her mind was on him, wondering if he would recover, when the door scraped open. Head swiveling, she was startled by the sight of a robed figure standing in the shadows of the archway, his face hidden in the depths of a cowl.

An ancient castle, flickering light, a mysterious figure. It was the stuff of Gothic legends. But even before he spoke to her in a gentle voice, Jennifer knew she was being foolishly imaginative. There was nothing diabolical here. And of course he wore a robe with a cowl. This was a monastery, after all.

"What is it?" he inquired kindly. "Have you lost your way in the storm?"

"Please, I need your help. I have an injured man in my car, and I think he may be in a bad way."

Chapter Two

Heat radiated from the glowing core of the peat fire. Huddled on a stool close to the wide hearth, Jennifer tried to keep warm without scorching herself.

There was apparently no central heating in the castle. Either funds didn't permit it, or the good brothers were obeying a spartan existence dictated by their order.

The room they had given her was a testament to that. Its thick stone walls were unadorned except for a plain wooden cross. The furnishings were sparse and simple, though the bed looked comfortable enough even in the poor light. There was a single lamp on the bedside table, which made her think that the electricity must be limited to essential uses. But even with the menacing shadows in the corners, Jennifer was glad to be out of the storm, which had worsened since her arrival. She could hear the snow being driven against the window by a raging wind that battered the ancient walls.

Looking up from the fire, she cast a nervous glance in the direction of the closed door that connected her room with the one that adjoined it. Jennifer wondered what was happening behind it.

"We'll let you know as soon as Brother Timothy has examined him," she had been assured.

The monks assumed she was concerned about her unconscious passenger who had been installed in that other room. Although it was true that his condition mattered to her, they didn't know that she was equally worried about his identity.

She had sacrificed an opportunity at the scene of the accident to search him, suppressing her longing to know who he was. Since he could be in a critical state, it had been far more important to get help for him without wasting a moment of time.

Jennifer regretted that lost opportunity now because she still knew nothing. She was certain of only one thing, that the man she had rescued was no one she had ever met before.

But whoever was with him now might be learning not just his identity but why he'd been pursuing her. And if he was carrying anything on him that implicated her in Guy's murder, then—

Jennifer started at the sound of a knock on the hall door. Leaving the stool, she crossed the room to answer it. When she opened the door, a tall, almost gaunt figure stood there in the dimness of the passage. The habit he wore of coarse, undyed sheep's wool identified him as one of the brothers. He bore a tray with covered dishes on it.

"I've brought you some supper," he said. "If I might come in…"

"Please."

She stood aside in the doorway. He glided on sandaled feet into the room where he paused to look around.

"In front of the hearth, I think. If you'll just hold the tray for me, I'll drag the table there into place."

She took the tray from him, watching him as he drew a small table over to the fireplace. When he'd placed a chair at the side of the table, he recovered the tray from her and carried it to the table. Satisfied with the arrangement, he turned to her.

"I hope you don't mind eating in your room. We do have a dining parlor for our guests, and tomorrow you'll be able to have your meals there. But what with the weather and all, we're in rather a muddle tonight. This seemed to be the most expedient way of seeing to it that you didn't go hungry."

"I don't mind in the least. I'm just grateful to be here at all."

"Yes, I understand you had rather a bad time of it out on the road. It's Miss Rowan, isn't it?"

"That's right, Jennifer Rowan."

"I'm Father Stephen, the abbot of Warley Monastery."

Jennifer was surprised by his identity. She wouldn't have expected the abbot himself to serve her like this. Nor was there anything about his robe, except perhaps for the heavy cross that dangled from the cord around his waist, to distinguish him from the other monks.

He must have sensed her confusion. "This was an opportunity for me to meet and welcome you to Warley," he explained. "I'm sorry I was unable to come to you sooner, but there were other matters that needed my attention. Have they made you comfortable?"

"They have," she assured him, though he needn't have concerned himself.

The brother who had answered the bell in the courtyard and the monk he'd summoned to help him, had been efficient from the moment of her arrival. Taking charge, they had managed between them to move both her and her unconscious passenger into the area of the castle reserved for guests, delivered their luggage to the connecting rooms and even saw to it afterwards that her car was garaged in one of the old stables.

"In that case I'll leave you to your supper."

He started to move toward the hall door, but Jennifer stopped him.

"Father, before you go…"

"You have questions. Yes, that's understandable." He hesitated. "We'll visit then for a few minutes."

He waited until she was seated at the table before he placed himself on the stool across from her.

"You'd better eat your supper before it gets cold."

Whatever his garb, she should have known he was a figure of authority. It was evident in his voice and manner. He had that kind of face, too, beneath his tonsure. It was narrow with deep grooves from his hawklike nose to his thin mouth. It would have been austere if it hadn't been softened by a pair of cheerful blue eyes.

Jennifer uncovered the dishes on the tray, exposing a simple fare of thick vegetable soup, bread, slices of cheese, and a small bowl of stewed apricots. The soup was steaming and smelled delicious. Tasted delicious, too, when she began to spoon it into her mouth.

"Now for those questions," he said.

She reached for a slice of bread, her gaze slewing in the direction of the connecting door that remained closed. He understood.

"You're wondering about the condition of our patient."

"Is he awake, Father?"

The abbot shook his head. "Not yet, no. But I had an encouraging report from Brother Timothy who saw him earlier. Brother Timothy doesn't think his injuries are serious."

"And Brother Timothy is…"

"Our healer in charge of both the infirmary and the dispensary. He's quite knowledgeable."

"Does that mean he was in medicine before he joined the order?"

Father Stephen chuckled. "Brother Timothy was a prize fighter before he came to us. By his own admission, not a very good one. But he claims that all the punishment he suffered in the ring has turned out to be quite beneficial. There aren't many injuries he didn't learn how to treat, the external ones in particular."

The abbot paused, glancing down at her hand. Only then did Jennifer realize she'd been unconsciously crumbling the bread into bits. It was a result of her tension over the man in the next room. She'd have to be more careful. She didn't want Father Stephen to suspect that she was worried about more than the health of Brother Timothy's patient.

She took a fresh slice of bread and went on with her soup.

"Of course," the abbot continued, "capable though our Brother Timothy is, whenever there is any question about an injury or an illness, we don't hesitate to consult with a doctor in Heathside. Unfortunately, that won't be possible in this case."

"Oh?"

"Both the phone and power lines are down. It happens more often than we'd like with our situation as exposed as it is, which is why we have a generator. It's enough to operate our water pump, as well as permit us a reduced number of electric lamps."

That explained the poor lighting in the castle. The generator *was* obviously unable to provide anything but essential power during any outage.

"Will the lines be restored tomorrow, Father?"

He shook his head. "Doubtful with this storm. By morning the road will be blocked with heavy snow. I've seen it happen before. And the forecast promises more of the same for the next few days."

"So we're cut off until the weather clears."

"It's the price we pay for the seclusion we prize."

Jennifer knew about that seclusion. She thought again of the story Guy had told her that explained the monastery's unlikely existence in a castle. How, at the time of the Dissolution in the sixteenth century, the brothers had been driven out of their abbey, their properties stripped from them. Warley's devout owner had risked his life and his own wealth by offering them the castle, which had been abandoned by his titled family in the previous century for a more convenient location. The order had managed to survive at Warley only because its extreme isolation drew no attention to them.

And now Jennifer was stranded in all this vast solitude. It could work for her, give her the time she needed. Or it could be a disadvantage. She thought of the man lying in the room next door. Everything depended on him.

Wanting to be in no suspicious hurry about what she was so anxious to know, she tried the cheese but found it too strong for her taste. She finished the soup, then framed her question in what she hoped was a casual tone as she laid down her spoon.

"I've been wondering, Father, whether anyone managed to find some identification on the patient."

"Yes, I'd forgotten that I was told you mentioned when you arrived you have no connection with this man. You happened to be passing when you saw his car in the ditch, wasn't that it? Well, he was fortunate you were on the road and found him."

Jennifer didn't correct him, allowing him to believe it was all just by chance.

"Since he owes his life to you, he shouldn't remain a stranger. Brother Timothy was able to learn his identity from both his driver's license in his wallet and the passport he carries. His name is Leo McKenzie. An American like you, I believe."

Leo McKenzie. No, she didn't recognize the name. It meant nothing to her. "I wonder. Did Brother Timothy happen to find anything else on him?"

She had gone too far in her desire to know whether Leo McKenzie was connected somehow with the London police. Jennifer realized that immediately when Father Stephen gazed at her thoughtfully. Was there a hint of suspicion now in those intelligent blue eyes?

"Did you have something particular in mind?" he asked her slowly.

Hoping to cover her mistake, she turned to the dish of stewed apricots. "Only," she replied nonchalantly, "that he probably has family or friends somewhere who could be worried about him, and if we knew who they were—"

"They should be contacted. I see what you mean. No, Brother Timothy said nothing about any evidence on him of family or friends. We'll have to wait until Leo McKenzie is awake to learn that. In any case, nothing can be done in that direction until we can communicate again with the outside world."

Jennifer began on the apricots. They had a sour flavor, but she didn't feel she could leave them uneaten, as she had the cheese. It would look as if she didn't appreciate the meal.

"In the meantime," the abbot said, getting to his feet, "you and our patient are safe here. I can only give thanks that providence led you out of the storm to our door."

Jennifer could have left it at that, but she knew that Father Stephen would have to be told at least a part of the truth at some point. It might as well be now.

"I'm afraid it wasn't anything like that, Father."

"Then you weren't lost out on the road when you found us?"

"No. Warley Castle was my destination all along."

"I see." Puzzled, the abbot lowered himself again on the stool. "But, of course, I don't see at all."

Jennifer tried to explain without telling him what she couldn't afford to reveal. "I came to see one of the brothers. It's something that…well, I need his help. I'm not at all certain he can provide it, but I'm hoping he can."

"One of our order, you say." He was understandably surprised. "And this would be?"

"Brother Anthony. He is here, isn't he?"

"He is, yes," the abbot admitted, sounding suddenly reluctant now. He had to be wondering just why she needed to speak to Brother Anthony. Maybe his position even entitled him to know, but he remained polite. "However, I'm sorry to tell you that you won't be able to see him."

"May I ask why, Father?"

"Brother Anthony is cloistered in his cell under a self-imposed vow of silence."

"I don't understand."

The abbot hesitated, looking at her solemnly. Her disappointment must have been all too evident, because in the end he relented.

"I don't suppose there's any reason you shouldn't know. Brother Anthony recently came back from London where he met with an old friend."

On behalf of the monastery. The abbot probably wouldn't tell her that, but then he didn't have to. Jennifer knew all about it.

"This morning," Father Stephen continued, "Brother Anthony learned of the death of that friend."

Guy's murder, Jennifer thought.

"I think you can appreciate just how shocked and upset our Brother Anthony was. His friend was very dear to him."

"But to restrict himself to his cell…"

"You think it extreme. It isn't, you know. Not when you understand, as we do, that there are times when one of our order needs absolute solitude for prayer and meditation."

"I can respect that, Father, but I was just wondering…"

"What?"

"Whether Brother Anthony was troubled even before he heard of his friend's death."

Jennifer knew that the monk had, in fact, been worried when he visited Guy in London. Guy had confided as much to her. And this, among other reasons, was what had brought her to Warley Castle. But she couldn't tell the abbot this without disclosing her connection to Guy. That would be a dangerous admission that could destroy her chance of getting answers.

Or maybe she had already lost her opportunity. She could see by the guarded expression on the abbot's face that her probing had again been a mistake. He was definitely uncertain about her motives now.

"That isn't something I can tell you."

Because he didn't know, she wondered. Or because he was being protective of Brother Anthony? It was understandable. His role must require him to safeguard all the members of his community.

Jennifer heard the slow tolling of a bell somewhere off in the distance.

"You'll have to excuse me," the abbot said, coming to his feet again. "I need to be in the refectory for vespers and our evening meal."

Jennifer didn't think it was her imagination that his tone was on the severe side when, crossing the room to the door, he turned to address her again.

"We'll let you know when Brother Anthony is able to speak to you. I can't say just when that will be. Until then, you're welcome to move around the castle. With one exception. I must ask that you not try to visit the wing occupied by the monastery itself."

A warning because he didn't trust her not to try to see Brother Anthony in his cell? Or because the brothers' domain was off limits to any secular outsiders, especially women?

"I'll remember that."

"Don't concern yourself about the tray. It can be collected in the morning. Good night, Miss Rowan."

He slipped out of the room. She gazed at the door that closed silently behind him. Whatever his wariness with her in the end, she decided that she liked Father Stephen, even though his formal manner and mode of speech struck her as oddly old-fashioned. But then, from the moment of her arrival at Warley, Jennifer had felt as though she'd gone back in time to another age. One in which the innocent battled dark forces. And didn't always win.

IT HAD BEEN a long and daunting day. Jennifer's exhaustion should have guaranteed her a solid, uninterrupted sleep when she climbed into bed. It didn't work that way.

She found herself awake and restless, listening to the mournful wind outside. At some point she heard the soft tolling of the bell again that measured the canonical hours of devotion.

Another hour must have passed before Jennifer realized how cold the room was. The fire had dwindled to smoldering embers. Turning on the bedside lamp, she pushed back the covers and swung her legs over the side of the bed. She shivered when she came to her feet. Her robe was draped over the chair. She reached for it, hugging its thick folds around her as she padded on bare feet to the fireplace where she fed the grate with fresh peat chunks from the basket beside the hearth.

Safe, she thought as she crouched there, feeling the heat from the glow that slowly developed. That's what Father Stephen had told her. That she was safe now in the sanctuary of the monastery.

The abbot had meant she was safe from the harsh weather. He didn't know she was threatened by something far worse than the elements.

And right now, she thought, gazing at the connecting door, that something was not only in the monastery with her but inside the room behind that door.

Father Stephen had informed her that Leo McKenzie's identity had been established by his driver's license and his American passport. Nothing had been said about a discovery of anything that would give her a reason to be alarmed. But what if there was something?

It was no use. Jennifer knew she wouldn't be able to sleep until she had satisfied herself that Leo McKenzie wasn't carrying something that incriminated her. If not, she might at least be able to learn how he had traced her to Yorkshire. And why he'd been hunting for her.

She crossed the room and put her ear against the connecting door, listening. Silence. She tried the door. It was unlocked.

Opening the door slowly and carefully, hoping she wouldn't find him awake, she entered the room.

A single lamp burning on the bedside table revealed that the chamber was similar to her own. What she could see of it, anyway. The light here was also weak, leaving the corners in darkness. But it was sufficient to show her the man on the bed.

He lay on his back, his eyes closed. It wasn't his face, though, that immediately captured her attention. The blanket that should have fully covered him had somehow gotten tangled down around his waist, exposing his chest. A sleekly muscled chest that was naked except for some kind of white band wound tightly around the lower part of his rib cage.

Riveted by the sight of the powerful shoulders above that wrapping, Jennifer was suddenly nervous about approaching the bed. She went on standing there just inside the door. Then, directing her gaze elsewhere, she discovered his belongings that had been removed from his clothing. They had been dumped on the seat of a chair beside the bed. His wallet was among them.

The temptation to search those personal belongings was as strong as ever, but she hesitated. If there was anything in that collection that incriminated her, wouldn't Brother Timothy have discovered it and alerted the abbot?

Now that she thought of it, it didn't make sense that Leo McKenzie had been sent by the London police to find and arrest her. If she was a wanted woman now, then the local police would have been asked to handle it. Wouldn't they?

But Jennifer was no longer certain of anything. She had to *know*. Summoning her courage, she started to move in the direction of the chair. And was halted by the sound of Leo McKenzie mumbling in his sleep as he stirred on the bed.

"Lad's restless."

Jennifer whirled around with a startled gasp.

The voice, like gravel, went on speaking to her from one of the dark corners of the room. "Keeps throwing off his covers. I've given up trying to keep them up about his chin where they belong. Don't think he minds the cold at all."

A chair creaked as the man whose silent presence she'd been unaware of until this moment rose and moved forward into the light.

"Still, it's a good sign he's restless," he said. "Tells me he's not gone and sunk hisself into a coma. You'll be Miss Rowan, is it?"

"Yes," she murmured.

"Brother Timothy," he introduced himself. "They'll have told you I'm minding the patient."

In spite of the robe he wore, he looked more like the hefty prize fighter he'd been than the monk he was now. His round, ruddy face with its broken nose also belonged to a boxer. But his grin was good-natured.

"Gave you a bit of a start, did I?"

"I didn't know you were still with him."

"Thought I'd better spend the night here. With a bump on the head like that, there's always the chance of a concussion, you see. Have to be watchful for that. I expect you came in to check on him yourself."

"Yes," Jennifer lied, "I was worried about him."

"Mind you, he's not out of the woods," Brother Timothy said, bending over the bed, "but he'll come around yet, stout lad like him."

"That's good."

"Grumbled about his ribs being sore when I examined him. I'm of a mind he's just bruised there, nothing broken, but I taped him up. Can't be certain that it isn't a cracked rib. No trouble breathing, anyway."

"And he is sleeping."

"Sleep is the ticket all right, and I gave him something to be sure he did just that." Brother Timothy chuckled. "But he's been fighting it. Not a man who likes to be helpless, I'm thinking."

Scratching the fringe of graying hair below his tonsure, the monk gazed at her, as if wondering whether she had anything further she wanted to know.

There was a great deal that Jennifer *did* want to know about Leo McKenzie, but Brother Timothy wouldn't be able to provide that information. Nor, while the monk remained here keeping his vigil, could she attempt to learn it on her own. She would have to wait for her answers.

"Well, since he's in such good hands…"

Wishing Brother Timothy a good night, Jennifer retreated to her room.

Tomorrow, she promised herself as she closed the connecting door behind her.

IT WASN'T DAYLIGHT, however, that awakened her some hours later. Nor was it the desire for those answers. This was something else. And though Jennifer initially resisted the summons as she drifted back to consciousness, in the end she could no longer ignore its urgency.

She needed a bathroom.

You might as well give in, because it's not going to go away.

"Fine," she muttered, fully awake now as she emerged from the covers under which she was burrowed.

But, of course, it wasn't fine at all. Not when it was the middle of the night. The blackness at her window told her that even before she peered at her watch, after almost upsetting the lamp when she fumbled for the switch. And the room was frigid.

When her feet hit the icy floor, she couldn't slide them into her slippers fast enough. She reached for her robe and bundled into it, snugging the belt around her waist.

Better, but a hotel accommodation equipped with its own

bathroom would have been better still. This was not a hotel, she reminded herself. It was Warley Castle, and private bathrooms were nonexistent.

There was a single bathroom reserved for guests. That is, if she could remember how to get to it. One of the brothers had conducted her to the facility shortly after her arrival. Jennifer had hoped not to have to visit it again before morning, but the call of nature wasn't going to be denied.

The wind continued to snarl outside, muffled by the thick walls. She could barely hear it in the passageway that stretched away in front of her, cold and gloomy in the dim light.

Warley Castle was a big place. Its stone-vaulted corridors seemed to meander in every direction from level to level, so medieval in character that flickering torches mounted on its walls would have been more appropriate than the electric lights that were located at inadequate intervals.

It was either by chance, or because her memory was served by necessity, that Jennifer found the bathroom. But once she had used the primitive plumbing and was on her way back to her room, that memory failed her.

She realized after several minutes of wandering that she must have taken a wrong turn somewhere. There was nothing familiar now about the route. She was lost. Coming to a stop beneath one of the weak lanterns high on the wall, she tried to get her bearings.

Jennifer thought of herself as a realist and not easily unnerved, even about things she couldn't readily explain. So maybe what happened next was simply because of the setting. The absolute stillness of this dim passage was certainly eerie enough to activate the imagination, making her suddenly aware of her aloneness here.

Except she wasn't alone, because without warning a figure appeared down at the end of the corridor that stretched away into the shadows, moving toward her. His long, pale robe identified him as one of the monks. Help at last!

"I can't seem to find my way back to my room," she called out to him. "Can you direct me, please?"

He must have heard her, but he didn't answer her. Didn't so much as pause as he continued to glide along the passage.

"Hello," she called again.

Still no response. How could he not be conscious of her presence? And his gait…there was something not right about his gait. It was so slow and smooth, as if he weren't walking but floating. Like a wraith.

Jennifer was no longer relieved by his arrival. In fact, she was far less than that when he turned and suddenly disappeared, as if he'd passed through a solid wall. Alone again, she shivered.

Not a ghost, she told herself firmly. There had to be an explanation, probably a cross passage down which he had vanished. But she was in no mood to investigate that likelihood. All she wanted was to get away from here and back to her room.

Swinging around with the intention of retracing her route, Jennifer slammed into a wall. It was a barrier composed not of stone or timber but of hard flesh.

Uttering a little cry of alarm, she threw up her hands in a gesture of self-defense. Her palms came into searing contact with a warm, naked chest. Although he had managed to sneak up behind her without a sound, there was no question of any apparition this time. He was very real.

Her gaze collided with his, and for a long moment she found herself trapped by a pair of whiskey-colored eyes that burned into hers with a disarming intensity. She wasn't sure at what point she realized it wasn't only his gaze that held her. A pair of strong hands grasped her by the elbows, locking her against him.

Her palms, still flat against that tantalizing chest, seemed to sizzle. She removed them with a breathless "Let me go."

But he didn't release her. He went on staring at her with a harsh expression in his eyes. Then, in a slow, gruff voice, he warned her, "It won't do you any good to run. Wherever you go, I'll find you."

There was something about the way he said it, something in his entire manner that—

It struck her then. Leo McKenzie didn't know what he was saying, probably didn't know how he had managed to slip away from Brother Timothy and catch her here. He was disoriented. Was it the result of whatever kind of sedative the monk had given him, or—

Disassociated fugue.

A condition caused by a trauma, like a blow to the head. It could leave the victim confused, not responsible for his actions or his words, even rob him of any memory of his behavior afterwards. Leo McKenzie had suffered such a blow in the accident.

Was he dangerous like this? Maybe not, but the situation was far too intimate for comfort. She was suddenly conscious of things she hadn't noticed before. *Unsettling* things, like the stubble on his jaw and the tattoo of a salamander that wrapped itself halfway around his right bicep. They made him look tough.

And, admit it, sexy.

Uh-uh, much as she longed for the answers, this was definitely not the time to ask him how and why he had pursued her to Yorkshire. Even if she wasn't afraid of him, and that was not a certainty, he was in no state for any rational conversation.

"I'm not going anywhere," she promised him as gently as possible, "so you don't need to hang onto me any longer."

Those hypnotic, whiskey-colored eyes continued to search her own eyes, narrowing now as if he were wondering whether he could trust her.

"Please," she added softly.

For a moment she wondered whether he understood her plea. Then his hands on her elbows slowly relaxed. Taking a deep breath, Jennifer removed herself from his grip and put several safe feet between them.

He looked so suddenly bewildered that she felt sorry for him. Especially when, able to look down his full length now, she saw that he wore nothing but a pair of pajama bottoms that Brother Timothy must have dug out of his suitcase.

Jennifer was no expert on what the modern man wore to bed. From her limited experience, guys either slept in the raw or in T-shirts and boxer shorts. But Leo McKenzie's hard body in those bottoms could have started a whole new craze for pajamas.

"Aren't you cold?" she asked him, noticing that his feet were bare against the stone-flagged floor.

He didn't answer her.

"You must be cold. Come on," she coaxed him, "let me take you back to your room."

Would he go with her, or would he resist? He hesitated for a few seconds when she started to edge away along the passage, but then he willingly fell into step beside her. Good. Now she had only one other problem. Exactly where were their rooms?

She needn't have worried. Dazed or not, his sense of direction was better than hers. *She* ended up following *him,* and by some instinct she didn't understand, maybe the same one that had led him to her, he took them straight back to their rooms.

A worried Brother Timothy burst out of Leo's room when they arrived. "Praise the saints, you found him!" he welcomed Jennifer. "I went and dozed off in that chair, I'm ashamed to say, and when I opened my eyes again he was gone."

"I ran into him on my way back from a visit to the loo," Jennifer said, using the British term for a bathroom for the sake of clarity. She didn't feel the need to offer any further explanation about the whole episode. Brother Timothy looked worried enough.

"He's all right then, is he?"

"I think so. Just…well, not with it yet."

"That'd be the medicine." He turned to his patient. "Come on, matey, you've been busy enough for one night. Let's get you back to bed where you belong."

Silent and docile now, Leo permitted the monk to take him inside the bedroom. Brother Timothy thanked Jennifer, wished her a good night, and closed the door behind them.

Jennifer entered her own bedroom, threw more peat on the smoking remains of the fire in the grate and crawled into bed. She, too, had had enough for one night.

Her brain refused to shut down, though. It was infuriatingly busy with the image of Leo McKenzie. That encounter with him in the passage had impacted her far more strongly than she cared to admit. Her hands still tingled from their contact with his chest.

Damn. This wasn't good. Not good at all.

Chapter Three

No more midnight spooks, Jennifer thought with relief, opening her eyes to the first gray light of morning seeping into the room.

Or maybe she wasn't relieved. A glance in the direction of the window showed her that the snow was still coming down. Just how bad was it?

Very bad, she decided when, leaving her bed with her robe clutched around her, she went to the glass and looked out. Or tried to look out. The snow was so thick that she could barely glimpse the savage, white landscape. Father Stephen hadn't exaggerated when he'd told her the storm would leave them isolated, perhaps for several days.

Jennifer was tempted to climb back into bed and bury herself again under the warm blankets. Except...

Turning her head, she gazed at the closed door to the room that connected with hers. If this should turn out to be the opportunity she'd been hoping for, she couldn't afford to waste it.

Crossing the room, she listened at the door. She could hear nothing but the eternal moan of the wind. The hour was very early. Chances were the occupants of that room were asleep. It was worth the risk. But this time she wouldn't make the mistake of sneaking in there and getting caught by an alert

Brother Timothy, who might not regard a second visit as innocent.

Jennifer's rap on the door was soft enough not to rouse anyone but loud enough to be heard if one of them was awake. There was no response.

Turning the iron ring that served as a handle, she inched the door open and peered around its edge. Like her own, the room was murky with shadows. But the light from the window, feeble though it was, revealed that Brother Timothy had departed. He must have determined that his patient no longer needed his presence.

Leo McKenzie was not restless this morning. His tall figure stretched out on the bed never stirred as Jennifer crept across the room. Reaching the chair at his bedside, she looked down at him, wanting to be sure he was as deeply, peacefully asleep as he appeared to be.

That was evident with a glance. There was no reason for her gaze to linger on his face, to be interested in those square-jawed, craggy features softened by a wide, sensual mouth. She hadn't noticed it before, but there was a small, crescent-shaped, white scar high on his left cheek. A result of what? she wondered.

What was she doing? This man could be her enemy, probably was, and here she stood being susceptible again to his masculinity while wondering about a scar on his cheek. What difference did it make how he had come to have the scar?

Just get on with it.

Crouching down beside the chair, she considered the collection of his personal belongings spread out on the seat. A handful of coins, a comb, a belt, a set of keys, sunglasses tucked into a case, his passport and his wallet.

The wallet seemed the likeliest prospect. Jennifer started to reach for it, and then hesitated. She hated this. Hated the necessity of having to mine someone's privacy, to dig out whatever secrets he might be concealing. But that was the whole point, wasn't it? It *was* necessary.

Smothering her guilt, she snatched up the wallet and opened it. It was a bulky thing that carried his American driver's license along with the usual credit cards. Folded among them were two kinds of currency, American bills mixed in with British pound notes of various denominations.

But what was this?

Tucked between the bills were several identical business cards, probably ignored by Brother Timothy who must have looked no further after satisfying himself with the information provided by the passport and the driver's license. Jennifer removed one of the cards and read the bold print.

Leo McKenzie, Private Investigator.

Apprehensive now, her gaze flashed from the face of the card to the face of the man asleep on the bed beside her.

Leo McKenzie was a P.I.? But what was an American P.I. doing over here in England? More to the point, why should he be after *her?*

She supposed she could have waited until he was awake and then demanded an explanation from him. Assuming, that is, he would be in any state today to make sense. Or that he would be willing to tell her.

But she was in no mood to wait. She had waited long enough. She wanted answers now. Still hoping that the wallet could give them to her, she turned her attention back to its contents.

There was a series of plastic windows, the kind that displayed insurance cards and photographs. Jennifer rapidly flipped through them, passed the only photograph they contained and then, seized by something familiar, came immediately back to the solitary picture.

The once clear plastic was clouded from long use, blurring the photo. Removing it from the sleeve for a better look, she stared at it. It was a snapshot of two young men still in their teens, their arms draped over each other's shoulders as they gazed into the lens of the camera.

The taller of the two wore a cocky grin. Jennifer judged that nearly two decades must have passed since he'd posed for that snapshot, but she was able to recognize him. It was Leo McKenzie. And the other one...

She sucked in her breath and then released it slowly.

Oh, yes, she was able to identify him, too. Guy Spalding, the man whose murder back in London she feared that sooner or later she could be charged with.

Leo and Guy. This was the connection. They'd known each other. But how could Leo McKenzie have—

"Just what the hell do you think you're doing?"

She'd been so intent on examining the snapshot that she'd forgotten to be cautious. Had failed to be aware that the man on the bed had awakened and discovered her investigating his wallet.

Alarmed, her gaze shifted from the young face in the photograph to its mature, coldly angry counterpart.

"If you're through snooping," he said, his voice early-morning husky, "then I'd like to have those back."

His hand shot out, plucking the wallet and the snapshot from her fingers. With both of them back in his possession, he shoved himself up against the headboard, those mesmerizing, whiskey-colored eyes wearing a challenge as they glowered at her.

"Satisfied yourself, have you?"

"I haven't even begun to be satisfied." Jennifer herself was angry now as she got to her feet. "I saw one of your business cards in that wallet, and unless you're licensed to operate here in the U.K., and I very much doubt that you are, then you have no right to investigate me, much less the authority to follow me to Yorkshire."

"You think that's what I've been doing and that it entitles you to answers?"

"You bet I do. And you can start with the snapshot. You obviously knew Guy, but I can't believe you were friends, longtime or otherwise."

"Why not?"

"Because, frankly, I don't see how you could have had anything in common with him."

"Meaning that he had cultivated tastes and I'm some kind of a lout who wouldn't know Chinese Chippendale from Chinese checkers? Maybe you're right. But we had something in common all right. Our mother."

Jennifer stared at him in disbelief. "Are you saying you were brothers? But how is that possible when—"

"He was a Spalding, and I'm a McKenzie? *Half* brothers, Jenny."

No one called her Jenny, but she didn't bother to correct him. "I didn't know," she said.

Not that Guy would have had any particular reason to mention it to her. Their relationship hadn't reached the stage of intimate confidences, whatever his efforts in that direction. But she was still very surprised.

"Didn't you?" he said.

She didn't like the way he looked at her, as if she weren't to be trusted about anything she said.

"So, okay," he relented, "I guess it's understandable he didn't tell you about me. Why should he when Guy and I didn't see a whole lot of each other after our mother died. We were separated when her first husband, who was English, took him back to London, and my own father kept me in the States. But there was always a bond between us, maybe because we were the only family each other had after our fathers were gone."

All of which meant he must be determined to bring his brother's murderer to justice, and if he was somehow convinced that she—

But she didn't know that was his reason for following her.

Not for sure. She wasn't even certain that he had recovered his memory of yesterday's events, though he seemed entirely lucid this morning.

"Do you know where you're at, or how you got here?"

"Testing me?" His slow smile wore something of the cocky grin in that photo. "I've a pretty good idea, yeah."

Brother Timothy must have explained it to him at some point. But whether he had any recollection of his encounter with her out in the passage last night was another matter. Maybe not. Maybe it had just been some P.I.'s instinct kicking in so that, dazed though he'd been, he'd left the room to search for her. Whatever the explanation, she had no intention of reminding him of that uncomfortable episode.

"What are you wondering now, Jenny? Whether I'm going to be okay, or whether I'm a candidate for the nearest hospital?"

He was observant all right. He had caught her eyeing the injury on his forehead, where the swelling was considerably diminished, and the tape wrapped around the lower half of that sinewy bare chest.

"I hate to disappoint you, but it's like this…."

Swinging his legs over the side of the bed, he sat up on its edge. There was something provocative about the way he leaned toward her so earnestly, his dark hair tousled, his unshaven face flushed, as though he'd spent a long night doing more than just sleeping.

Damning her treacherous imagination, she backed several inches away from him. There was no question of it. Leo McKenzie was a threat to her on more than one level.

"There's nothing wrong with me," he finished informing her emphatically. "Nothing that a monk's medicine and a night in bed haven't already fixed. So, while I'm grateful for both your rescue and your concern, if you think I might be too helpless to keep you from running again—"

"Why?" she demanded. "Why are you after me?"

"My brother was murdered. I'd kind of like to see that his killer pays for that."

"And you think that I'm the one who murdered him?"

"It occurred to me that you might know something about it anyway, especially after what Barbara had to tell me."

"Barbara?"

"Yeah, Barbara, his wife. Or do you want to pretend that you didn't know Guy was married?"

"I didn't, not until the day before his death."

"Funny, because Barbara seemed to think you knew all about her. She was in a bad state when she called me at home and begged me to fly over to try to talk some sense into Guy."

"What did she tell you?"

"Enough to worry me. I got the full details on the way into London when Barbara picked me up at Heathrow the night before last. How Guy had told her he was crazy about you and that he wanted a divorce. How you were already so wildly possessive of him that you'd do anything to have him, including breaking up his marriage."

Jennifer was dumbfounded. She knew that Guy had been in love with her, or foolishly claimed to be, but to tell his wife such outrageous lies...

"And you believed what she told you?"

"I believed *she* believed it. As for me, I wanted to talk to Guy before I got real serious about it. Only I never got the chance. The police were there to meet us with the bad news when Barbara and I got to his shop."

Guy's esteemed antique business on Great Brompton Road where he had been murdered. The scene haunted Jennifer.

"And you immediately assumed I was the one who killed him? How could you? Or weren't you told that the police questioned me and were satisfied I wasn't a suspect?"

"Neither Barbara or I assumed anything. And, yes, I was told you weren't a suspect. But a P.I. likes to ask his own questions, especially when they concern the death of his brother. Went to your mews cottage the next morning, Jenny, to ask those questions. You weren't there. A neighbor told me you were in a big hurry when he saw you coming away with your suitcase. Said you went tearing up the street in a small, green Ford. Kind of suspicious to run away like that, wouldn't you say?"

"And that made me guilty?"

"Not guilty. Not yet. Let's just say your action makes you a strong possibility. After all, you were involved with Guy. But if you're so innocent—"

"I *am* innocent."

"Then why are you on the run?"

"I have my reasons. *Good* ones." But Jennifer wasn't ready to share them. She still wanted answers. "Just how did you find me?"

"You were careless, Jenny. You must have called directory assistance and then jotted down the number they gave you."

On the back of an old bill next to the telephone. She remembered that and how afterwards she had crumpled up the bill and tossed it into the wastebasket.

"I called the number," he said. "Turned out to be the King's Head Inn in Heathside. I took a chance and told them I was Jennifer Rowan's husband just checking to be sure they had my wife's reservation for a room. It paid off. They were happy to verify your reservation."

"You broke into my cottage and went through my wastebasket? You had no right," she accused him, resenting the man's total brashness.

"Now how else could I look for some evidence of where you might have gone?"

"And, of course, you didn't share that evidence with the police."

"Didn't think they'd like hearing I entered your cottage." His eyes narrowed. "Besides, it had become very personal by then."

So personal, Jennifer thought, that she realized Leo Mc-
Kenzie would go to any length to see his brother's killer con-
victed of his murder. And if she was his chief suspect, maybe
his *only* suspect at the moment, then maybe he was prepared
to wring the truth out of her, no matter what it cost either of
them. And the police be damned.

Guy and Leo. She was still shaken by the revelation that they
had been half brothers. There was nothing about their characters
or looks that were alike. Except for one thing. Guy, too, had been
single-minded in his determination to go after what he wanted.

"I'm waiting, Jenny," he said, sounding patient about it.

But she knew he wasn't patient at all. He had given her his
story, and now he demanded hers.

"What's the point?" she said, unable to keep the bitterness
from her voice. "Haven't you already condemned me?"

"I don't remember saying that. Hell, I'm a reasonable man,
willing to listen to all the arguments. Maybe you've got a good
one. So, go on, tell me, and if I like what I hear—"

"What?" she cut him off sharply. "You'll reconsider your
judgmental opinion of me?"

"Depends on how well you explain what made you run to
Yorkshire. And while you're at it, don't leave out the Warley
Madonna."

He had surprised her again. "You know about the Madonna?"

"It's no secret it's missing. What do *you* know about it,
Jenny?"

But whatever she told him, *if* she decided to tell him anything
at all, would have to wait. They were interrupted by a tap on the
hall door. Before either of them could answer it, the door opened
and the cheerful face of Brother Timothy poked around its edge.

"Looks a rare treat, this does. The both of you awake, and
my patient sitting there like he no longer needs me. Feeling
better, are you, lad?"

Leo grinned at the monk. "The cure would be complete, friar, with a cup of strong coffee."

"If you're up to it, I'm thinking we can do better than that." Brother Timothy came into the room. "There'll be breakfast waiting for the two of you in the guests' dining parlor. Or a tray here for you, lad, if you're of a mind to keep to your bed for a bit."

"No trays," Leo said firmly. "I'm ready to join the living."

"That's the ticket. Give you a chance to meet the others in your dining parlor."

"There are other guests in the castle?" Jennifer asked him.

"There are."

This was certainly unexpected. Maybe it was what Father Stephen had meant last night when he'd mentioned that other matters had delayed him in welcoming her to Warley. Had he been attending to those guests?

"The lot of you will make a regular party," Brother Timothy said. "Now, they've had their turns in the bath, so I'm guessing you'll want your own, and then I'll take you down."

Not only unexpected, she thought, but another complication.

A SHOWER AND A SHAVE had Leo feeling halfway human again. Getting the meal inside him that Brother Timothy had promised them would be even better.

Not that breakfast was the most important thing on his mind, he thought, eyeing the closed door to the room that adjoined his as he tucked the tail of a fresh shirt inside the waistband of his jeans. *She* was on the other side of that door, waiting for the monk to come back and conduct them to the dining parlor.

Yeah, she was on his mind all right. More than he wanted her to be, and that worried him.

Jennifer Rowan was not what Barbara had led him to expect. The treacherous seductress who had stolen her husband. Oh, maybe she did physically fit the image, with that shoulder-

length hair the color of rich mahogany, a pair of jade-green eyes
and a body that a man would eagerly welcome into his bed.

He could see why Guy had been captivated by her. He was
susceptible to that allure himself, and if he didn't watch
himself...

The thing of it was, though, nothing else about Jennifer
smacked of a conniving woman. She struck Leo as being intelligent, independent, not lacking spirit and scared. Scared
with good reason, considering the circumstances.

Okay, maybe all that vulnerability, the kind that made a
man want to be protective of such a woman, was nothing more
than an illusion. Her face alone could be responsible for that.
He remembered that his ex-wife had angelic features like that.

But there had been no angel underneath, he sourly reminded
himself, dragging a sweater over his head.

Leo hadn't trusted a sweet face and a hot body since then.

Anyway, he knew from his work that what people were on
the outside seldom matched what they were inside. Look at
how he had caught her going through his things. Maybe just
an act of desperation. Or maybe she was guilty of something.
Because if she were so damn innocent, why had she run? He
kept coming back to that.

Sliding his feet into a pair of loafers, he looked at the closed
door again.

He could swear Jennifer had been relieved by Brother
Timothy's interruption, and afterwards she couldn't escape into her own room fast enough. Why? Had she been panicked by
Leo's demand to hear her version of her involvement with Guy
and the explanation for her flight from London the morning
after his murder? Had she needed to get away from Leo long
enough to put together a convincing story?

He wasn't certain of anything at this point except his frustration. As hungry as he was, breakfast meant a delay, and he
wanted to hear Jennifer Rowan's story. *Needed* to hear it.

Only that wasn't completely true. There was one other certainty. He couldn't stop thinking of that enticing mouth of hers and how they were stranded here together.

Hell, none of this was going to be easy.

"YOU'RE SURE of it now, are you?" Brother Timothy asked as he escorted them along the corridor.

"I'm sure, friar," Leo answered, trying to be patient with the monk's excessive concern. "No headache and no chest pains. Just a little tenderness around the ribs." He didn't add that he was relieved to be rid of the tape in that area, which he had removed before his shower. Brother Timothy might not be happy with him if he knew about that.

"You'll do then."

The monk played guide as they continued along the route to the dining parlor, pointing out things and telling them there were many areas in the castle that the monastery rarely used. Leo could believe it. The place was immense, and probably rooms like the great hall would be impossible to keep comfortable in weather like this.

Jennifer beside him was quiet, offering no comment. She was close enough to him that he could catch whiffs of her fragrance, something subtle but seductive. Damn. It was bad enough that he had to be aware of everything else about her that was desirable.

She didn't look at him, but Leo sensed that she was equally aware of him. And nervous about it.

"Turned real nasty again, it has," Brother Timothy observed as they paused at an embrasure where a window in the stone wall looked down into a courtyard. There was a snow-covered sundial in its center surrounded by a formal arrangement of elevated beds framed by clipped hedges.

Or at least that's what Leo thought he was seeing. It was hard to tell through the curtain of driven snow that had resumed after a brief lull in the storm. Even in this enclosed place the wind had the force of a gale. Not the kind of weather you'd choose to be out in, and yet there was a solitary figure down there pacing the paths. Head bent inside his cowl, he seemed oblivious to the conditions. Strange.

Leo noticed that Jennifer was intently watching the small, stoop-shouldered figure, whose habit identified him as one of the monks. "He doesn't seem to be minding the cold," she murmured.

"Not even noticing it, I'm thinking," Brother Timothy said. "Our Brother Anthony has a deal on his mind these days. Only permits himself to leave his cell to exercise a bit in the cloister yard there or to pray in the chapel on the other side."

"That is Brother Anthony then?"

"It is."

Jennifer obviously knew about this Brother Anthony and was interested in him, though Leo couldn't imagine how or why. And it didn't look as though either she or Brother Timothy was going to bother to explain it to him.

So just what was that all about? Leo wondered as the three of them moved on along the passage.

He was to ask himself the same thing a moment later about another mystery when, pausing as they arrived at the top of a spiral stairway, Jennifer turned to the monk with a sober "Brother Timothy, I have another question for you."

"If it's about my days in the ring..."

"No, nothing like that." She hesitated before asking what was clearly a self-conscious "Have there...well, ever been any tales about Warley Castle being haunted?"

Leo stared at her. Hell, was she serious?

The monk looked amused. "A ghost at Warley? Never heard of any ghost being sighted here. But if one was to turn up, I don't see our Abbot Stephen tolerating him. Mind the stairs now. They're a bit steep."

There had been her interest in Brother Anthony, Leo thought

as they descended the coiling flight. And now she was worried about a ghost? She seemed too levelheaded for that one, but something was up.

Okay, this made two more questions, among all the rest, that he intended to put to her when they were alone again. He just wished that, breakfast or not, he didn't have to wait to ask them.

When they reached a landing less than halfway down the flight, Brother Timothy opened a door on the right and led them through a stone archway into the guests' dining parlor. Leo could see why it was named that. There was a sitting area at the far end of the long room. It was furnished with easy chairs and a sofa.

The seven people who occupied the room were all gathered at this end, which served as the dining area. Some of them were busy helping themselves from a breakfast buffet laid out on a sideboard while others were already seated with their plates at a long trestle table.

Leo was surprised. Considering the weather, he hadn't expected to find these number of guests at the castle. Or maybe it was just because of the weather that they were here. He could feel glances of curiosity directed at Jennifer and him.

"No need to go and worry about names," Brother Timothy assured Jennifer and Leo. "Time for that when you're settled with your plates."

Of all the company, only one of them hovering near the sideboard wore a habit. Leo noticed, however, that he lacked a monk's tonsure. Brother Timothy asked the young man to join them.

"Here now, this is our Geoffrey," he said. "A novice, Geoffrey is, who has yet to take his final vows."

Which explained why the young man with his fair hair and pale, melancholy face didn't have a tonsure yet, Leo guessed. But it didn't explain why he looked so unhappy when Brother Timothy turned them over to him with a hasty "I'm off to prime."

"Prime is one of our daily communal prayers," Geoffrey said

when the monk had departed. "I'm excused. It's because of Patrick." He indicated another young man who waited for him at the sideboard. "Patrick is here because he wants to join our order, but he isn't permitted into the monastery side of the castle until he's certain of his calling. Father Stephen has asked me to look out for him."

And Geoffrey, Leo decided, isn't any more happy about playing nanny to Patrick than he is about Jennifer and me.

"Don't worry, Geoffrey, we can take care of ourselves."

An introduction to the breakfast buffet wasn't a problem anyway. There were more than enough dishes to choose from when he and Jennifer helped themselves at the sideboard. Oatmeal, scrambled eggs, sausages, toast and fish. Why the English had a taste for fish at breakfast was something Leo had never understood. He took some of everything but the fish and the oatmeal. Jennifer, he noticed, had very little on her plate.

An introduction to the others when they joined them at the table was another matter. They struck Leo as a quirky bunch. Edgy, too, if he wasn't mistaken, and his work as a P.I. had taught him to be fairly accurate in his observations about people. But the weather was probably responsible for that edginess.

"Any of you have a working mobile phone?" the woman seated across from him asked. "Mine absolutely *refuses* to cooperate."

The others shook their heads.

"Well, there you are. We're not only stranded here, we're stranded without communication."

"Have a battery-operated wireless," a man down the table said. "A lot of crackle on it, but I was able to raise a weather forecast. More of the same filthy stuff on the way, I'm afraid."

"Then we might as well make the best of it."

Ignoring Jennifer, she smiled at Leo across the table. A smile that was more than just polite. Hell, was the woman flirting with him? Well, she was attractive enough, if you went for the brittle, consciously elegant type. He wasn't interested. And wouldn't have been, even if she wasn't wearing a wedding ring.

"Sybil Harding," she introduced herself. "And this is my husband, Roger."

She indicated the man beside her. He had a moustache and wore a stolid expression on his lined face.

"Once upon a time Roger was one of the brothers here," she went on to explain, "which is why he comes back to the monastery on retreat twice a year. A bit excessive, but I think he regards it as a holiday from me. One can only imagine his disappointment when, after dropping him off, a blocked road forced me to turn back."

Roger Harding's face reddened. "These people aren't interested in hearing this, Sybil."

"Dear heart, we're all in this together, so why not be friendly?" She turned her attention back to Leo. "Let me see now. You've already met Geoffrey and Patrick, haven't you?"

Leo glanced in the direction of the two young men. He hadn't noticed it before, but the novice had shadows under his eyes, as if he'd slept badly. His charge beside him, skinny, round-shouldered and with a face suffering from acne, looked equally miserable. Maybe because he was painfully shy or because Geoffrey pointedly ignored him.

"And the other couple there," Sybil went on, "are the Brashers. Fiona and Alfred, I believe."

A timid-looking pair, they nodded by way of acknowledgment.

"If they have an exciting tale of their own," Sybil said, "then we have yet to hear it."

Alfred Brasher cleared his throat before responding with a quiet "Just travelers on our way to the coast and caught on the road like the rest of you."

The group seemed to have already been told beforehand

who he and Jennifer were, Leo thought, helping himself to more coffee from the pot on the table. And maybe how they had ended up at Warley themselves. No one asked, anyway.

"And our friend with the battery-powered wireless," Sybil continued, gesturing toward the balding, thick-waisted fellow at the end of the table, "is—"

"Harry Ireland," he introduced himself. "In sales. I call at the monastery every few months to take orders on goods the brothers like delivered to their gate, then move on to the next place. Some people still like the old-fashioned door-to-door service." A laugh rumbled out of him. "Couldn't move on this time, what?"

All of us trapped here in this isolated place, Leo thought, finishing his eggs. Was there something just a little too coincidental about that, or was he imagining it? And the edginess in the company he had noticed earlier…he was sure now he wasn't imagining that. You could almost smell the tension in the air. Just the weather, or was there another explanation?

He didn't have to wonder about the tension of the woman at his side. He already knew. Jennifer hadn't spoken a word since they'd entered the dining parlor. But those wary green eyes of hers said a lot whenever he caught her watching him. She was definitely worried.

"Have I left anyone out?" Sybil wondered. "No? Then Mr. Ireland concludes the introductions."

"Just Harry," he insisted.

"Yes, just Harry. Well, it makes us a cozy party, doesn't it? Although," she added, looking around the room, "one could have wished for a cheerier setting."

Leo hadn't paid much attention to the surroundings before this. He had to admit that the time-worn, dark paneling made the room a somber place. But then the whole castle was like something out of a vampire movie. Count What's-his-name would have felt right at home here.

"Roger told me that in centuries past this used to be the solarium where the family gathered after meals," Sybil informed them, "which is why it has a good fireplace. I suppose one must be grateful for that, although that chimneypiece is a horror."

This was something else that Leo hadn't noticed until now. Carvings on the stone chimney breast depicted strange beasts and leering monsters, all of them crowded together and tumbling over one another. Not exactly what you'd expect to find in a monastery. Nor was the grotesque mask fitted into the paneling of the wall adjacent to the fireplace.

Jennifer, noticing him gazing at the hollow eyes of that stone face, spoke up for the first time. "It's a squint," she said.

Leo turned to her. "A what?"

"If this used to be the solar in the medieval days," she explained, "then the great hall must be on the other side of that wall. A squint permitted the lord of the castle to look through those eyes down into the great hall."

"A spy hole? Why?"

"It was a method for checking on the activity of his household to be sure they weren't getting too boisterous in his absence."

Leo had forgotten that Jennifer would know about this stuff. His brother's wife had told him that, like Guy, Jennifer was connected somehow with the antiques trade.

"Aren't you clever to know that?" Sybil cooed, then abruptly dismissed Jennifer with a casual "I'm not interested in solariums, but I do care about loos. And the scarcity of them in this place, along with the state of the plumbing, is not my definition of comfort."

"Sybil, please—" her husband murmured pleadingly.

"Dear heart, it's true. I don't know how all of us will manage."

If any of the rest of them had any feelings on the subject, none of them bothered to contribute them. There was a long, awkward silence while they concentrated on their plates.

Sybil Harding, looking around the table, ended the silence

after a few moments with an exuberant "I do hope some of you play bridge."

Leo could sympathize with her husband. The woman was an embarrassment.

"Sybil, perhaps—"

"Roger, hush. If we're to be stuck here, we must pass the time somehow." She leaned provocatively toward Leo. "Roger refuses to play, which always leaves me looking for a partner."

"I don't play bridge. Poker is my game." Leo had had enough. He wanted out of here. Scraping his chair back, his hands on the table to support himself, he got slowly to his feet. "But right now," he muttered, "I think I need to go back to my room."

"You feeling off again, old man?" Just Harry asked him.

"Yeah, maybe a bit."

"Bloody shame."

Jennifer looked up at him, this time with concern. "Would you like me to find Brother Timothy?"

"Not necessary. But if you'd go with me…"

He left the rest unsaid, knowing she would be convinced that someone should be with him in case he started to black out on the way back to his room.

She came immediately to her feet. "Of course. Excuse us, everyone."

Jennifer waited until they were out of the room before she started to fuss at him. "You pushed yourself too far too soon."

"I'm not having a relapse," he assured her.

"Well, you need to rest."

Leo didn't argue with her. She waited until they gained the corridor at the top of the stairway before asking him, "Are you feeling light-headed? That climb—"

"No," he growled, feeling guilty for worrying her.

She was silent again until they passed the window embrasure.

"You're going too fast," she complained.

But Leo was in too much of a hurry to slow his long-legged

stride. Nor did he offer an explanation for his urgency until they were back inside his room with the door closed behind them. Then, a grimness in his voice, he swung around to challenge her.

"All right, we've wasted enough time with that bunch downstairs. I want the truth, Jenny, and I don't want to wait any longer for it. So go ahead and convince me that you didn't murder my brother before you helped yourself to the Warley Madonna."

Chapter Four

In the slow, measured voice Jennifer used whenever she was very angry and trying not to show it, she confronted Leo with his deceit. "You tricked me. You're not feeling ill at all."

"Interesting," he said. "I'll have to remember that about you."

"What are you talking about?"

"That purr in your voice just before you go and blast someone. I noticed it earlier. Dangerous."

He didn't miss much, Jennifer thought. And she didn't want him to be so observant about her, reading her moods and then analyzing them. It meant she would have to be on guard with him every minute. She had enough to worry about with the idiotic way he affected her whenever he got anywhere near her. Like now.

"Come on, Jenny," he coaxed, moving in close, "you know you're going to have to tell me your story sooner or later. Might as well be now, huh?"

The way he said it, his voice low and husky, he could have been urging something far more intimate than that.

"I can't figure you out, McKenzie."

"What's that?"

"Whether you're playing good cop here or bad cop."

"Whatever gets me answers." He jerked his thumb in the direction of a small table that was identical to the one in her room.

"Suppose we get comfortable over there while you give them to me."

Jennifer eyed the table and the two chairs on either side of it. "Now why do I get this feeling of an interrogation room in a police lockup?"

"We could use the bed."

"I don't think so."

Since there was no other safe place to sit, and nothing to be gained by delaying the inevitable, she crossed the room and seated herself at the table. Leo took a moment to fuel the fire and then joined her, slinging the chair around on his side of the table and straddling it. They were face to face now, with only a few feet between them. He lessened the gap by leaning toward her expectantly.

"Praying?" he asked, looking down at her hands folded together on the table, fingers steepled.

He had caught another of her habits, one she unconsciously used when she found the need to steady herself in a strained situation. This was definitely one of those times.

"It's called collecting my thoughts."

And, damn it, she was not going to have him think she was nervous by hastily hiding her hands in her lap. Whatever he thought about their position, she kept them right there in front of him on the surface of the table.

"Those thoughts collected yet, Jenny?"

"Enough to tell you," she informed him emphatically, "that whatever Guy told his wife, we were not having an affair."

"What *were* you having?"

"A friendship. I thought. And stop looking at me like that."

"Like what?"

"Like you think I'm either lying or was incredibly naive about Guy's feelings for me."

"I don't see you as being naive, Jenny. I see you as being a pretty smart woman. Which leaves me wondering why you didn't guess at some point in this *friendship* that he was falling for you."

"How could I? I barely knew him."

One of those dark eyebrows of his—and, yes, she thought, even his eyebrows were disturbingly sexy—lifted, expressing his disbelief.

"It's true," she insisted. "We were together only a few times in the three weeks after I met him. Not enough for me to realize that he—"

"Wait a minute. You saying the friendship was a *new* one? That you were in the same trade, antiques, and that your paths never crossed until three weeks ago?"

"They had no reason to. Guy specialized in the more formal things. My specialty is pretty much English country pieces. He had a shop. I don't. He lived in London. I live there only part of the year and the rest back home in Boston."

"Then how do you sell the stuff?"

"I don't. I'm an overseas agent for American antique dealers. My clients tell me what they want. I try to acquire it for them and then arrange to have it shipped back to the States."

"Nothing to do with the retail end of the business, huh? And you didn't know Guy."

"I knew a little about him, his reputation for handling the best, that kind of thing. But nothing personal until he introduced himself to me at an estate auction."

"And after that?"

"He phoned me, asked me out to dinner. I went. It was a pleasant evening. And so were the handful of others we spent together. Nothing heavy. Oh, I'm not saying it couldn't have developed into something more. It might have, if I hadn't learned what Guy hadn't bothered to tell me."

"Being?"

"That he was married."

There went that incredible eyebrow of his again, registering his skepticism.

This time Jennifer did remove her hands from the table, clenching them in her lap where he couldn't see the evidence of her emotional agitation. "Why am I bothering? You're not going to believe me, whatever I tell you."

"I'm trying, Jenny. But you gotta admit—"

"All right, I should have made sure he was unattached before I went out with him. And that probably makes me nowhere near as smart as you think I am. But I just didn't make sure. Okay?"

"What comes next in this tale? After you heard he had a wife."

"Something I didn't like. Guy was waiting in his office for me behind his shop after closing. This was the evening before his death. We were supposed to go to a play."

"You didn't go to a play," Leo guessed.

"We didn't have to. We had one of our own. I told Guy I wouldn't be seeing him socially again and why. He said he was in love with me. I told him he was crazy. He said his marriage was finished, that he and his wife were separated. I asked him if his wife knew that."

"Sounds like a good play. You use that soft, calm voice of yours when you played this scene?"

"I wish I had. Then maybe there wouldn't have been a witness to my anger."

"Who?"

"Guy's charwoman. I didn't realize she was there cleaning the shop until I came away from his office. Judging by the look I got from her on my way out, I knew she must have overheard our quarrel. And probably misunderstood my anger with Guy, because that look wasn't a sympathetic one."

"Misunderstood how?" Leo pressed her.

He wasn't going to be satisfied with the essentials, was he? He wanted all the details. Wouldn't let up on her until he had them.

"I think she may have thought I was furious with Guy

because I wanted him and couldn't have him, when all I was really angry about was how he'd deceived me."

"This the same char who's in a coma in a London hospital?"

He would have learned about the coma from the police, Jennifer thought. Learned the woman had been found unconscious at the scene of Guy's murder.

"Yes, the same."

Those whiskey-colored eyes that could caress a woman with their unsettling gaze until they had her yearning for something more, or else have her squirming under the heat of their accusation, looked at her for a long, silent moment. Jennifer wasn't sure what she read in them, seduction or accusation. Maybe both, if that was possible.

When he spoke, it was in a slow, raspy voice that had her quivering inside. "And that's got you worried, hasn't it, Jenny? Why is that, I wonder?"

"Because when she wakes up from that coma, as she's expected to, and when the police who are waiting for that to happen question her, they'll learn—"

"What? What will they learn?"

This was it. Either she backed away now from the rest of her story, or she told him all of it. Everything that in the end had brought her racing to Yorkshire. And if she told him the rest, then she was sure he would no longer question her guilt. He would be convinced of it.

The truth. Remember, you've committed yourself to it.

"That," Jennifer went on with more resolve in her voice than she felt, "I wasn't just in Guy's office the evening before he was murdered. I was there again the next night standing over his body."

Leo's reaction wasn't what she expected. He laughed. There was no mirth in that laughter, though.

"You've got guts telling me that. But I'm guessing this isn't a confession you killed my brother. What is it exactly?"

"An explanation. And, no, I didn't go to Guy's shop to kill him. I went there by request."

"Guy's?"

"Yes."

"Feeling as you claim you did by then, why would you do something like that?"

"Because he promised it was strictly business and not some excuse to try to win me back. All right, I was willing to be convinced. Probably because I couldn't resist the opportunity."

"For what?"

"Before I tell you that, there's something you need to know about me."

"Which is?"

"I have this…well, kind of gift, I guess you'd call it. I can sense things about antiques, sometimes by just touching them. It doesn't always work, but a lot of the time it does. It's one more tool that helps to make me good at what I do."

"I'll take your word for it. What kind of things?"

"Mostly whether there's something not right about a piece."

"A fake, you mean?"

"Any antique expert can tell that, usually after a careful examination. This is more. This is a feeling for the honesty of a piece, not just whether it's genuine but whether it's everything it's supposed to be. It's hard to explain."

"I get the idea." Leo shifted restlessly on the chair he continued to straddle. "Let's get to the good part. I've heard the *why*. Now suppose you tell me the *what*."

"What do you know about the Warley Madonna?"

His broad shoulders lifted in a shrug. "Just what the cops and Barbara were able to tell me. That it came from here, it's worth a fortune and it's missing. Theory is it was taken from Guy's office by his killer. I think that's a solid theory. What do you think?"

"That I didn't murder Guy or steal the Madonna, even if I

was drooling over the chance to see and actually touch it. What antique lover wouldn't."

"Yeah? What's so special about it?"

"What isn't? Legend says it was carved from a section of the true cross sometime in the first or second century after the crucifixion. The earliest known depiction of the Madonna and Child."

"Holy sh—" Leo caught himself. "Sorry. Bad choice. So, how did the monastery come to have it?"

"It was a prize of war. A crusading Warley baron carried it back from the Holy Land in the twelfth century. The brothers eventually received the Madonna along with the castle. They kept it safe all these ages."

"Until it ended up with Guy."

"Did your sister-in-law tell you how Guy came to have it?"

Leo shook his head. "Barbara might have told the cops when they questioned her separately, providing she knew. All I got was it's gone. But I bet you know, don't you?"

She hated that cynical sting in his voice, the way he pushed her for a truth he probably wouldn't accept. It left her wanting to push him right back. But all she said was a quiet, "It was because of Brother Anthony."

"The monk Brother Tim identified for you down in the courtyard?"

"Yes."

"Uh-huh. And you're interested in this Brother Anthony. Why is that?"

"Because he brought the Warley Madonna to Guy the day before his death. Guy told me all about it on the phone when he called and asked me to come by the shop the night he was murdered. How he and Brother Anthony were old friends and that the monastery was badly in need of funds and had to sacrifice the precious relic."

"That mean Guy was going to buy it from the monastery? Or maybe he did buy it."

Jennifer shook her head. "It wasn't the kind of thing he carried. But Guy had the connections to find a buyer for it. Brother Anthony trusted him to do that when he left the Madonna with him before turning around and going back to Yorkshire."

Leo was silent for a moment. She could see he was thinking about what she'd just told him. She could also see the way the pulse was beating in the hollow of his strongly corded throat. Mesmerizing. And far too alluring.

"Two and two make four," he muttered.

"Is that supposed to make sense?"

"That's what I'm wondering, Jenny. Guy had the Warley Madonna. That's a two. You tell me you have this gift for sensing when an antique isn't all it should be. That's another two. Now if they do add up to four, it's gotta mean Guy asked you to come by his shop because there was something about the Madonna that bothered him and he wanted this gift of yours to go to work on it."

"He was a little mysterious about it on the phone, but I did get the impression he wasn't altogether satisfied," Jennifer admitted. "Of course, with a piece like that, he would have sent it out to be authenticated, probably had it submitted to tests, that sort of thing, but in the meantime—"

"He wanted your opinion. So, if we have a four, why do I keep getting a five?"

Because you're suspicious of everything I'm telling you. Probably not willing to believe any of it.

Maybe the expression on her face gave her away. Or maybe he was just reading her again when he said, "Suspicion comes with the P.I. territory. Want to try to rid me of that by telling me just what happened that night? Your version of it, anyway."

Restraining her resentment, she gave him that version.

"It was after hours when I got there. The shop was closed. I went around to the service door at the side. Like the front entrance, it has a security code."

"You knew the code?"

"I did not, and I don't know who did besides Guy. Probably the charwoman and I suppose his wife."

"Then how would you get inside?"

"By ringing the bell and having Guy let me in. Only this time…"

"Yeah?"

"The door was already unlocked. Even though Guy was expecting me, I thought it wasn't like him to be careless like that."

"But you didn't feel anything was wrong?"

"Not then. I let myself in and called up to him. You probably know—"

"That his office is at the top of a short flight of stairs, yeah."

"He didn't answer me, but the office door was open and the light on. I went on up still calling to him, and when I entered the office—"

The scene was still so fresh and awful in her mind that Jennifer found herself unable to describe it. Leo, who must have had an account of it from the police, described it for her.

"Guy was dead on the floor. Shot with a bullet from one of a pair of antique dueling pistols. Cops couldn't figure out why they should both be out on his desk like that and loaded."

Jennifer knew, but she couldn't bring herself to tell him. Not yet.

"Barbara said he collected the things," Leo went on. "Even had the skill and tools to repair them. Something I didn't know about him, maybe because he had this illegal firing range down in the cellar of the shop where he'd test them out on a target."

"Yes," Jennifer murmured.

"According to Barbara, if they were really valuable, he'd keep them locked away in this big safe in the office. The Warley Madonna being worth a fortune, that must have been in the safe, too. But the safe was wide open and not a sign of the Madonna anywhere. You notice all that, Jenny?"

"Yes," she said.

"Then what happened? After you found him dead? After you saw the Madonna was gone?"

"The charwoman," she said, forcing herself to go on. "She must have let herself into the shop after me. Must have come upstairs to clean the office. I didn't hear her. Too busy trying not to be sick while bending over Guy, wanting to make sure he wasn't still alive, even though I knew he had to be dead. I didn't know she was there. Not until she let out a shriek behind me."

"Then?" Leo urged.

"I tried to go to her. Tried to tell her I didn't kill Guy. She backed away from me. Lost her footing and went over backwards down the stairs. I ran down to help her. She was unconscious. That's when I heard the wail of a siren. When I realized," she finished breathlessly, "that someone, a neighbor maybe, must have heard the gunshot and called the police."

"But you weren't there when they arrived."

"No, I—" Jennifer paused, inhaling slowly to restore the air in her lungs "—I did a foolish thing. I panicked. I knew help was on the way for the charwoman, but if I stayed…"

"You'd be hauled in for questioning, maybe even charged with Guy's murder when the char was recovered enough to tell the cops all she'd seen and heard on those two nights. So you got out of there, huh?"

"And went back to my mews cottage, yes."

"Not a very smart decision, Jenny. Kind of got guilt written all over it. From a cop's point of view, that is," he added dryly.

She glared at him, hating the tone of implication in his every word and look. "All right, I wasn't thinking clearly. I was scared. But I realized how wrong I was. It took me hours of being huddled there in front of a gas fire to realize it, but I did. I knew I had to turn myself in for questioning before they came for me."

"But that never happened."

"It would have. I was on my way out when an officer turned up at my door. I thought he was there to arrest me. All he wanted was information." Jennifer remembered her vast relief in that moment, but she didn't try to tell Leo about that. "The detectives on the case were talking to all of Guy's friends and associates, hoping for some lead in his murder."

"Because they would have known it couldn't have been a thief who'd broken into the shop to rob the place," Leo pointed out. "There was no sign of that. Guy had to have let the killer into the shop himself. Must have been someone he knew, maybe someone he was expecting."

Like you.

Leo didn't say that, but Jennifer knew he was probably thinking it.

"You could have given that officer the lead they were looking for. Could have told him you were on the scene. That's what you meant to do, isn't it?"

"I—I lost my nerve. And also…"

"What?"

"He told me about the charwoman. I suppose because by then the media must have gotten hold of it, so it was no secret. Anyway, that's when I learned she was in a coma. Although, like I said, the hospital expected her to regain consciousness, they couldn't say when. I saw it as a chance to clear myself before she told the police everything, and they ended up believing— Well, I needed something to convince them I was innocent."

"By chasing all the way up here to Warley Castle? Now why do I think that's a little excessive?"

"Okay, so it's a long shot. But when you're desperate, and there seems to be only one hope—"

"What hope?"

"Brother Anthony."

"You think this monk has answers?"

"I don't know. I'm praying he does."

"Why should he?"

"Because Guy told me on the phone that Brother Anthony was relieved to turn the Madonna over to him. He wasn't specific about it, but Guy had the impression he was concerned about its safety."

"Understandable."

"And that its sale might be opposed."

"Less understandable."

"I wanted to know Brother Anthony's reasons for being so worried. And I didn't trust a phone call. He might have refused to speak to me. But if I turned up in person—"

"He'd be willing to give you the answers, if he has them. The ones that are going to clear you. Tell you who could have killed Guy and why. Why hasn't he?"

Jennifer explained about Brother Anthony's vow of silence.

Leo nodded. "Got another question for you," he probed. "A simple one. Why didn't you let the cops interview Brother Anthony?"

"Would they bother after the charwoman talks? Why would they when they'd already have their killer?"

"I don't know, maybe just because they're thorough with their investigations."

Jennifer shook her head. "I can't count on that."

Leo sat back on the chair, the fingertips of his big hands absently tapping the top rail. "You tell a good story, Jenny."

"But?"

"I'm still getting that five when I should be getting a four. All that you've told me so far about the murder scene…see, there isn't enough solid evidence to convince the police you're their likeliest suspect. Got a feeling there's a missing piece. You care to provide it?"

He was perceptive, and he was persistent. Just as the police would be. She knew it would come to this. That she would have to tell him about that missing piece.

"My prints are on the pistol that killed Guy."

His fingers stopped tapping on the chair rail. He leaned forward again, eyes narrowed. "This a confession after all, Jenny? You telling me the gun was in your hand when the char caught you standing over his body?"

"I never touched the pistol that night. But I handled both it and the other pistol before then. My prints must be all over them, unless Guy cleaned them thoroughly when he repaired them, and even then there could be traces of my prints."

"Why would you have handled those guns?"

"Because they belong to me, and sooner or later the police will learn that. And when they do, and assuming the killer left no prints of his own because he was either wearing gloves or wiped the grip clean, then—"

"Whoa. Back up. The guns are *yours?*"

"Yes. The estate auction I told you about where Guy and I met…that's where I bought them."

"Yeah, I remember. I also remember you told me your specialty is English country pieces. How does a pair of dueling pistols qualify?"

"They don't. I bought them as a gift for my father. He collects old firearms himself. But he likes them in working order, and since these weren't…"

"Think I get it. Guy offers to fix the pistols for you, and you hand them over to him."

"That's right. It wasn't just the Warley Madonna I went to see that night. Guy had finished repairing the pistols and was going to return them to me."

"Loaded?"

"He was going to show me how they worked down in his soundproof firing range. Instead of which—" She broke off, shuddering over the memory.

"Yeah," Leo said grimly, "one of them was used to murder my brother."

Did he believe it was she who had seized that pistol from Guy's desk and shot him through the heart? Jennifer wondered. Had she, by telling him everything, made him no longer question the possibility of her guilt but convinced him of it?

She was suddenly far too aware of him as he sat there considering her, arms folded across the rail of the chair. Conscious of how good he looked in that bulky, oatmeal-colored sweater. Of the intriguing, crescent-shaped scar high on his angular cheek. Of his wide, bold mouth and that intense gaze focused on her so tightly, so deeply that she knew he had to be equally aware of her. Aware on a level that couldn't be defined as anything but a risk to both of them.

"And now you're sick with worry," he said in a low, thick voice loaded with sensuality. "Afraid that if you don't find the answers, you'll stand trial for Guy's murder. But, Jenny…"

Getting to his feet, he scraped the chair off to one side, planted his hands on the surface of the table and bent toward her. His face was so close to hers that she could see the way his smoldering gaze dropped, lingering for a few seconds on her mouth before lifting again to meet her eyes, searching them with a breath-robbing intimacy. So close that his warm breath mingled with her own when he spoke again.

"It's still not enough," he went on. "Even with the pistols, it's probably not enough for the police to build a tight case against you."

There was a surprising gentleness in the way he said it. It heartened her, making her think he was no longer her enemy. Until, that is, he added a slow, mocking "Unless you *are* guilty, which could be the actual explanation for your desperation. And if that's true, it makes you one hell of an actress, doesn't it?"

The brief magic of the moment shattered like ice struck with a heavy hammer.

Fool.

That's what she was. A terrible fool for letting him woo her into believing he was on her side now. Well, not again.

Shoving her chair back from the table, from *him,* Jennifer surged to her feet and headed for the connecting door to her room. He didn't try to stop her. He had that much sense anyway. Because in her current mood, if he had tried to prevent her from leaving, she would have been capable of smacking him.

As it was, it cost her an effort not to slam the door behind her when she stormed into her own room. She wasn't going to give him that satisfaction, because she knew, *just* knew, that he would have chuckled over that kind of dramatic exit. But she did make certain that she shut the door firmly behind her.

For a moment, Jennifer stood there, striving to calm herself. When her worst anger had ebbed, she crossed the room to the window where she gazed out at the storm.

The wind continued to wail around the stone walls, like a chorus of voices in a ghostly lament. Even in daylight, there was that kind of eerie quality about the castle. Maybe just because the blizzard left it so isolated.

Still no sign of a letup either.

She watched the snow pelting against the glass and thought about Leo McKenzie. He'd made it clear that he had yet to believe her, hadn't he? Just how serious was his mistrust? Enough to have him go to the abbot about her? If that happened, it could destroy any chance she had of getting the answers she needed.

Jennifer hugged herself, suddenly aware of how cold the room was. The fire had gone out. It was like a freezer in here. Leaving the window, she went to the wardrobe and snagged her coat from the hook inside. She put it on over her sweater and started for the fireplace, intending to build a fresh blaze on the hearth. She never got there.

No.

She wasn't going to stay here in her room and brood about her situation, give Leo the opportunity to sabotage her mission.

She'd had enough of this unnerving delay. She wanted action, results.

More than anything, she wanted what she'd come to this place to learn so that she'd be ready, when there was a break in the storm, to get away from Warley Castle.

Be honest about it.

This wasn't just about proving her innocence. There was also her need to flee from Leo McKenzie and the infuriating effect he had on her senses.

With a renewed urgent purpose, Jennifer left her room and headed along the empty corridor. She didn't care what the abbot had said about not violating Brother Anthony's vow of silence. She intended to find the monk and get him to tell her what he knew.

Chapter Five

All right, so he'd been a jerk.

Hands plunged into the pockets of his jeans, Leo gazed regretfully at the door that Jennifer had closed behind her so emphatically, shutting him out.

Yeah, definitely a jerk. He shouldn't have treated her like that. But he'd been angry with her. Angry because, whether it was intentional or not, she ignited a fire inside him whenever he got anywhere near her. A heat that made him want to take her in his arms and promise her anything in exchange for that full mouth under his, that soft, fragrant body welcoming his hardness.

He didn't like his self-control threatened like that. It never failed to bitterly remind him of Kimberly, his ex-wife, and how she had used her own lush body to get what she wanted. And Leo had always given it to her, hadn't he? Until she'd dumped him for someone who could offer her more.

Kimberly had been a lesson. But maybe not as effective as it should have been, because here he was battling another temptation in the shape of Jennifer Rowan. And what she wanted was to win his support.

Face it, McKenzie. The truth is, you're not as angry with her as you are with yourself for being so damn susceptible to her.

Okay, so maybe he was being unfair. Maybe Jennifer wasn't another Kimberly. Maybe she was— What?

But Leo knew what she was. At least in part. He had already seen and admired her courage and spirit, her need to have him believe in her innocence. That long confession of hers couldn't have been easy.

Better watch it. This isn't smart.

No, because it always came back to Guy, didn't it? Leo couldn't forget his brother and his resolve to catch his killer. Nor could he shake the possibility that Jennifer could have murdered him and stolen the Madonna. As far as he'd been able to determine, anyone else who might have had a motive had a solid alibi, including Guy's wife who'd been at the airport at the time of the murder.

Except…

Yeah, there was something that didn't make sense. If Jennifer was guilty, why come here, of all places? It was an irrational place to hide. Unless everything she had told him *was* the absolute truth.

This was nuts. Standing here seesawing back and forth like this, hardening himself about her in one minute and in the next softening. It was getting him nowhere.

What was he going to do about her? About *them?*

Removing a hand from his pocket, he plowed it through his hair and went on staring at the connecting door.

Maybe it was time for an apology along with a willingness to help her find the answers, even if he did think it was unlikely they were here. But, hell, he was a P.I., wasn't he? He could at least try, for Guy's sake if not hers.

Leo crossed to the door, knocked on it. No answer. She was probably not in any mood for his apologies. He didn't let that stop him. He tried the door, found it unlocked and opened it. There was no sign of her in the room. She was gone, but where?

Warley Castle was a big place. She could be anywhere. To go looking for her didn't make sense. What made sense was to wait here for her until she got back.

That's what Leo told himself. He was still thinking it as he left the room and strode along the corridor in search of her. There was something else he thought about. He had learned from Jennifer why she was so interested in Brother Anthony. What he hadn't learned was an explanation for that earlier business about a ghost. Probably nothing that mattered. It could wait.

WHERE IS EVERYONE? Jennifer wondered.

She had hoped to encounter someone who could direct her to the area of the castle where the brothers were quartered. But she met no one along the corridor.

Confusing though the network of passages was in this vast structure, she was at least confident about the route to the dining parlor. She'd decided by now to make this her first stop. If any of the other guests were there, maybe one of them could tell her how to get where she wanted to go.

She was passing the window embrasure that overlooked the courtyard when she had an idea. Brother Timothy had earlier indicated that the figure exercising in the yard below was Brother Anthony. Cloistered as he was, the monk wouldn't have ventured far from his cell. That had to mean the courtyard was adjacent to the wing occupied by the brothers.

All she had to do, Jennifer decided, was get down to the courtyard and she would have reached her destination. Hopefully.

To that end, she paused at the window in an effort to judge the location of the courtyard in relation to where she stood. She was committing its position to memory when she caught the fleeting movement of a figure down there.

Her glimpse was too brief and the falling snow too thick for any identification, but she didn't think it could be Brother Anthony this time. Possibly one of the other monks then. In any case, he was gone.

Satisfied that she could find her way, Jennifer moved on to the spiral stairway that coiled down to the ground floor. No need to bother now with the dining parlor midway along the flight.

Reaching the bottom, she found herself in a broad, stone-floored gallery that stretched away into the dimness. Her footsteps echoed on the flags as she traveled its length. There were little puffs of cold air that stirred around her. She could swear she actually heard them whispering to her.

Creepy. And silly. Had to be her imagination triggered by the gloom of this place. That and her aloneness. Again she met no one.

There was a closed door down toward the end of the gallery. She could see a hatch in the top of it covered by a grille. Ah, this had to be it! The entrance to the monastery itself!

Now all she had to do was knock on the door and wait for one of the brothers to slide the panel open behind the grille. If she was earnest enough with her appeal, Brother Anthony would be summoned to the hatch. Of course, her plan to convince him how imperative it was that he violate his vow of silence would be far more difficult.

And useless, as it turned out. At least for the moment. She'd been too sure, and too fanciful, because the door wasn't the entrance to the monastery. That was immediately evident when she reached it. A gothic script in faded gold marked it as the infirmary.

And the hatch? Well, maybe just a method for safe communication should a patient, or patients, be contagious and need to be quarantined inside. Or was her imagination at work again?

If this was Brother Timothy's domain, he wasn't here to help her. No one answered her rap on the door.

There was another door on the opposite side of the gallery. The abbot's office, according to the gilt lettering. Jennifer crossed the gallery. The door stood ajar, but when she opened it fully Father Stephen was nowhere in evidence.

Infirmary. Office. Had to mean the refectory, cells and workshops were somewhere close by. How about off the far end of the gallery where it turned a corner?

A few yards along brought her to the corner. When she rounded it, she saw on the left an arched doorway. The heavy, oak door stood wide open. She went and looked inside.

It was the chapel. Hollow and dim, it was almost large enough to qualify as a church. It was also very beautiful. The stonework was incredible. And so were the murals high on the walls. Medieval in character, faded and peeling, they must have been painted long before the brothers came to the castle.

One of the life-sized figures, a tall, lean pilgrim in a religious procession, seemed to gaze down at Jennifer where she stood in the doorway. There was something familiar about his laughing eyes and sardonic smile, something that reminded her of...

An unwanted image chased through her mind. Leo. The good-looking figure faintly resembled Leo. Damn him. Did he have to haunt her even in this peaceful place?

Tearing her eyes away from the painting, she focused on her errand. The chapel was deserted, but it occurred to her that if the brothers had a direct access to it from their cells, which seemed likely, then somewhere in its depth must be what she was looking for.

Before Jennifer could investigate, she became conscious of a current of frigid air. It originated from behind her. Swinging around in the archway, she saw another door on the other side of the gallery. It had drifted open a few inches. Snow was blowing through the crack, evidence that it was a door to the outside. The courtyard?

She watched it for a few seconds as it stirred back and forth. Then, shivering in the cold air, she went to shut it. And didn't. Curiosity demanded a look outside. Pulling the door inward, she gazed into the courtyard she'd anticipated.

Satisfied, she started to retreat. That was when she saw the courtyard was occupied. Sheltered under the far side of the arcade that framed the four sides of the yard was a stone bench. There was a solitary figure seated on it.

It was hard to tell through the swirling snow, but his long robe told her it had to be one of the monks. Even at this distance and seated like that, she had an impression of someone as small and slight as a child. Like Brother Anthony. And if this was Brother Anthony…

Jennifer no longer hesitated. She stepped into the courtyard, not bothering to close the door behind her in her excitement at the prospect of winning an interview at last. Hugging the inner wall in an effort to protect herself from the worst of the wind and snow, she headed along the arcade, her breath smoking in the cold air.

It wasn't until the arcade turned, carrying her to the other side of the yard, that she noticed the bench was positioned to face a simple shrine on the wall. Mounted on a recessed ledge was a stone figure with his hand raised in blessing. One of the saints, she supposed. For all she knew, it was the patron saint of the monastery.

The monk on the bench had his back to her from this angle. Head bowed, hands looking as though they might be folded in his lap in an attitude of concentrated prayer, he never stirred as Jennifer approached. She hated disturbing him at his devotions, but this could be her only chance to speak to him.

"Brother Anthony?"

She expected him to raise his head, turn to her. But he remained motionless on the bench. That was when she remembered Guy mentioning to her that the monk was hard of hearing.

Reaching him, she raised her voice. "Brother Anthony, I know I'm not supposed to bother you, but if I could just have a few words. It's very important."

There was no response. Was he more than just hard of hearing? Deaf perhaps?

Jennifer rounded the bench so that he could see her. When he still failed to lift his face to her, she leaned over him, touching him on the shoulder. His head rolled to one side, the cowl on his robe falling back to expose his tonsured head. Revealing, too, the raw, red welt on his throat. And his bulging eyes locked in a sightless, frozen gaze.

If she gasped or cried out, she wasn't aware of it. She was just barely conscious of backing away from the bench. That was when she realized she was no longer alone in the court-yard with Brother Anthony. Another figure stood there now behind the bench. Leo McKenzie.

She watched him bend over the monk, silently examine him without touching him. When he came erect again, his eyes sought hers. For a few, terrible seconds there was no other reality, just Leo's hard gaze pinned on her.

JENNIFER HUDDLED in one of the pews inside the chapel where Leo had left her. Presumably, he had gone off to play private investigator after seeing her settled here. But she wasn't certain of that. She was still so numb that she barely remembered anything that had happened since her gruesome discovery.

Something had gone very wrong with her world. First Guy, now Brother Anthony.

As the worst of her shock eased, Jennifer recalled she wasn't alone in the chapel. One of the other monks sat just across the aisle from her. She could hear him softly praying. For the soul of Brother Anthony?

She dimly recalled the monk solemnly telling her that Father Stephen and Brother Timothy were being summoned. He had said nothing else to her. Except for one brief thing. That Leo had taken him aside and asked him to stay here with her until he returned. That she wasn't to be left on her own.

Jennifer didn't want to question the explanation for Leo's request to the startled monk they had encountered in the gallery after leaving the courtyard. She was afraid of the answer.

Seeking some image of comfort, she looked up at the murals on the walls. Her gaze went almost automatically to the tall, lean pilgrim who reminded her of Leo. But his eyes were no longer laughing down at her. They seemed instead to be hot with accusation. Like Leo's eyes burning into hers out in the courtyard. There was no comfort here.

Quickly lowering her gaze, she turned her head and stared instead at an intricately carved stone pedestal. It supported a fluted stoup for the holy water. Both the pedestal and the basin were very old. Handsome pieces that should have been a safe subject for her attention. They weren't.

Jennifer kept seeing Brother Anthony's contorted features stricken with horror. Kept remembering how the killer must have afterward arranged his hands in his lap in that attitude of prayer. It was an obscene thing to have done, hideously irreverent.

The uninterrupted sound of the monk across the aisle droning his prayers was getting on her nerves. That and this endless waiting. Fully recovered now from her shock, angry with the wickedness of Brother Anthony's death, she wanted answers. Determined to get them, she started to rise to her feet.

It was in that moment that Leo strode back into the chapel. She slid over, making room for him as he joined her in the pew. Turning on the seat to face him, she saw that he looked tired, as if he had just survived an unpleasant ordeal. She didn't let that stop her from demanding an explanation. Hadn't she suffered her own ordeal?

"Where have you been? What's happening?"

"I was helping the abbot and Brother Timothy deal with Brother Anthony."

"Father Stephen identified him? It is Brother Anthony for certain?"

"No question of it."

"It didn't seem possible it could be anyone else. But having never met him, I could have been wrong. I don't suppose there's any chance that he's still…"

Jennifer couldn't bring herself to say it. Not that she had to. Leo understood what she was asking.

"No, he's dead all right."

"How?"

"Garroted."

She couldn't stop herself from thinking about it. The monk's bulging eyes and twisted features, his open mouth gasping for air, the angry welt on his throat where whatever instrument that was used had bit into his flesh. Yes, they were all clear evidence of strangulation. Jennifer shuddered over the cruelty of it.

"I looked around for the weapon, the cord or whatever," Leo said. "There was no sign of it. No footprints either. The blowing snow would have covered them."

"You disturbed a crime scene?"

"What would you have had me do? Hell, with the weather being what it is, the police might not be able to get up here for days, and by then there'd be nothing to see. Better I should check it out while it's still fresh, even if there wasn't anything to find."

She could understand the wisdom of that. "And Brother Anthony…"

"Crime scene or not, the abbot refused to leave him there like that. We carried the body into the infirmary where Brother Timothy examined him. Any burial will have to wait."

There was a silence in the chapel. The monk across the aisle was no longer chanting his prayers. He must have stopped to listen to their exchange. Leo turned to speak to him.

"Thanks, Brother. I'll stay with her now."

The monk nodded and slipped out of the other pew. Jennifer

watched him disappear through a door at the side of the chapel. That had to be what she'd been searching for earlier, she decided. The way into the cloistered part of the monastery.

"He was guarding me, wasn't he?" she asked Leo. "You left him here to make sure I didn't get away."

"That'd be a good assumption. If it made any sense."

"Do you suppose it hasn't occurred to me what you've been thinking since you found me there with Brother Anthony in the courtyard?"

"No. Why don't you tell me."

"That I could have murdered Brother Anthony, just as I could have murdered Guy. That what I told you back in your room, about my reason for coming here, was wildly improbable." She knew her voice, too, became a little wild as she rushed on, unable to stop herself. "That my actual reason for being here was to silence Brother Anthony. Because I was afraid he knew something that would convince the police I had killed Guy."

"All that, huh?"

"It's true, isn't it? You had to think it when I was standing there over his body, just as the charwoman discovered me standing over Guy's body."

Out of breath now, she gazed at him, her insides churning as she waited for his reaction. He took his time in providing a response.

"Yeah," he said gruffly, "you could have wanted to kill Brother Anthony. Only you didn't."

"How can you be sure of that?"

"What are you trying to do, Jenny? Convict yourself? I'm sure because you left the door to the courtyard open, which is how I managed to find you. No killer intending to murder his victim would have been careless like that. I'm sure because I was inside the courtyard and saw you when you approached Brother Anthony. And I'm sure because you didn't have any weapon in your hands or a chance to hide one by the time I reached you. Is that enough, or do you need more?"

It was a relief that Leo didn't think she had murdered Brother Anthony. More than a relief. That he was on her side, at least where this situation was concerned, had her feeling all warm and weak. And that was dangerous.

Needing to hide her vulnerability, she murmured quickly, "All right, I was wrong. Then why did you have the monk stay close to me?"

"Because leaving you all alone with a killer on the loose would have been a risk I didn't want to take."

Leo McKenzie was protecting her? She had trouble believing it, and yet…

There went that treacherous warmth again, not just deep inside her this time but flowing out through her limbs. It was accompanied by an awareness of his big, solid body squeezed close against her. Before her senses went out of control with his nearness, she edged away from him.

"What happens now?" she asked him, forcing her thoughts in a safer direction.

"The abbot wants to meet with us in his office. He'll send for us as soon as he's free."

Leo didn't say, but she guessed that Father Stephen must be busy now making arrangements for Brother Anthony. Some kind of service maybe. And when he'd dealt with that…then, yes, he would have questions for Leo and her. Things he had the right to know. Until then, they had to wait.

Not easy to wait with Leo here at her side. With her mind in a turmoil of possibilities. She needed to express those possibilities.

"Brother Anthony," she said, hoarseness in her voice. "Why was he murdered?"

"You tell me."

"I don't know. Unless…"

"Go on."

"What if it was because he knew something that was dangerous to his killer? Something maybe connected with his uneasiness about the safety of the Warley Madonna."

"That same mysterious something Guy told you about, huh? The thing that brought you here to Warley Castle."

"More than that. Brother Anthony could have suspected who Guy's killer is, just like I was hoping he might. And if he did, and the murderer realized this…"

"He'd want to make sure Brother Anthony kept his vow of silence forever. If you're right, that means Guy's killer is here in the castle."

It was a chilling thought, something that hadn't occurred to her until now. And it brought another sudden realization. One that had her hopes sinking into a state of despair.

"I'll never learn now what Brother Anthony was so troubled about! He took that with him when he died! He can't help me clear myself!"

Jennifer must have sounded as desperate as she felt. It seemed to worry Leo, arousing a kind of tenderness she wouldn't have believed him capable of. He reached for her hands, his strong fingers closing around them. She should have immediately withdrawn her hands. She didn't.

"You're not going to go hysterical on me now, are you?" he asked her softly. Before she had a chance to assure him she had no intention of hysterics, he went on rapidly, "Because if you are, I have a remedy for that."

"You don't need to use it."

Those lethal eyes of his searched her face. They seemed to darken, smoldering with something she was afraid to define. Something that suddenly deprived her of oxygen. She was still much too close to him, but she couldn't seem to move.

"Oh, yeah," he said slowly, his voice deepening to a sensual huskiness, "I think maybe I do."

Carrying her hands to his mouth, he began to demonstrate

that remedy, nibbling on her fingers, placing kisses in each of her palms.

This is the time to stop him. Now before it's too late.

But Jennifer found she had lost the will to do anything but submit to his attentions. No, that wasn't true. Because when he released her hands in order to slide his arms around her waist, she did more than just comply. She leaned into him, becoming an active participant in his embrace. Betraying her eagerness for what they both wanted. *Needed.*

Drawing her tightly against him, a growl low in his throat, Leo angled his mouth across hers. His kiss was deep, demanding. Infused with the flavors of him, his clean, masculine scent, the taste of his wet tongue on hers.

Jennifer's senses rioted on her. Threatened to go out of control. And might have, if there hadn't been the deliberate sound of someone clearing his throat behind them, making them aware they were no longer alone.

Pulling away from Leo, she twisted around on the seat to find Brother Timothy framed in the doorway of the chapel. She felt her cheeks flaming with guilt, wondered if her mouth was swollen with the evidence of Leo's hot kisses. What must the monk think to find them locked together like that in a holy place?

She glanced at Leo. No sign of embarrassment there, damn him. If anything, he was amused.

"Friar?"

"Father's ready now for the two of you, laddie."

They left the pew and joined the monk where he waited for them in the doorway. This was a different Brother Timothy, Jennifer realized. A sober one. She understood. It couldn't be easy losing one of your own. Not in that way certainly. Murder.

Chapter Six

The abbot's office wasn't what Jennifer expected. There was no evidence of pious images, only a prie-dieu facing a simple cross. The walls were a stark white, the floor bare. The compact room might have qualified as austere had it not been for the clutter. Books and papers were everywhere.

The gaunt figure of Father Stephen rose from behind his desk at their entrance. Jennifer remembered his visit to her room last night and how she'd noticed the cheerful blue eyes in that narrow, holy face. The eyes suited these surroundings. Except they weren't cheerful this morning. They were very grave.

"I regret that I kept you waiting," he apologized, "but I'm sure you understand that in the circumstances…"

He didn't finish. It wasn't necessary. She knew this had to be a very difficult time for him.

He indicated a pair of comfortable-looking chairs. Jennifer was careful not to look at Leo as they seated themselves. She didn't want to be reminded of those reckless moments in the chapel. How he had devoured her mouth with his own, his hardness strained against her while she had clutched at him in a mindless daze.

His kiss had left her deeply confused, and right now she needed a clear head.

Father Stephen brought his own chair from behind his desk and settled in it, facing them. This was not to be a formal meeting then. Exactly what it would be she refused to guess. Maybe because she feared the outcome.

"Mr. McKenzie has given me the essentials," the abbot began. "How he followed you into the courtyard and how the two of you found Brother Anthony dead. What I have yet to learn, Miss Rowan, is why you went to the courtyard."

He fixed his gaze on Jennifer, his eyes reproachful.

He knows already, she thought. He's too intelligent not to have realized why I was there. He just wants to hear me admit it.

She could no longer avoid the truth. She would have to tell him everything.

"I know you asked me not to try to approach Brother Anthony while he was under his vow of silence. I'm sorry I disobeyed you, Father, but it was urgent that I speak to him. I'm in a lot of trouble, and I need—*needed* his help."

Hands steepled in her lap, she gave him the whole story from the beginning, the same one she had shared with Leo back in his room. Leo didn't contribute to her tale. Neither man said anything until she was finished. Then the abbot looked perceptively at Leo.

"And you, Mr. McKenzie? It wasn't just by chance that you were on the road last night, was it?"

"Afraid not, Father. Brother Anthony's friend, the man who was murdered in London, was my half brother. Guess you can figure out why I was tailing Ms. Rowan."

The abbot was silent, but Jennifer could tell by the severity of his expression how displeased he was that they'd misrepresented themselves.

"Do I have the whole truth now?" he finally asked them.

"As much as we know of it," Leo said.

From the glance Leo slid in her direction, Jennifer wondered if what he really wanted to say was: "As much as *I* know of it. I'm not sure about her yet."

She made no issue of it, though. There was something else she wanted to pursue. "The Madonna, Father," she asked him, leaning earnestly forward in her chair. "Did you know it was missing before I told you that part of my story?" She thought he must have heard about it because he hadn't expressed any alarm when she'd mentioned the theft.

"I did, yes," he said. "Brother Anthony learned of it when the call came from London informing him of his friend's death. It was a great blow to us."

"A big loss, huh?" Leo said.

The abbot nodded solemnly. "So serious that—" He hesitated, looking uncertain. Then he must have decided there was no reason why they shouldn't know. "I was meeting with my prior to discuss what we should do about it when you arrived yesterday evening."

And that, Jennifer realized, was what he must have meant about being occupied with "other matters" when he brought the supper tray to her room last night. His delay in welcoming her had had nothing to do with the other guests.

"Not," Father Stephen went on, "that there is anything we *can* do. We're a poor order, I'm afraid. Our only wealth is the castle and the Madonna. Now half of that wealth is gone and at a very critical time."

"Critical in what way, Father?" Jennifer wanted to know.

"We need repairs. The roofs alone are in a bad way and want replacing. Much as we hated parting with the Madonna, its sale would have provided essential funds."

"Wasn't the Madonna insured?"

The abbot shook his head. "Nothing like its value. Insurance at that level is very costly."

"So," Leo said, "the recovery of the Madonna would be pretty important to you, wouldn't it?"

His tone was too casual, Jennifer thought. *Deceptively* casual. Father Stephen must have thought the same thing, because he regarded Leo suspiciously.

"It would mean everything. What are you trying to tell me, Mr. McKenzie?"

"That it's possible, *just* possible, a solution to Brother Anthony's death could mean a recovery of the Madonna."

The abbot waved his hand in a gesture of dismissal. "*How* is that possible when it was stolen in London?"

"Because there's a connection with what happened in London to what happened here. Too much of a coincidence otherwise."

Leo went on to explain how he believed that Guy's killer may have murdered Brother Anthony because he feared the monk's knowledge.

"If that's true, Mr. McKenzie, it would mean your brother's killer is here at Warley."

"Looks like it. I want my brother's killer, Father, and you want the Madonna. And since that killer must have taken the Madonna from Guy's office…" Leo sat back in his chair, stretching his long legs out in front of him, crossing them negligently at the ankles. "Let me try to solve Brother Anthony's death, and maybe we'll both get what we want."

"This is the business of the police, Mr. McKenzie."

"When? Maybe days from now? Losing time in a case can cost you the answers."

"You have a point, but you're hardly qualified to—"

"Investigate a murder? That would be true if I were an amateur. I'm not. Turns out, Father, that what I am is an experienced professional. Don't believe me?"

Leo reached around behind him, pulling a small folder out of one of the back pockets of his jeans. Flipping it open, he handed it to Father Stephen. The abbot gazed down at it in silent bemusement.

Jennifer knew it must be Leo's private investigator license, something Brother Timothy seemed to have overlooked when he'd undressed his patient last night. Leo's passport and driver's license had apparently been enough to satisfy the monk. But not Jennifer, which is why she had discovered the business cards when she'd searched Leo's wallet this morning. She hadn't found the ID folder, however.

"Of course," Leo said, taking the folder the abbot returned to him and tucking it back into his pocket, "I'm not authorized to operate here in the United Kingdom, but under the circumstances…"

Father Stephen shook his head, undecided. "I don't know. That this should be happening, any of it, *all* of it, is…" He spread his hands in a gesture of helplessness.

Jennifer felt sorry for him. She knew he had to be struggling to come to terms with something that was totally alien in his isolated world. In the end, though, the chance to recover the precious Madonna, together with bringing Brother Anthony's killer to justice, was a temptation he plainly couldn't resist.

"Very well, Mr. McKenzie, in lieu of the police, I accept your offer. You may take charge of the investigation."

"Beginning where, how?" Jennifer wondered.

"By eliminating suspects. Let's start with the brothers."

The abbot shook his head emphatically. "Impossible."

"Men of God have killed before, Father," Leo said bluntly.

"I'm not so unworldly, Mr. McKenzie, that I fail to realize that. I say *impossible* because all of the brothers except Anthony were in the workshops at the time of the murder. I can guarantee this because I was there with them. Only Brother Michael left the scene in order to fetch something for Brother Timothy from the infirmary. Indigestion pills, I believe. He was on his way to the infirmary when you met him in the gallery."

"Yeah, well, the brothers weren't very likely candidates anyway, especially if it does turn out that whoever killed Guy also killed Brother Anthony. *All,* Father? You sure that all of the order was there in the workshops?"

"Yes, everyone." The abbot paused, frowning in consideration before adding, "With the exception of Gregory and Patrick. I'm not absolutely certain where they were."

Gregory was the novice, Jennifer remembered. And Patrick was? Yes, the other young man who wanted to join the order.

"Looks like that leaves us with either one of them or one of the guests," Leo said. "Gonna be fun trying to learn where they all were at the time of the murder. But there's something else…"

Whatever it was, Jennifer's attention was diverted from it. She'd been seized by a sudden recollection. A fleeting image she'd forgotten about in all the horror that had followed. A thing that had seemed at the time in no way important. But now…

She must have vocalized her realization, made some kind of startled sound, because she became aware that the two men had stopped talking and were looking at her.

"What is it?" Leo asked.

"Something I forgot about until just now. I think I may have seen Brother Anthony's killer."

"You *what?*"

Jennifer explained how, on her way to the ground floor, she had stopped at the window overlooking the courtyard to get her bearings. "There was someone down there. I had only a fast glimpse of him crossing the yard before he moved back under the arcade out of sight. Or it could have been her. The snow was too thick for me to tell."

"But surely," Father Stephen said, "it was Brother Anthony himself you saw."

Jennifer shook her head. "I don't think it could have been Brother Anthony."

"Why?" Leo asked.

"I'm not sure. It was just… I don't know, an impression I had. Sort of like the thing I get when an antique isn't right."

"*Think,* Jenny. Was it size, shape? Maybe clothing?"

Tapping her finger against her lips, she made an effort to bring the elusive image into focus. Nothing. "It's no use. I can't say who it was."

"Some little detail," Leo pressed her. "Anything."

"I just don't know. It was all too quick, and there was the snow."

Frustrating. She could have actually seen the murderer. Chilling thought. But it was of no value. Whoever it was, he remained a phantom figure.

"I'm sorry."

"Okay," Leo said, "maybe something more will come back to you. Maybe it won't. But for now…"

"Something else," Jennifer reminded him. "You were starting to tell us about something else when I interrupted."

"That I want to do, yeah."

"And that would be?" the abbot wanted to know.

"I want to search the rooms of the other guests. All right, Father, I can see how much you don't like that idea, but I think it's necessary. Never know what could turn up." Leo swung unexpectedly in her direction. "You agree this is something you and I have to do?"

For a moment Jennifer was too surprised to respond. Then, with disbelief, she asked him softly, "You want me to work with you?"

"We both have an investment in this whole thing, Jenny."

The intense way he said it, the way he looked at her… had her remembering again the searing kiss they had shared in the chapel. She also remembered his earlier distrust. Why? Why did he want to keep her close to him? To protect her? Or to watch her?

What did it matter? He was right. She still had a need to prove her innocence. And if that meant being thrown together to achieve it, making a bargain with a man capable of both firing her senses and destroying her…

"All right," she said, recklessly accepting his challenge, "I'll help you search those rooms. Just one little thing. How do we manage to go through them without the occupants finding us there?"

"Perhaps…" the abbot started to say, then hesitated before overcoming what had to be reluctance to participate in their intention. "Perhaps," he continued, "I can provide a solution to that risk."

Leo looked at him expectantly. "Father?"

"I'm conducting a memorial service for Brother Anthony in the chapel this afternoon. The entire order will attend. I'm sure that if I urge it, all of our guests will join us there."

"Leaving Jenny and me free to search their belongings. It's a plan, Father."

"Uh, there's a little problem here," Jennifer said dryly. "You and I are also guests. The others are going to think it funny if we're not in the chapel with them."

"I think," Leo said after briefly considering the problem, "that I'm about to have another relapse like the one I had at breakfast. Say, just after lunch?"

"And, naturally—"

"You'll volunteer again to stay with me."

"Because you can't be left alone in that state."

"Not when I could take a turn for the worse."

The man was devious, Jennifer thought. Willing to do whatever it took to get results. She had further evidence of that when, everything settled, the three of them got to their feet. Leo had one last request for the abbot before they left the office.

"For now, Father, I'm going to ask that we keep my P.I. identity to ourselves. I want to be on the inside, able to freely observe these people. But if they learn I'm an investigator…" He shrugged. "Well, they could close ranks, leaving me outside. I've seen it happen before."

The abbot agreed.

Devious. Jennifer was still thinking that about Leo on the way back to their rooms. It was why, when they got to her door, she turned on him decisively. "Let's get something straight."

"Yeah?"

He leaned toward her, arms stretched out on either side of her, hands planted on the stone surround so that she was trapped against the closed door. Daunting, but she didn't let it stop her.

"You don't fool me. We both know that, even if I didn't kill Brother Anthony, you're still not certain I didn't kill Guy."

"And?"

"We don't trust each other."

"Then why are you working with me?"

Why? Because she had no other choice. Trying to operate on her own made no sense when she could benefit from Leo's experience as a private investigator. But she knew theirs was an uneasy alliance made more difficult by the sexual tension that thrummed between them like a high-voltage wire. As dangerous as the intoxicating nearness of his hard body that had her pinned against the door. And that kiss in the chapel...

"You're the smart detective. You figure it out. I'll see you at lunch."

Abruptly swinging around, she went into her room, closing the door in his face.

DAMN!

Leo went on standing there in the corridor, staring at the door she had so firmly closed, shutting him out. Only he wasn't seeing the door. He was seeing Jennifer in that pair of dark woolen slacks that hugged her hips so provocatively and the burgundy-colored sweater stretched over the swell of her breasts. Seeing, too, the silky, mahogany-colored hair she'd brushed impatiently back from her cheeks, along with the fire in those jade-green eyes when she'd laid into him.

Nor could he shake the memory of that wanton kiss in the chapel and how he'd wanted it to be much more than a kiss.

What the hell was he doing? He should be grieving for his brother, not lusting after the woman Guy had been in love with. And whose innocence, just as she'd said, he had yet to totally accept.

She resented him, of course. That was what her anger just now had been all about. She resented him because she needed him, and she didn't want to need him. And *he* didn't want to lose his head over her, but he was beginning to fear it might already be too late for that.

"THAT QUESTION YOU HAD for Brother Timothy this morning," Leo probed. "About Warley being haunted. Care to explain that?"

He *would* go and remember that, Jennifer thought. Maybe because they were on their way to lunch in the dining parlor, and it was along about here that she'd mentioned the subject to Brother Timothy. This could have reminded Leo of her interest in a ghost. Or maybe it was just because the man had a mind like a trap and forgot nothing.

Either way, Jennifer regretted that she'd ever asked the question. Her encounter with a possible ghost late last night seemed absolutely silly now. An unreal experience she didn't want to discuss.

"There's nothing to explain. I'm into old things, remember. Castles are old things, and in England that usually means legends about ghosts."

"And that's all it was?"

"That's all."

She was grateful he didn't pursue it, although the way he turned his head and gazed at her made her wonder if he was dissatisfied with her response. Maybe even suspicious.

In any case, they both had something else that claimed their attention. They were starting down the spiral stairway when they heard what sounded like a quarrel in progress on the landing below them.

"We have a right to know!" A woman's voice, high with emotion.

Leo put his hand on Jennifer's arm, checking her descent. She knew what he intended, only it seemed wrong to her to hang back like this in order to eavesdrop on what was obviously a private conversation. But if this was in any way connected with what was happening here at Warley Castle…

"Why won't you tell us? Why do you insist on keeping it from us?" A man's voice this time, intense, insistent.

Jennifer didn't know enough about the other guests to recognize these voices. She strained to hear the reply from whomever they were addressing, but it was too low, no more than an indistinguishable murmur drifting up to them.

"This is bloody unacceptable, and I won't stand for it!" The man's voice again.

Leo must have been as eager as Jennifer was to identify the speakers, because he motioned for her to continue their descent. If they could creep down just far enough to glimpse the trio without being caught…

"Please, if we could only hear how it was for him at the end, it would mean everything. You must see that." The woman pleaded.

Jennifer and Leo edged around a turn in the coiling flight.

"I warn you," the man said, "if you won't give us what we want, then—" He broke off abruptly.

As careful as Jennifer and Leo had been to approach the landing without a sound, one of them must have scraped his foot against the rough stone of a tread. Alerted by the noise, realizing they were no longer alone, the trio below them went silent.

No point now in concealing ourselves, Jennifer thought.

Leo obviously agreed with her because he took her arm and

hurried her on down to the landing before the three people standing there could slip away out of sight.

Rounding the last turn, they came face to face with Fiona and Alfred Brasher. Jennifer remembered them from breakfast. The timid couple. Except there had been nothing timid about their quarrel with the young man with the spotty face hovering by the closed door to the dining parlor. His name escaped Jennifer for a second, and then she recalled it. Patrick, who was visiting the monastery because he wanted to join the order. Or so he'd claimed.

"Hello, folks," Leo greeted them casually, just as though he and Jennifer hadn't heard a word of their conversation.

It was impossible to tell whether they either resented their arrival on the scene or were embarrassed by it. They stared at Jennifer and Leo with wooden expressions on their faces. Then, with no more than nods of acknowledgment, at least from Alfred Brasher and his wife, the three of them turned and passed through the stone archway into the dining parlor, leaving the door ajar behind them.

Left alone on the landing, Leo turned to Jennifer. "And wouldn't I love to know what that was all about," he said softly.

"Something that the Brashers felt they were entitled to know from Patrick and which he refused to tell them. That much was plain anyway."

"Uh-huh. Remember what the Brashers said at breakfast. About being travelers caught on the road and having to take shelter here. Makes you wonder, doesn't it?"

"That it isn't just by chance they're here, you're saying."

"They seem to know Patrick, don't they?"

"Which means Warley could have been their destination and not somewhere on the coast, as they said. Do you think any of this might be connected with—"

"Two murders and a theft? Let's not go there until we know more. Lunch," Leo reminded her.

Jennifer felt it the moment they entered the dining parlor. The climate of anxious stress, like a noxious gas hanging in the air. Unlike the faint undercurrents among the group at breakfast, this was something strong and definite. Decidedly unpleasant. And this time it couldn't be blamed on the weather.

They *know,* she thought. They know Brother Anthony was murdered in the courtyard. It wasn't surprising. The word must have traveled through the castle like a fire of control.

All of them were here in the room, she noticed. The Brashers and the young Patrick. The novice, Geoffrey, with his fair hair and pale, melancholy face. The traveling salesman, Harry Ireland. The elegant, brittle Sybil Harding. And her husband, Roger, who'd once been a monk here and had returned on retreat.

Were any of them just what they appeared to be? Or did they all have secrets? If Leo was right, *one* of them certainly had a horrific secret.

Geoffrey spoke to them when she and Leo arrived at the sideboard. "It's like breakfast. We serve ourselves from the buffet."

Just that. A brief instruction. Then, taking his plate, he joined the others, who were already seated at the long table.

Jennifer watched Leo suspiciously eye one of the dishes on the sideboard. "Smoked eel," she informed him. "An English treat."

"I bet it's real tasty." But he passed it by, helping himself instead to cold salmon and peas.

Their plates filled, they found places at the end of the table. There was very little conversation in the group. Understandable, considering this morning's tragedy. Nor did any of them seem to have much of an appetite either, including Jennifer herself. Harry Ireland was the only exception, eating his meal with gusto.

Jennifer was aware of Leo at her side stealing glances around the table between bites. She knew he was watching the company, hoping for any scraps of enlightenment. She, too, tried to be observant. Not that there was much of anything to see.

Geoffrey had settled next to Patrick, but there was no exchange of conversation. The young men weren't on friendly terms. Maybe just because the novice resented having to be responsible for the glum Patrick. Was Patrick unhappy because of this, she wondered? Or was it because of his unexplained issue with the Brashers?

Jennifer's attention shifted to Fiona and Alfred, who were seated farther along the table. They picked at their food with disinterest, seldom looking up from their plates. Nothing to be learned there.

Nor were the Hardings of much interest. Sybil toyed with her potato mash while Roger pulled at his mustache. The lines in his face seemed to have deepened since breakfast. As a former member of the monastery, he must be especially feeling Brother Anthony's loss.

It was the balding Harry Ireland who finally broke the uneasy silence. The salesman leaned toward Leo with a hearty "Feeling better then, are we, old man?"

"For now. It comes and goes," Leo said, laying the foundation for another relapse.

"But isn't it convenient," Sybil cooed, with an eager smile for him that turned sweetly spiteful when she looked at Jennifer, "that you seem to have acquired a nurse capable of caring for you?"

Her husband's face flamed with embarrassment. "Sybil, don't."

"Oh, Roger, don't be so tiresome."

Pushing her plate aside, she leaned down to recover a handsome alligator bag from the floor. Opening the bag, she produced a gold lighter and a packet of cigarettes.

"Darling, you know you can't smoke in here."

"I don't see that it matters, what with that fireplace over there smoking like a dragon. They're all in the castle like that."

And we wouldn't survive without them, Jennifer thought. It was bad enough in the unheated areas of the castle where the temperatures couldn't be much above freezing. At least the fireplaces, wherever they occurred, provided an adequate warmth. And there seemed to be no shortage of peat to burn. The baskets were kept filled, just as food appeared magically on the sideboard. It wasn't magic, of course. The brothers were conscientiously, if not visibly, taking care of their guests.

The unpleasant Sybil Harding should have been grateful for that, but at least she had the courtesy to shove the cigarettes and lighter back into her bag.

"Why wouldn't I be nervous," she complained, "when we're caught here like this with a murderer loose in the place? And it could be one of us."

"Sybil, no, you mustn't—"

"Dear heart, I don't see why I mustn't. It's what we're all thinking, isn't it?"

There was a tense stillness at the table. It lasted for a few seconds, ending when Fiona Brasher dropped her fork. The fork clattered loudly against her plate. Eyes wide with shock, she gazed at all the faces around her.

"That can't be! It just *can't* be! It—it's a wicked thing to suggest!"

"Oh, come now, sweetie, you can't be so innocent that it hasn't occurred to you one of us has been very naughty."

Fiona's husband loudly voiced his indignation. "My wife and I have nothing to do with this sad affair, Mrs. Harding!"

The salesman leaned toward Alfred Brasher. "That's what we're all claiming, old man. At least I imagine we are."

"What's that supposed to mean?"

"Just that *someone* had it in for the old padre, what."

"But not one of us!" Fiona cried. "Tell them, Alf, that it couldn't be one of us!"

"Why not?" Harry Ireland insisted. "When it comes down to it, do any of us have a decent alibi?" There was a taut silence again. The salesman chuckled. "Well, there you are."

"One of the monks!" Fiona said, clearly desperate to rid

herself of the fear that someone in this room could have killed Brother Anthony. "It had to be one of the monks!"

Geoffrey spoke up in their defense. "That's not possible. They were all accounted for at the time of the murder."

Jennifer had been quiet during this emotional exchange, knowing that like Leo beside her it could be far more informative to listen than to contribute. She would have gone on being just that if Sybil hadn't pounced on her.

"Is it true that it was you who found the monk?"

Jennifer's reply was a cautious "Yes."

"But whatever were you doing in the courtyard?"

"Just—getting some exercise."

"Really? In a snowstorm? One wonders what form of exercise that could have been."

That tears it, Jennifer thought. She'd had enough of Sybil Harding's nasty innuendos, which probably had as much to do with the woman's obvious attraction to Leo as it did with her bitchy character.

"I hope you're not implying I could have had something to do with Brother Anthony's death, Mrs. Harding," she began softly. "Because if you are—"

But Leo, who was familiar by now with the slow, measured speech that signaled she was about to launch an attack of her own, cut her off quickly. "I'm feeling a little rotten again. Think I need to get back to my bed. Sorry, folks."

Shoving back from the table, he got to his feet. "Coming?" He looked down at Jennifer with a pathetic little smile meant to communicate to the others that he couldn't possibly make it back to his room without her support. Considering the man looked as fit as an athlete in peak condition, this had to be a lot to swallow.

But he was right, Jennifer thought, coming to her feet. There was nothing to be gained by getting into a battle with Sybil Harding. And probably nothing more to learn by staying here listening to a conversation that had deteriorated into a lot of pointless squabbling.

They were still at it, arguing and accusing, when she and Leo left the dining parlor.

Leo expressed his disgust on the way back to their rooms. "What a bunch. Everything but a food fight."

And one of them *is* a murderer, Jennifer remembered. What other explanation could there be?

Chapter Seven

It was hard to believe that through all the thickness of walls and doors, Jennifer could hear the distant bell. But its slow, mournful tolling seemed to echo down the countless passages, penetrating the farthest reaches of the castle.

The bell was a summons, calling monks and guests alike to the chapel where Father Stephen would perform the memorial service for Brother Anthony.

Jennifer found it an unnerving, ghostly sound, not just because of its connection with murder but because it was a signal for the search she and Leo were about to conduct. She was uneasy about that as she perched rigidly on the edge of her bed, waiting for Leo to come and collect her. Anything could go wrong.

To her relief, the bell finally stopped pealing. There was nothing now but the muffled wail of the wind buffeting the ancient, outer walls.

Where is he?

Maybe something had already gone wrong. She resisted the temptation to go and look for him. Leo had asked her to be patient, but if he didn't come soon…

Restless, she left the bed and went to the window. The storm was still in progress. Would it never let up?

She stood there at the glass for what seemed like forever,

watching the snow. Outside was all that fury, but in here there was nothing but stillness. It felt ominous.

He was taking too long. She'd had enough of this vigil. Turning away from the window, she was prepared to go after him. There was no need. A knock sounded on the connecting door. Before she could tell him to come in, his head poked around the door.

"Ready?"

"I've been ready since lunch. Where have you been? I thought you were never coming."

"Had to give them all enough time to leave their rooms and get down to the chapel. Let's go."

Now he was in a hurry? The man was maddening.

Jennifer followed him out into the corridor, trying to keep up with his long-legged gait.

"Uh, mind filling me in? I know we're supposed to be on the way to their rooms, but just how do we find those rooms and how do we know who's occupying what when we get there?"

"Got it all here." Extracting a slip of paper from the pocket of his jeans, he came to a stop and waved it under her nose. From what she could tell, it was a hastily sketched map.

"Where did you get it?"

"From Father Stephen down in his office."

"And that's where you went after you left me. I don't suppose it occurred to you that you were supposed to be in your room having a relapse. What if you'd run into one of the others?"

"But I didn't. I was careful. We go this way."

He led them along the passage in the direction away from the route to the spiral stairway. Jennifer had realized the other guests weren't quartered in the vicinity of the rooms she and Leo occupied, or she would have been aware of their coming and going.

But she hadn't known, until Leo conducted her along a series of turning corridors, that they were lodged in another wing entirely.

They passed a flight of stairs to the lower level. Not a spiral stairway this time. Something that was broad and direct in its descent. Jennifer had a fuzzy memory of being led up this stairway from the front door on the night of her arrival. Or one like it.

They moved on.

"Where are we now?" she asked.

"Opposite side of the castle. Almost there."

"Leo?"

"Yeah?"

"What if one of them didn't go to the service? What if he's in his room and challenges us?"

"Relax. Father Stephen said he'd manage to get word to me if any of them didn't show, which was also what I was waiting for. But he didn't, and you worry too much."

"Can't help it. Stuff like this reminds me of a game called Spooks that we played as kids on our block. I always hated it when the spooks jumped out at you with these bloodcurdling screams."

"Wouldn't have thought your neighborhood was into that kind of thing."

Jennifer came to a stop. "What's that supposed to mean?"

Aware that she was no longer on his heels, Leo turned to face her. "You know, Boston. Old money."

"Where did you ever get the idea that I came from the Beacon Hill crowd? Or anything like that?"

"Just an impression I got. Maybe because of all those expensive antiques you acquire."

"Wrong impression, detective. I grew up in a middle-class neighborhood in West Roxbury, and the only old money my family ever heard about belonged to a few clients my dad handled as an insurance agent."

"Okay."

"And while we're comparing histories—"

"I didn't know we were."

"I suppose you'll tell me you grew up on the mean streets of—where?"

"Philadelphia."

"Well, there you are. Both places have a reputation for old money. But Philadelphia doesn't have to mean the Main Line, anymore than Boston—"

"Actually…"

Jennifer stared at him. "Are you telling me that you *do* come from the Main Line?"

"Not that close, but not bad. My old man was a criminal lawyer. Made plenty of money. Lost most of it, too, in poor investments."

"So how did his son end up as a P.I.?"

"The old man had this detective agency he used on some of his cases. I got interested in them, and they got interested in me. It's where I trained." Leo glanced at his watch. "Now if we're through trading backgrounds, maybe we can get on with it before those spooks you're worried about start getting restless in the chapel and wind up back here."

Leo swung around and headed along the corridor again.

Philadelphia, huh? Jennifer thought, hurrying to catch up with him. Not the tough streets either. But he must have acquired that scar he carried on his cheek somewhere. And what about the tattoo of a salamander she had noticed when he'd accosted her last night?

Okay, be honest with yourself.

Neither the scar nor the tattoo were of real interest, even if they had been visible at this moment. What did command her attention as she trailed behind him around another corner was his well-defined backside in those snug jeans. Jennifer was absolutely riveted by the sight.

Stop it! You're practically salivating!

So what if Leo McKenzie was on the A-list when it came to sexual appeal. It wasn't like she hadn't met plenty of guys who qualified in that area. There was no good reason for her to behave like an idiot with this one. He couldn't be that special.

It was just the situation, she told herself. Being stranded like this in a blizzard, having to work together so closely. That kind of intimacy was bound to have an effect on your hormones. But it didn't make it something substantial.

Right. Just remember that.

It was a piece of sensible advice, except it failed her when Leo came to a sudden halt and she bumped into the enticing backside that was giving her so much trouble.

"Sorry," she mumbled, drawing quickly back from the contact.

"You hear me complaining?"

She wisely responded with a question of her own. A safe one. "Um, why are we—"

"Because we're here. I think."

She watched him consult the map the abbot had given him. The corridor that stretched in front of them was silent, deserted. She hoped there was nothing deceptive about that. That Leo was right and they were alone here.

A thought occurred to her as she waited for him to decide which door belonged to whom. There were no locks on the ancient doors of the rooms she and Leo occupied, but these doors along here had keyholes. She pointed that out to him.

"What if we can't get in?"

But he had already anticipated that potential problem. And solved it. He produced a key from the same pocket that had contained the map. "It's a master key. Courtesy of Father Stephen. Let's see if we need it."

They didn't. When he tried the first door on their right, it opened without resistance.

If they're all like this, Jennifer thought, then maybe their occupants had nothing to hide. Or maybe in a place like this it would have looked odd if any one of them had locked his door. After all, this wasn't a hotel.

"This one should belong to Harry Ireland," Leo said, leading the way into the room.

For all Jennifer knew the salesman might be a master of organization where his work was concerned. His personal habits were another matter. Jennifer surveyed a room where articles of clothing were strewn across the bed and on the backs of chairs. The doors of a plain, sturdy wardrobe, the kind that once would have been found in the servants' quarters of an Edwardian house, gaped open.

"It's a mess," she said.

"Yeah, and let's leave it and the others exactly as we find them. We don't want any of them guessing someone was snooping in their rooms. You take the wardrobe, and I'll look through the suitcase there," he said, indicating a piece of scuffed luggage which lay open on the foot of the bed.

Jennifer approached the wardrobe with misgiving. She hated having to paw through someone's personal belongings, knowing how much she would have resented an invasion of her own privacy. But since this undertaking was necessary…

There was a faux leather case on the floor of the wardrobe. She lifted it out and raised the lid. It was the salesman's sample case. The contents consisted of various catalogs accompanied by order blanks, a selection of over-the-counter type drugs, condiments and what looked like packages of organically grown dried fruits and vegetables. It was an odd assortment, but there was nothing harmful or particularly unusual.

"Find anything interesting?" Leo called from the bed.

"Not so far."

She spent another couple of minutes carefully checking the case while making certain she replaced each item exactly where it belonged. Satisfied, she put the case back in the wardrobe and turned her attention to the garments inside hanging care-lessly on pegs. A search of their pockets rewarded her with nothing but an old ticket stub.

"I'm not having any luck at all over here," she reported. "How about you?"

Leo didn't answer her. Puzzled by his silence, she backed out of the wardrobe. He was still there at the foot of the bed, holding a packet of letters he must have removed from the suit-case. His head was bent over one of those letters.

"Leo?"

She got a response this time in the form of a long, low whistle.

"What is it?"

"Hot stuff. Come over here and see."

She joined him at the bed. He handed her the letter. Jennifer could feel her face growing pink as she read it, and she wasn't easily embarrassed. The writer, some woman the salesman was involved with, recounted in graphic detail their last meeting together and how she longed to get naked with him again at the first opportunity.

"Sounds like old Harry is a real stallion, huh? And the other letters are even hotter."

"We shouldn't be reading them." Jennifer thrust the letter back into his hand. "They can't have anything to do with what we're investigating."

"Probably not. Except in one of them the lady writes about leaving her husband to run away with Harry. If only they had the money. A lot of it."

"That's just talk. It's nothing incriminating."

"Trying to tell me Harry Ireland has to be just what he says he is? The old-fashioned traveling salesman, down to and in-cluding…well, not the farmer's daughter in this case but somebody's wife he's met on the road." Leo shook his head. "Doesn't satisfy me."

"Why?"

"He isn't right. Haven't you noticed the way he talks? Like some British colonel out of an old movie."

"It's just an affectation."

"Maybe. But it's as much of a cliché as the image of a traveling salesman. Think I'll be keeping my eye on Harry."

He reached for the letter's envelope he had laid on top of the open suitcase. Jennifer wasn't sure whether it was an accident or intentional when his hand brushed against the side of her breast. She *was* certain about her reaction. A tongue of fire streaked through her, setting off an alarm.

Stepping away from him, she tried to be casual about it. "There's nothing more to be seen in here, is there? Can we get on to the next room?"

"Just give me a second. I want to make sure these letters are all in the same order I found them."

She was relieved when they left Harry Ireland's room and moved on to his neighbor. The door here was also unlocked.

"Map says this one belongs to Fiona and Alfred Brasher," Leo said, again leading the way inside.

The Brashers' room proved to be as tidy as the salesman's was messy. There was no sign anywhere of clutter.

Leo leaned down, peeking beneath the bed. "Yep, they slid their suitcase under there. What do you want this time? The suitcase or the wardrobe?"

"I'll take the suitcase."

Dragging the single piece of luggage out into the open, she heaved it up on a chair and lifted the top. There was no disorder here either. All of the garments the suitcase contained were precisely folded.

This was going to require extra care, Jennifer told herself as she began to search through the contents. She had to leave everything looking undisturbed.

Leo had to be having the same problem. "Talk about a challenge," he grumbled from the direction of the wardrobe. "I swear they must have measured the distance between the clothes they hung in here to make sure none of them touched each other. A real pair of neat freaks."

It was down near the bottom of the suitcase that Jennifer discovered the picture. She took it out for a closer examination.

"No secrets in here," Leo said, closing the doors of the wardrobe. "You find anything?"

"Maybe. Come and have a look at this."

He joined her by the chair. "What have you got?"

What Jennifer had was a photograph of a group of young men. The way they were dressed indicated a team posed for the camera at some kind of sports event.

"I don't see that it means anything," Leo said.

"Here." Her finger pointed to one of the faces in the back row. It was the face of the young man who wanted to be a monk.

Leo looked closely at the figure, seeing now what he had missed with his first glance. "Yeah, it's Patrick all right."

"Why would the Brashers have a picture of Patrick?"

"Guess we could speculate about that."

The husky way he said it, and the way he stood beside her, so close that she could feel the heat of his body, made her even more aware of the danger she had felt back in Harry Ireland's room. There was a long moment of pure sexual suspense.

Jennifer ended it with a brusque "Let's not. We need to move on."

She quickly occupied herself with returning the photograph to the suitcase, making sure everything was left as she'd found it, then closing the suitcase and placing it back under the bed.

"Proves one thing anyway," Leo said. "The Brashers *did* know Patrick before they came here. But exactly what that connection is and how it relates to the argument we overheard outside the dining parlor is still a mystery. And maybe nothing to do with the mystery we're trying to solve."

Or maybe it did, Jennifer thought, although she was unwilling to discuss it when she was anxious to leave the scene. And not just because they couldn't afford to lose time. Leo was too much of a temptation. She promised herself that she was going to avoid getting too close to him in the two rooms they had yet to search.

The next room on the map was Roger and Sybil Harding's, which was also unlocked. Unlike the first two rooms, this one had a long bench situated under the window. There were two suitcases sitting on it side by side. Jennifer presumed that one of them belonged to Sybil and the other was her husband's. Both of them were open, their contents in plain sight. That could mean their owners had nothing to hide. Maybe.

"Suitcases or wardrobe?" Leo asked.

"I'll start with the wardrobe."

Jennifer found it was a good choice. There were several interesting items in the massive cupboard.

The first to catch her eye was the monk's robe suspended from a peg in one corner. It was identical to the robes worn by all of the brothers at Warley. Had Roger Harding worn it when he was himself a member of the order? Clad himself in it whenever he returned to the monastery on his periodic retreats? Possibly, but on the two occasions she'd been with him, Roger had been dressed in ordinary clothes.

Most of the other garments hanging in the wardrobe belonged to Sybil. They were stylish and looked expensive. So did the vanity case placed on the floor of the wardrobe. She removed it from the cupboard for a better look. It was crafted of fine leather. It also had an impressive family crest on its lid.

It seemed Sybil Harding not only had money, she had rank. Unless, of course, the case was secondhand. Which it probably was, since Sybil was the kind of woman who would make certain you knew she had a title. And she hadn't done that.

Jennifer opened the vanity. It held the usual toilet articles, creams, lotions and every makeup imaginable. She poked through them. No, nothing else.

She was replacing the case in the wardrobe when she found a bottle tucked behind a row of shoes. She took it out and held it up to the light. The bottle was half full.

"One of them likes gin," she said, waving the bottle in Leo's direction. "A lot, if you go by the level."

Leo looked up from the suitcases he was examining. "Beats anything I've found over here. Unless you count the lady's fancy underwear, which I don't."

No, he wasn't the sort of man to appreciate lingerie. Not without the right woman wearing it for him anyway.

Jennifer returned the bottle to the wardrobe and closed the doors. Her search may have been interesting, but it had provided no useful clues. Leo was equally disappointed.

"Nothing else in these bags but a pile of reading material," he reported. "Dull stuff. Most of it religious. Guess that's understandable, with old Roger coming here on regular retreat."

"It makes you wonder though, doesn't it?" Jennifer said, moving close enough to Leo to talk about it but not close enough to risk any further intimacy.

"What does?"

"Just that with Roger Harding being as devout as he is, why did he ever leave the order?"

"Easy. He married an attractive woman, didn't he?"

"Meaning?"

"He couldn't take the celibacy. There are monks and priests who can't."

While that was true, it was perhaps unfair to judge Roger by so simple an explanation. After all, there were such things as crises of faith.

Leo cast his gaze around the room. "Looks like there's nothing else to see in here. You ready to tackle Patrick?"

Jennifer was more than ready to move on to the last room. Their investigation had taken more time than she'd imagined it would. She was beginning to be very nervous about that.

What if the memorial service had ended? That could mean the guests were even now leaving the chapel and on their way back here.

But the corridor still lay in silent gloom when they reached Patrick's door. Leo's hand closed on the handle. And met resistance.

"Locked?"

"Yeah," he said, digging the master key out of his pocket.

"And none of the others were. Do you suppose that could mean…"

"That our Patrick does have something to hide? Could be," he said, using the key to admit them into the room.

But the young man's quarters turned out to be even more of a disappointment than the other three rooms. Patrick had brought very few belongings with him. Leo reported after looking through the wardrobe that it contained nothing but several changes of clothes and an extra pair of shoes.

"What about you?" he asked Jennifer, who was going through the simple, solitary bag perched on the wide window ledge.

"I'm not doing any better. A couple of books, that's all. Religious, like Roger Harding's material. But that's no surprise if he's thinking of joining the order."

"Guess the kid just likes his privacy," he said, referring to the locked door. "You ready to call it quits?"

Jennifer didn't answer him. She had found something wrapped in a T-shirt at the bottom of the bag. Something that alarmed her.

"What is it?" Leo asked, her silence telling him she had made a discovery. He swiftly crossed the room to her side.

"This," she said, holding out a wicked-looking knife for him to see.

Leo took it by the handle, turning it in his hand. "It's no penknife, is it? More like a weapon."

"An ugly one. Why would he bring something like that here, of all places?"

"Who knows. Maybe the kid is paranoid about his safety. Maybe that's why he locks his door."

And maybe Patrick had a particular need to protect himself, she thought, unable to forget the nasty quarrel they had over-heard outside the dining parlor.

"It wasn't a knife that killed Guy and Brother Anthony, so we have no reason to take it with us," Leo said, giving the knife back to her.

Even though Jennifer would have preferred to confiscate the thing, she knew he was right. Removing it would tell Patrick that someone had been in his room. She wrapped it up again in the T-shirt and tucked it back in the bag.

"This has all been worthless," she said, piling the other contents of the bag on top of the knife, making certain she left them looking undisturbed. "There was nothing in any of the rooms to tell us who the killer might be or what happened to the Madonna."

"Did you think it would be that easy? It never is. But it wasn't a wasted effort. If nothing else, it's given us a better handle on our suspects. And that's always worth something in an inves-tigation."

Was it? She wasn't convinced, although she wasn't about to stop here and discuss it with him. All she wanted was to get away before they were discovered. But she ended up having to wait impatiently for Leo, who insisted on a last look around the room.

Satisfied that they had overlooked nothing, he led the way out into the corridor. There was another moment's delay while he searched for the master key.

"Thought I stuck it in—no, here it is in the other pocket."

"Please hurry," she urged him.

"Relax," he said, relocking the door and testing it to make sure it was secure. "We're almost in the clear."

But *almost* wasn't enough. The words were scarcely out of his mouth when Jennifer heard the sound of approaching footsteps. They came from back around the corner in the direction of the stairway. Her uneasiness had just been justified.

"Someone's coming," she whispered.

"I hear."

This was no time to panic, she told herself, looking in the opposite direction for an escape route. There was none. The corridor dead-ended in a blank wall less than ten yards away. They were trapped! *Now* was a good time to panic!

"What are we going to do? Whoever it is is going to come around that corner in another second, and if he finds us here—"

"This way," Leo said, drawing her swiftly in the direction of the dead end.

That was when she noticed it, realized what he intended. Daylight. That meant a window along this side of the corridor, and with the walls of the castle being as thick as they were...

They reached the source of the light. It was better than just a window with a wide ledge that might, or might not, have accommodated them. It was a floor-to-ceiling alcove deep enough to conceal them. Providing, of course, no one wandered to this end of the corridor.

She and Leo backed into the alcove. The trouble was, it was a very narrow alcove with just enough space for them to fit. Jennifer found herself squeezed so tightly against Leo's hard body that his warm breath mingled with hers.

This couldn't be good. Not that she had any choice about it since whoever was coming had already arrived. She could hear him passing the doors in the corridor. Then the footsteps stopped. There was the sound of a key scraping in a lock. Patrick. It had to be Patrick. His was the only door that needed to be unlocked.

The door opened, closed behind him. There was silence now. Prepared to flee down the corridor, Jennifer started to steal away from the alcove. Leo pulled her back, his hand on her arm.

"Wait," he whispered in her ear. "He might be stopping in his room just long enough to get something."

The seconds passed. Tense seconds, and not just because she feared discovery. The intimacy of their situation, her awareness of Leo pressed against her side with all the heat of a lover's embrace, had every nerve in her body on alert. It was all she could do not to squirm.

"Careful," he warned her softly.

For a brief moment Jennifer thought he was cautioning her about the danger of his nearness, something that was totally unnecessary. She was all too conscious of the risk here. Then she realized he was alerting her to the sound of Patrick's door opening again.

Leo had been right. Apparently the young man had returned to his room only long enough to collect something. She heard him emerging into the corridor, and in that instant something entirely unexpected happened.

The storm clouds parted just long enough to permit the sun to break through. Jennifer could feel its warmth on her back, was dazzled by its light streaming into the alcove. A brilliance that threatened them.

The shadows of their bodies were cast out across the floor of the corridor. A silent but clear betrayal of their presence. All Patrick had to do was glance in the direction of the alcove, and he would know they were there.

Rigid with apprehension, she listened to the sound of Patrick relocking his door. If it was going to happen, it would happen now. But the startled challenge she anticipated never occurred. All she heard was the sound of his footsteps retreating down the corridor. Safe. They were safe.

The clouds must have closed behind them. The alcove was plunged into gloom again.

There was nothing but silence now from the far end of the passage. The threat was gone. They could emerge from the alcove. But for some reason she would never understand, or perhaps she did understand it and refused to admit it, they lingered there.

A long moment passed, and then she turned slowly to face Leo. And met his breath-robbing gaze.

Struggling for air, she managed a weak "He didn't see us."

"No," he rasped.

"We can leave now."

"Yeah."

"We should leave before someone else comes along."

"Right."

But neither of them stirred. They went on standing there, scant inches apart while his dark gaze continued to search her face. And then even those few inches closed into nothing as she swayed toward him, helpless against the force that pulled her into his waiting arms.

His mouth sought her own without hesitation. She would have sworn that the sun had managed to burst through the heavy clouds again. But it wasn't the sun that blinded her. It was his kiss, as strong and primal as anything the elements could deliver. And as molten as the kiss they had shared in the chapel. With a not-so-small difference. This time, upright as they were and with Leo clasping her body tightly against his solid length, she could feel the hard ridge of his arousal strained against her groin.

What had she tried to tell herself earlier? About Leo not being all that special? She'd been wrong. He *was* that special.

He took his slow, sweet time plundering her mouth, his tongue savoring hers. Which should have left her satisfied, not disappointed when he finally released her.

"You ready to go back?" he said gruffly.

Just like that. No aftermath of endearments or caresses. She could have smacked him, whatever wisdom he might be exercising in a situation that, admittedly, was potentially treacherous.

"Yes," she agreed.

She was still in such a mindless state from that kiss she didn't remember going back to their rooms. It just seemed that they were suddenly there, standing in the passage outside her door.

"Are we going down for tea with them?" Jennifer asked him.

He looked puzzled.

"This is England," she reminded him. "Whatever happens, no one misses afternoon tea. The others will be gathering before long in the dining parlor."

Leo shook his head. "I don't think it would be smart of me to show up there that soon when I'm supposed to be feeling rotten again."

"You're probably right. And since they believe I'm up here taking care of you, I'd better not turn up there either. Well…"

Jennifer opened her door, waiting for him to indicate he would join her in her room. That they would sit down and talk both about what they had learned and hadn't learned in their search. But he was plainly not interested in doing that.

"I'll see you when it's time for dinner," he said. "I ought to be able to risk an appearance by then."

She could see that he wanted her to go into her room and close her door, that he was only lingering here long enough to make sure she was safe inside. He left her no other choice but to oblige him. She went into her room and shut the door.

For a long moment she stood there with her back against the door, wondering what had just happened, unable to deny her hurt over his abrupt parting from her. Did he regret that scene in the alcove?

It was cold in the room. She left the door and crossed to the hearth. There were just enough embers in the grate to revive the fire with the chunks of peat she scooped out of the basket. Reasonable or not, she was angry with Leo, angry with herself as she fed the flames.

What on earth was the matter with her?

It wasn't until she had a good blaze going and was benefiting from its warmth, that Jennifer was able to acknowledge exactly what was wrong with her. Not anger, no. It was fear. A fear that she was falling in love with Leo McKenzie.

Couldn't be. All right, she *had* fallen in lust with him. She would admit that much. But not love. Love took time to develop. It didn't happen this soon, and it required a lot more than just sexual attraction to make it genuine. Things that to her they didn't seem to share, like the same basic values, common interests, the capacity to fully enjoy each other's company.

And, most important of all, trust. Trust was missing from their relationship. Because she knew that Leo had yet to decide for certain that she hadn't killed his half brother. On that level anyway he was still her enemy.

He had been right to leave her at her door before both of them lost their heads again. She silently thanked him for that.

WHAT THE HELL was the matter with him? Leo asked himself, raking a hand through his hair as he prowled restlessly around his room. He couldn't seem to keep his hands off her.

Good thing he hadn't gone into her room with her. He'd had that much sense anyway. Because if he *had* gone into that room, he wouldn't have been able to trust himself. He would have lost his last shreds of restraint.

This was nuts. Okay, so he wanted her. He was even willing to admit that it was more than just a physical need. He liked being with her, admired her courage, the way she was ready to stand up to him. Everything that could mean something more was going on between them than just sex. Everything except—

Yeah, there was the possibility she could have killed Guy. Slim now though that possibility was, it still gnawed at him. And as long as it was there, a shadow divided them.

Chapter Eight

Jennifer didn't know how many more of these meals she could take. They weren't pleasant affairs, and dinner was no exception. There was the same nervous climate in the dining parlor as there had been at both breakfast and lunch.

To be fair about it, however, she couldn't blame the company for her mood. Not entirely. Not tonight. It was because of Leo. Although he had been nothing but agreeable with her all the way down to the dining parlor, there was a difference in his manner.

She was aware of it as they filled their plates from the buffet and joined the others at the table. He might be at her side, physically close, but emotionally he was keeping his distance. As if he had promised himself that, yes, he was going to be there for her if she needed him. And, yes, he'd be friendly about it. But no more intimacies.

Well, everything considered, he was probably right. It was better for them to resist any further romantic involvement. Just like she'd told herself earlier.

Then why on earth was she so unhappy about it?

"Can't complain about the food, what?" Harry Ireland said, tucking cheerfully into a slice of roast beef.

"Brother Gabriel does well by us," Geoffrey informed the table. "He was a chef in a *cordon bleu* restaurant in Manchester before he joined the order."

"Smashing."

They weren't going to discuss the memorial service, Jennifer thought. Or the reason for it. Nor were they firing accusations at one another tonight either. But the tension was still there, just waiting to erupt all over again.

Fiona Brasher couldn't have considered the weather a topic to be avoided. She attacked it peevishly. "I have no argument with the food. It's that snow out there. Filthy stuff never lets up. I call it a bad omen when for two days one can't catch even a glimpse of the sun."

"Fiona's a bit superstitious," Alfred mumbled, excusing his wife.

Sybil Harding put up a carefully manicured hand to fluff her ash-blond hair. "It's Britain, dear, where the sun is always shy, especially in a blizzard. You ought to make your peace with it, as I've done."

Fiona glared at her.

Sybil laughed. "Such fun to be trapped here like this, when one is willing to look at it that way. Like a party really."

Her tone of sweet cynicism was more artificial than usual. She's been drinking, Jennifer thought, remembering the gin bottle in the Hardings' wardrobe.

"The snow will quit," Roger said. "We just have to be patient about it."

"We don't know that, dear heart, now do we? It's much more jolly to party."

Pushing her plate aside, she reached for her bag and brought out a flask. Uncapping it, she poured a generous measure of gin into her empty coffee cup.

"You really shouldn't, Mrs. Harding," Geoffrey tried to caution her. "This is a monastery, after all, and alcohol—"

"Medicinal, dear boy. Purely medicinal."

Roger squirmed in an agony of embarrassment. "Sybil, please, not here."

Eyes narrowed, she turned on her husband with a soft, savage "If you want to preach, then why don't you just put on your robe and go off to the other side of the castle with your precious brothers? It's where you want to be, isn't it?"

The woman was some piece of work all right, Jennifer thought in disgust. She didn't know how her husband could put up with her. On the other hand, she supposed that if you loved a person enough, even someone like Sybil, you could endure just about anything.

Defying the objections, Sybil raised her cup in a toast. "Good health, everyone. Hoping, that is, one of us isn't next."

Her allusion to Brother Anthony's murder couldn't be plainer. Or more brazen. Fiona gasped. The others merely sat there in a stunned silence and watched Sybil toss back the gin in her cup.

It was Patrick who ended the silence with a quiet "It did, you know."

Geoffrey frowned at him. "*What* did *what?*"

"The sun. It did come out for a moment."

Jennifer's nerves tightened on her. Leo beside her must have sensed her alarm. His hand reached down under the table and closed over her knee. His light squeeze was meant either to steady her or as a request to keep still. Either way, she said nothing.

"When was this?" Alfred Brasher wanted to know.

"This afternoon when I left the service long enough to get my sinus medicine from my room. I think it might have been the smoke from all the votive candles in the chapel that was bothering me."

"Have to get used to that if you're going to join the order," Geoffrey said.

"Anyway, that's when I saw it, the sun streaming through a window out in the hall as I came away from my room."

Patrick avoided looking at her and Leo, but Jennifer was sure he was letting them know he *hadn't* missed their shadows on the floor, that he'd been aware all along of their presence in the alcove. Would he tell the others?

Sybil gave him no chance. She leaned toward Fiona with one of her spiteful smiles. "There, that lovely glimpse from heaven you've been wanting, and you had to miss it. Such a pity."

There was another uncomfortable silence. A taut Jennifer expected Patrick to fill it, but he said nothing. It was Harry Ireland who, clearing his throat, spoke up with a change of subject, maybe to forestall a further dose of Sybil's brand of acid.

"So, old man," he addressed Leo, "feeling more like yourself again, are you?"

"A lot better, thanks."

Jennifer relaxed. The bad moment seemed to have passed. Whatever his reason, it appeared that Patrick wasn't going to betray them. She and Leo were safe. For now at least.

"Looks like that nasty bump you were sporting on the old noggin has—what do you Americans say? Called it quits?"

"Yep, swelling's down to almost nothing."

"I expect that long rest you had in your room this afternoon did the trick, hey."

"But he wasn't in his room resting," Patrick said matter-of-factly. "He and Ms. Rowan were in the other guest wing of the castle. *Our* wing."

This time he did train those mild brown eyes on Leo and her. And Jennifer realized just how premature her relief had been. She ought to have known Patrick would never have mentioned sighting the sun if he hadn't meant to expose them.

He must have been waiting all along for this opportunity. Or maybe he had just needed to find sufficient courage to challenge them. If so, that courage deserted him when he met Leo's steely gaze head-on. Flushing, the young man looked away.

Again there was an uneasy silence. Harry Ireland ended it with a snort of laughter. "Those pills you took. More than just sinus medicine, are they?"

"I don't do drugs, and I wasn't seeing things," Patrick muttered stubbornly. "The two of them were there hiding in the window alcove. I saw their shadows on the hall floor."

"Ah, then you didn't actually see them. You saw only a pair of shadows that—"

"It *was* them. It couldn't have been anyone else when all the rest of the castle was in the chapel."

"Lurking in an alcove? A bit hard to swallow, old man."

Leo spoke up then with a forceful "Okay, let's stop giving the kid a hard time. He's right. Jennifer and I were there."

Fiona was bewildered. "In our wing? Outside our rooms?"

"Not just outside, Mrs. Brasher. Inside, too. All of them, including yours, Patrick. Had the loan of a master key for that one."

Her husband was outraged. "What bloody cheek!"

He wasn't alone in his censure. Reproachful eyes from every side of the table locked on Leo like lasers. All but Sybil's. The gin had finally deflated her. She sat there slouched in her chair, immune now to the agitation around her.

Leo ignored the angry gazes and looked at Jennifer. She understood what he was silently telling her. *They'll have to find out sometime. It might as well be now.* She nodded her agreement.

The salesman expressed his disappointment in them. "I say, that's a bit much, isn't it?"

"A bit much?" Alfred raged. "It's a violation of our rights, is what it is! What are you? A pair of hotel thieves?"

"We didn't take, Brasher. We looked."

The storm came from every direction, all of them demanding explanations at the same time. It was Roger Harding who, lifting a hand, finally silenced them.

"Please," he said calmly, "let's give them a chance to tell us what they were looking for."

"Evidence," Leo said.

"Of what, Mr. McKenzie?"

He smiled at them. "Come on, you know what. One of the

brothers was murdered. And, uh, like most of you were saying yourselves at lunch, someone in this room must be responsible for his death. Right?"

No one answered him. The company avoided looking at one another. Worried, Jennifer thought. They had to be worried about what we might have turned up in our search. All those things that, while not incriminating in themselves, they wouldn't have wanted anyone to see. She felt guilty all over again for having invaded their privacy.

Alfred Brasher was the first to recover. "And why should you be the one to take on the role of a police officer?" he asked snidely.

"Experience, Alf. See, it comes from being a private investigator. Don't believe that's what I am? Ask Father Stephen. He authorized me to try to solve the murder and for Ms. Rowan to work with me. Any more questions?"

"Yes," Brasher said, still fuming. "Why Ms. Rowan?"

"I imagine," Geoffrey said, "it's because she saw the killer."

The attention that had been focused on Leo shifted. Jennifer felt their shocked gazes now riveted on her.

"Is this true?" Roger asked her in disbelief.

"If it were, Mr. Harding, we wouldn't have had a reason to search your rooms."

"Then what is Geoffrey talking about?" Fiona demanded.

"Why don't you ask Geoffrey?" Jennifer suggested. *Because I'd like to hear myself just how the novice came to learn what only Leo and Father Stephen were meant to know.*

"It *is* true," Geoffrey insisted. "I overheard Father Stephen tell the prior as much."

"That's a little unlikely, isn't it?" Leo said dryly. "That the abbot would leak a piece of information like that?"

"Father Stephen has to share everything that happens in the monastery with the prior. It's a rule of the order."

"Why?"

"Because if anything should happen to the abbot, then the prior assumes his duties."

"Okay, so the prior has to know what's going on. But *you* weren't meant to listen in on whatever it was Father Stephen told him, were you, Geoffrey? And if you couldn't help overhearing it, you sure as hell have no business broadcasting it. Especially if it's only conjecture."

Backed into a corner, the novice eyed the others, looking for support. "If they're all suspects," he mumbled, "then they have a right to know."

Jennifer realized that Leo was trying to discredit Geoffrey's assertion in an effort to prevent the murderer from being alarmed. But it was too late for that. She put a restraining hand on Leo's arm.

"Geoffrey's right," she said. "All of you do deserve to know what I saw." She went on to explain what she had observed from the window overlooking the courtyard, ending her account with an earnest "And that's all it was, nothing but a fast glimpse of a figure that might have been a man or a woman. Certainly no one I could identify, not through all that snow."

Eyes wide, fingers plucking at her napkin, Fiona tried to tell her she was mistaken. "But surely it was Brother Anthony himself that you saw."

"No."

"How could you know it wasn't?" Alfred scoffed.

"Just a feeling."

But it was more than just a feeling, Jennifer remembered. It was—

And then all at once she *did* know what it was that had made her so certain it wasn't Brother Anthony. That little something she'd been unable to name but which had been nagging at her ever since she had told Leo and the abbot that she must have seen the killer. She could name it now.

They were all watching her, waiting for her to go on.

She didn't name it. She said hurriedly, "That's all I can tell you. It isn't worth anything, and that's why an investigation is necessary."

They weren't satisfied, of course. But Jennifer had had enough of their emotional fireworks and was relieved to get away from them when she and Leo finally managed an escape from the dining parlor.

He was quiet on the way back to their quarters, both before and after a stop at the bathroom along the route. Whatever he was thinking, he didn't share it with her. But this time he didn't part from her when they reached their doors, as he had done so abruptly that afternoon. He strode into her room ahead of her, sweeping his gaze rapidly from side to side.

What was he doing? she wondered, shutting the door behind them. Making sure no menace was lurking in the shadows?

Apparently satisfied, he rounded on her with a brusque "All right, let's have it."

The man was a menace himself when he was like this with his brash, take-charge attitude. "Am I supposed to know what you're talking about?"

"You remembered something about the killer there at the table."

"How could you know that?"

"The way you hesitated, the look you had on your face. And if *I* could see it…"

Jennifer must have had another look on her face now, one of pure anxiety, because Leo nodded impatiently.

"Uh-huh, that's right. The killer, assuming he is one of us, could have guessed you'd suddenly gone and realized something that gives him a reason to be a little worried about you."

"But I couldn't have been that obvious." All right, she tried to reassure herself, so Leo seemed to have this maddening talent for knowing what she was thinking. But that didn't mean any of the others were anywhere near that perceptive. "And, anyway, what I realized amounts to nothing really. It couldn't possibly reveal Brother Anthony's killer."

"But *he* doesn't know that. Okay, so maybe I'm the only one at the table who noticed anything. Maybe I'm exaggerating a threat here. So are you going to tell me?"

"Yes, for what it's worth. It was simply that Brother Anthony was very stoop-shouldered. I noticed that this morning when Brother Timothy pointed him out in the courtyard on our way to breakfast, although I forgot all about it until just now at dinner."

"And?"

"The figure I saw later in the courtyard when I was on my way to find Brother Anthony had an erect posture."

"You sure about that?"

"It's the only thing I am sure about. Well, fairly sure, anyway. Remember, it was just a quick glimpse through all that snow, but that little bit did somehow register in the back of my mind. You see, it isn't anything that matters. It could have been anybody. All it proves is that it wasn't Brother Anthony in my line of sight."

"But if the killer thought it was more than that, then you're a danger to him."

"Providing he was able to tell I'd remembered something." Jennifer was still far from convinced any of the others at the table could possibly have realized that, even if Leo had. Not that she didn't plan to be cautious from now on.

"Yeah, providing…" His gaze looked beyond her in the direction of the hall door. She heard him mutter something under his breath that sounded like an obscenity.

"What?" she asked.

"Just remembering that *our* doors don't have locks on them."

Oh, great. Now he was making her nervous. "You don't think…"

"What I think is we need to be careful. Put a chair over there against the door before you go to bed. It won't keep anyone out who wants to get in, but it will make a noise if they try. And," he added, nodding in the direction of the connecting door between their rooms, "you leave that door cracked. You hear anything, anything at all, then you holler and I'll be here. Okay?"

"If you say."

"I do say." He regarded her thoughtfully. "You gonna be all right?"

"I *can* take care of myself, you know. I've been doing just that ever since a mugger and I came to an understanding on the Boston Common that didn't include his getting away with my purse."

"Sure. Better not just crack the door, though. Leave it open a good few inches. I'll see you in the morning then."

He started for the connecting door, but Jennifer had no intention of letting him get away from her this time.

"Whoa, detective."

He turned back, a dark eyebrow lifted in question. "Something?"

"Plenty. You don't walk out again until we've talked about what we found in those rooms this afternoon. I want to know what you're thinking."

One of his big hands came up to stroke the pugnacious jaw on that chiseled face. "What's to think. Like you said yourself, we didn't find anything to tell us who killed Brother Anthony and why."

Or to connect his murder with Guy's or the missing Warley Madonna, she thought. Which meant that, as far as what had happened back in London, she couldn't be eliminated as a suspect. It was a depressing realization, one that she knew must still be lingering in Leo's mind.

"All the same," she insisted, "we did turn up a few things that…well, if not downright suspicious, were at least puzzling. Like those letters in Harry Ireland's suitcase."

"Uh-huh."

"I keep remembering how his girlfriend wrote about needing

a lot of money and where was it to come from. Then I think about the Warley Madonna and what it's worth."

"Right."

"And then there's that photograph the Brashers have of Patrick and the argument we overheard outside the dining parlor and the connection the three of them have that they're being secretive about. Why? Are they involved in some kind of conspiracy?"

"Might be."

"And why would Patrick keep his door locked and have a knife hidden in his luggage? That's a mystery right there."

"Looks like it."

"And we've got Geoffrey, who doesn't seem to like Patrick. Maybe just because he resents having to babysit him, which I assume is why he has to take all of his meals with us, though I imagine he's quartered with the brothers."

"Probably."

"Father Stephen said he can account for all of the brothers at the time of the murder. But, technically, Geoffrey isn't a monk yet. I wonder where he was when Brother Anthony was killed. I suppose we ought to check with Father Stephen about that."

"Sure."

Jennifer stopped to catch her breath. She gazed at Leo in frustration. What was the matter with him? His responses to all of her speculations had amounted to little more than monosyllables. With a tone of disinterest at that.

"Well?" she demanded.

"Yeah?"

"Don't you think that these are all things that need explaining?"

"I never said they didn't. You got any idea how we go about getting those explanations?"

"You're the detective. Why don't we just ask them?"

"We could do that. Think they'd tell us the truth? There are reasons why people have secrets, Jenny. That's why they're called secrets and why they hang on to them."

"Then where do we go from here?"

"I don't know about you, but I intend to sleep on it. Always good for fresh inspiration. Don't forget that chair."

Tossing her a careless salute, he turned and went into his room, leaving the connecting door several inches ajar.

She hated that he had walked out on her again like that. As if he didn't trust himself to be alone with her. Not that it wasn't a wise action for both of them, of course, but still…

All right, it was foolish of her to mind being left on her own when he was right next door, when he would be here in an instant if she called out to him. Just the same, she was very aware of actually missing him.

And there was something else. A feeling of desperation because she wasn't getting the answers she needed. A sense that time was running out on her.

HERE WE GO AGAIN.

Like the night before, Jennifer found herself awake in the middle of the night with a need to relieve herself.

Come on, it isn't that bad. You can wait until daylight.

Wrong. The longer she lay there, trying to will herself back to sleep, the more urgent that need became. In the end, realizing it wasn't going to quit, she surrendered to the call.

Leaving the cocoon of her warm covers was bad enough. But not as shocking as her bare feet meeting the icy floor when she swung her legs over the side of the bed. She quickly slid her feet into her slippers.

Better, but she was still cold in her sleepshirt. And the cold wasn't helping her bladder. Where was her robe? Right. In the wardrobe, just where it shouldn't be.

The door of the tall cupboard creaked softly when she crossed the room and opened it. Her gaze went immediately to the connecting door. No light flared in the gap. It remained dark and the room beyond silent. The only sound was the ceaseless lament of the wind over the moors.

Grabbing her robe from a hook, she bundled into its thickness. Her attention was still fixed on the connecting door to Leo's room as she tied the belt around her waist.

There was no question of it. She would have to rouse him. After all his warnings, he would have a fit if she went off to the loo without him. Uh-huh, and she could also hear him complain about the necessity of the visit when, after all, they had stopped to use the bathroom on the way back to their rooms.

Well, maybe not. Maybe he would be very understanding about it. But why bother him when she could look out for herself. How much risk could there be in a quick trip down the hall and back? If she *was* in any danger from the killer, and that was only a possibility, she couldn't imagine him hanging around the corridors on the remote chance of catching her there. He'd have tried to get into her room by now.

Jennifer crept to the hall door and removed the chair that was blocking it. As careful as she was, the legs scraped a bit on the floor when she drew it back. She paused to listen. Nothing stirred from the direction of Leo's room.

Satisfied, she eased the door back just far enough to squeeze through the opening. And almost collided with the tall figure waiting for her out in the corridor.

"And just where do you think you're going?"

Jennifer swallowed a startled yelp and glared at him. Damn. All her cautious maneuvers had been for nothing.

"To the bathroom, and I don't need you to—"

"Oh, yes, you do. Or have you forgotten there's a killer loose in the castle?"

"How did you know I—"

"I would have had to be comatose not to hear you moving around in there."

"So, instead of just knocking on the connecting door, you go and ambush me out here in the hall."

"Didn't want to listen to some song and dance about you not being able to sleep, and why didn't I just go back to bed. Okay?"

No, it wasn't okay. He had not only scared her, he was now assaulting her senses. The sight of him in those pajama bottoms was devastating. Unlike last night, he'd had the sense to dig his feet into a pair of loafers and to shrug into his coat. But the leather coat gaped open, revealing the sleek muscles of his naked chest. That, plus sleep-tousled hair and a stubble on his jaw, contributed to his tantalizing image.

The sexual tension that had been smoldering between them since their first encounter was not just as strong as ever, it had shot to a new level. The problem was it was accompanied by her need for the bathroom, which had also reached a new level. One that was just short of an emergency.

"Uh, can we please not stand around arguing about this? I kind of have another priority here."

"In that case, you won't mind if I—"

"Fine, you can play bodyguard. Let's just move."

The trip down the dimly lighted passage and around a corner into another corridor where the bathroom was located had never seemed so long to Jennifer. Nor her relief greater when, reaching their destination, she dashed inside, leaving Leo on guard out in the passage.

"Thank you," she said, feeling more benevolent toward him when she emerged a few moments later from the facility, her desperation remedied.

He stood away from the wall against which he had been leaning, eyeing the antique plumbing behind her. "Might as well take advantage of it while I'm here."

Jennifer stood aside. "Be my guest."

"You gonna be okay while I—"

"I will wait right here," she promised him with an exaggerated emphasis on every word. "I will not move. I will keep a careful watch. Go."

He went, closing the door behind him.

Left alone, she thought longingly about the warmth of her bed. It was cold out here, with currents of glacial air stirring along the passage. As quiet as it was frigid. Here in the heart of the castle, a series of thick stone walls silenced the storm outside.

It was also far too gloomy for comfort. Blame the power outage for that. As she'd been told last night, the castle's generator permitted a minimum of lamps, and then only at essential intervals. The corridors were like sinister tunnels without the aid of daylight.

All right, so she was glad about Leo's presence on the other side of this door, though she would never have admitted it to him.

Obeying her promise to keep vigilant, she looked to the left down the long corridor that stretched away into the darkness. Nothing moved. Nor was there anything but the stillness when she turned her gaze to the right in the direction they had come.

Silly to be nervous like this, checking the shadows for bogeymen when—

Something registered in her peripheral vision. Swinging her attention to the left again, Jennifer saw it emerging from the blackness at the far end of the passage. The same pale, robed figure she had sighted last night!

It drifted to a halt and stood there, swaying slightly like a reed in a gentle breeze. She could swear it pulsed with a faint glow. But the nimbus had to be an illusion, a trick of the light. Didn't it?

She was dragging in a mouthful of air, making an effort to steady herself, when the bathroom door opened and Leo reappeared. The expression she was wearing as she turned to face him must have been all too evident.

"What's wrong? You look like you've seen a—"

"Don't say it," she said in an anxious whisper, "because I think I have seen one. I think I'm *still* seeing it!"

Her gaze swiveled in the direction of the distant apparition. Leo followed it with a scowl on his face.

"Jenny, it's only one of the monks."

"I know that. I just don't think this one is alive."

"Come on, you can't believe in ghosts."

"Logic says I don't. My eyes tell me something else. Look at him. He's floating!"

Leo scoffed at her assertion. "He's not floating. He's simply standing there."

"What for? And if he's not a ghost, then what's he doing wandering around the castle in the middle of the night?"

"Maybe for the same reason you're out here." Leo lifted his voice, hailing the figure. "Yo, friar, if you're waiting for a turn in the loo, it's free now."

There was no response, no indication that whatever it was was even capable of hearing a human shout. The form wavered for a few seconds more, turned slowly and glided away, melting into the wall.

"What did I tell you? People don't walk through walls. Ghosts do. He *has* to be a ghost."

"And I'm Prince Charming. Come on, Snow White, we're going after your ghost. I want to see what he's haunting and why."

Before she could object, Leo grabbed her by the hand and rushed her along the corridor. They reached the spot where the wraith had vanished. And found, not a solid wall, but a narrow archway into a cross passage.

"So much for his disappearing act," Leo said.

"All right, but then where is he?" she asked, peering down the cross passage. "There's no one in sight."

"Doors, Jenny. People use them to go places. And that one down there at the end is still stirring on its hinges."

She found herself being hurried in the direction of the cracked door. And without a defense when the door, once fully opened, disclosed a flight of stairs winding down through the gloom. How could she go on arguing in favor of a ghost now that she could hear the sound of sandals on flesh-and-blood feet slapping softly on the stone treads somewhere below them?

The stairway carried them to the ground floor and into a broad gallery that stretched away on both sides. Jennifer realized she had been here before but by another route, one somewhere off to the right where the offices and chapel were located. And in the other direction…

"There's your spook," Leo said, indicating the robed figure moving away from them on the left. "The one you were making such a mystery about this morning with Brother Timothy."

The light was a little better here. Strong enough to tell her that the monk was no specter, even if he was behaving like one. The light-colored robe, the pale complexion, the fair hair…they had all contributed to the illusion.

Leo was going to gloat about this, wasn't he? She just *knew* he—

It struck her then. Pale complexion. Fair hair. No tonsure.

"Leo, it's Geoffrey!"

"Yeah." He had also recognized the young novice.

"But why doesn't he know we're here? It's like we don't exist for him."

"I don't think we do."

Was that supposed to make sense? Before she had a chance to figure it out, Leo was urging her forward again in pursuit of the novice.

"I don't want to lose him. He's after something, and I mean to know what it is."

Closed doors flew past them as they raced along the gallery. Behind one of them Jennifer heard the low throbbing of machinery at work.

"Think it must be the generator in there," Leo said before she could ask him.

Geoffrey was no longer in sight.

"He's turned a corner up there," she said.

They headed toward the corner. But before they could overtake the novice, the gallery was plunged into a sudden blackness. And a silence that was absolute.

Chapter Nine

Jennifer hated to admit that she was scared, even to herself, but the complete darkness was damned eerie. Not to mention the awful silence.

It took her a few seconds, but she finally managed the courage to say fairly calmly, "If you've got an explanation for what just happened, this is the time to share it with me. Unless, of course, I've gone blind, and then I don't want to hear it."

"Generator has quit," Leo said.

It was a reasonable assumption, she supposed, since there was no longer a thrum of machinery. "Oh, good, then I haven't lost my sight. Well, maybe not so good, huh?"

"No, not so good. The whole castle must be out."

She could have sworn he'd been close beside her when the power failed. Now his voice seemed to come from several yards away.

"Where are you?"

"Over here against the wall. If we're going to feel our way out of here, we'll need the wall to guide us."

"Right. Stay put. I'll find you."

It was bad enough to no longer have the reassuring sound of the generator. She was not going to do without his comforting nearness as well, though she wasn't about to admit that either.

"This way," he said.

Hands out in front of her, Jennifer groped her way toward his voice. She sensed she was approaching the wall when someone brushed by her. At least she hoped it was a someone and not a *something*, though with a killer who might be prowling through the castle that was probably not the best hope for her to have.

Coming to a standstill, she called out to Leo. "Did you just move?"

"I haven't stirred. I'm still here against the wall."

"I was afraid of that. Leo, we're not alone."

"Didn't hear anyone."

"I didn't either. But I felt it. I swear that someone went past me."

"Maybe Geoffrey on his way back from wherever he was headed."

"Or a cat," she said hopefully, not wanting to imagine it was anything more ominous than either Geoffrey or a harmless feline. "I mean, with a place this big there's probably the threat of mice, so they'd keep a cat. Wouldn't they?"

"Makes sense."

But she knew by the sharp edge in his voice that he didn't think whoever or whatever had been here with them, and possibly still was, was either Geoffrey or a cat.

"Stay where you are," he instructed her. "I'll come to you."

Her hands were still out in front of her, which was why when he reached her with the speed and accuracy of someone equipped with night-vision goggles, her fingers came in contact with him. Not just the safe leather of his coat either. What she felt was warm, firm flesh. Judging by the whorls of hair in the vicinity of a depression that had to be his navel, what her fingers had met was his naked waist exposed by the low-slung pajama bottoms and the gap in his coat.

"In any other situation," he said, his voice so close she could feel his breath on her face, "I'd invite you to do a little exploring with those hands, but as it is…"

"Sorry," she mumbled, quickly withdrawing her hands.

"Interesting."

"What?" she asked, resisting the longing to connect with him again, so she kept her hands down at her sides.

"That the generator should quit when it did, with us just about to catch up with Geoffrey. And right after that someone rushes past you."

"You think it was deliberate?"

"Could be. I'd like to have a look at it."

"Uh, under the circumstances…"

"Yeah, no light, no look."

"A flashlight would be useful about now. I don't suppose…"

"Didn't equip myself with one. But hold on, because maybe…"

She heard a rustling that indicated he was searching through the pockets of his coat.

"Ah," he announced with satisfaction, "I do have one. A book of matches left over from the days when I smoked."

There was the sound of a match being struck followed by a flare of light. Although it was only a glimmer, it provided a welcome glow to counter the total blackness. Leo raised the flame above his shoulder, permitting them a better look. Jennifer cast her gaze nervously and rapidly on all sides. There was no sign of anyone in the immediate area but themselves.

"Whoever it was," she said, "he's no longer hanging around."
I hope.

The match went out. Leo lit another. "We'd better move. This isn't a full book, so these matches aren't going to last."

He had to burn several more of them and, if his muttered curse was any evidence, sear one of his fingers in the effort before they stopped at one of the doors.

"If my memory is worth anything," he said, "this should be where all the throbbing was coming from."

The door was closed, but it wasn't locked when he tried it.

And his memory proved correct once they were inside. Jennifer's quick glance, before the current match burned down and had to be extinguished, revealed an enormous metal monster crouched on the floor and hooked up to fat cables. The generator, she presumed.

Leo lit a fresh match and hunkered down to inspect the thing. "Doesn't look damaged."

"Would you know?"

"Probably not. I'm not much of a mechanic. On the other hand, if someone did want to temporarily shut down the power, it would be much easier to…" His head lifted, his gaze searching the walls.

"What are you looking for?"

"The breaker panel. There should be one."

"How about that box over there peeking through the stepladder?"

"That's it." He got to his feet and started for the panel fitted into the wall. Jennifer followed him.

When they arrived at the panel, it took a further match to enable Leo to reach behind the ladder and scrape its door open.

"Look," he said once he was inside. "Main switch has been turned off." His free hand closed over the switch. "Say a prayer that this is all it takes."

He snapped the switch over to the on position. The generator rumbled back to life. Light streamed through the door they'd left open behind them as the sparsely spaced lamps in the gallery bloomed again.

"What do you know, it works."

"Nice," she said. Having the power restored was a relief. Except for one thing. "What isn't so nice is knowing for sure now that someone was in here and did cut the power."

"And if it wasn't Geoffrey, then the question is still who and why." Leo clicked the door shut on the panel and withdrew his arm from behind the ladder.

"Maybe Geoffrey himself can tell us that. Or could if we hadn't lost him."

There was no sign of either the novice or the phantom when they emerged from the generator room. Except for the two of them, the gallery was deserted.

"I guess we won't be doing any more chasing after Geoffrey tonight," Jennifer said, gazing toward the chapel where nothing stirred.

Leo, who was checking the other direction, responded with a matter-of-fact, "Seems like he's just gone and saved us the trouble of that. Turn around and look."

Wheeling, she saw the robed figure of the young novice. Having reappeared from around the far corner where he had earlier vanished, he was now gliding in their direction. He seemed in no way worried by their presence.

"Leo, it's like you said before. He isn't even aware of us."

"Maybe because he's too busy searching for something that he's missing. But just what that could be…"

Geoffrey continued to advance on them with a slow, even gait. And then all at once it struck her. The explanation for her ghost, who had appeared to float like a wraith through the halls. Who had failed to hear them calling out to him. Who on neither occasion had been conscious of them.

Geoffrey was a somnambulist!

"I swear the kid's in a trance," Leo muttered as Geoffrey neared them. "He must be on drugs. Look at those glazed eyes staring at us."

"He isn't on drugs," Jennifer corrected him. "And those glazed eyes aren't seeing us at all. Don't you understand? He's sleepwalking."

"Sleepwal— I'll be damned, you're right!" he said as Geoffrey drifted past them without a glance or a pause. "Then it's time he wakes up and answers a few questions."

Jennifer clutched Leo's arm, holding him back as he started

to reach for the novice. "Don't! I've heard it can be dangerous to wake a sleepwalker. Anyway, if we took that chance, he'd probably be nothing but confused. He wouldn't know where he's at or what he's been doing and why, if there even is a *why*."

"Yeah," Leo reluctantly agreed. "But there has to be a *why*. Whoever cut the power to stop us from following him must have thought so."

It was a chilling reminder for her of the menace that gripped Warley Castle.

"Only this time he's not around to keep us from tailing the kid," Leo added. "Let's go. I want to see where he's headed now."

"Back to his bed, I imagine," Jennifer concluded a moment later when they caught up with Geoffrey in the chapel. He was just on his way through the entrance into the area of the monastery that was off-limits to anyone but the brothers.

"Looks like the show's over for tonight," Leo said regretfully as the door closed behind the novice.

"Leaving us with those questions you wanted to ask."

"Come morning, I will ask them," he promised.

But you won't get the answers, Jennifer thought. Not from Geoffrey anyway. He'll either be unable to answer them or unwilling. She wasn't going to argue with Leo about that, though. Not when she was too tired now after their adventure to want anything but her bed.

Leo had something else in mind, however. He lost no time informing her of his intention when they got back to her room.

"You're not spending another night in here."

"I'm not, huh?"

"No, you aren't. I don't want you on your own again. Not after what just happened. Shouldn't have left you alone in here even before that."

"So, we'll leave the connecting door wide open this time."

"No, we won't. You're coming into my room with me."

"I see. And, uh, I don't get any vote in this decision. Is that it?"

"That's about it, yeah."

She nodded slowly. "You are remembering, aren't you, that there's just one bed in your room?"

"That's no problem."

"It isn't?"

"No, because I'm going to take the mattress off your bed and put it on the floor next to my bed. You get my bed, and I get the mattress."

"I don't think so."

"Why?"

Why? Because she was probably in more danger from Leo McKenzie than their unknown assailant. Because having him that close to her all night, even if they weren't sharing the same bed, was a temptation she didn't want to risk. After those sizzling kisses in the chapel and the alcove, she was in enough trouble with this compelling man as it was.

Jennifer couldn't bring herself to tell him that, though. He already had more ego than he needed. All she could manage was a feeble "Why does it have to be your room? Why can't we drag your mattress in here?" It was a silly argument, but the thought of sleeping in his bed…

"Because if our killer should try to get at you, he'll come to your room. If he does, you won't be here. That might not stop him, but the delay could be enough to warn us. Makes you less vulnerable, see."

In the end, ammunition exhausted, she lost the battle. Ten minutes later, with her mattress deposited on his floor, the connecting door closed and her robe shed, she found herself crawling into his bed.

"We'll leave the lamp burning," he said from across the room where he was restoring the fire on the hearth. "It's safer that way."

No, she thought, the light wasn't safe. Not safe at all.

The warmth of the fire must have been too much for Leo, because he had peeled off his coat and dropped it on a chair seat. He was naked now from the waist up. The slabs of smooth muscle on his well-defined chest and upper arms gleamed in the glow from the flames. Jennifer was mesmerized by all that bold masculinity.

Uh-uh, there was no safety for her in the sight of him like that. But then she wouldn't have been any more secure without the lamp, not in this provocative situation when her treacherous imagination would have supplied what her vision couldn't in the dark.

And wouldn't you know he would look up at that instant and catch her staring at him.

"Something bothering you?"

Oh, he was bothering her all right. But she had no intention of letting him know that. She covered the awkward moment with what she hoped was a casual "Just wondering about the tattoo. Unusual."

He glanced down at the salamander wrapped halfway around the biceps of his right arm, as if he'd forgotten it was there. "Yeah, well, my ex-wife had a thing about salamanders at the time. She had a lot of nutty passions, none of which lasted for very long. Including me."

He had been married? "So the tattoo was something you did to please her?"

"Could be. I don't remember much about it. Just that we were out on the town celebrating one night. Don't ask me why. Kimberly was always ready to celebrate something. All I know is that after one round of drinks too many we ended up in this tattoo parlor."

"And the result was the salamander."

His broad shoulders lifted in a shrug. "People make mistakes."

"You could have it removed."

"Not the salamander. Kimberly was the mistake."

"I'm sorry."

"So was I. Trouble was, she craved excitement. I guess she

thought she'd get plenty of excitement being married to a private investigator. She was wrong, because a P.I.'s work is mostly routine, dull stuff."

His hand began to rub his chest in slow, lazy circles. She didn't think he was aware of his action, but it was arousing just the same.

"Anyway," he said, "I've got the salamander. I don't have Kimberly. Last I heard she was keeping company with a politician. Now there's excitement."

Jennifer knew she'd be in trouble if she went on being fascinated by that sensual performance with his chest.

"Personally, I've had enough excitement for one night. Think I'll try to get some sleep."

She slid down flat under the covers, closing her eyes against the image of him. It didn't work. Leo had slept in this bed, and though none of his warmth lingered, she could swear that the impression of his body was still here. That and faint traces of his musky scent.

She heard him kicking off his loafers, the rustle of the mattress as he stretched out on it, settling down for what remained of the night. How was she supposed to get to sleep when she was conscious of him being so close to her? When only inches separated them?

Aching for him was bad enough. Why did she have to go and make it worse by thinking about his ex-wife? From the tone of his voice, she'd been able to tell that Leo had been hurt by that marriage. Was he still hurting? And why should that possibility bother her so much?

LOCKED HANDS pillowing his head, Leo lay there on his back listening to the cry of the wind outside that told him the storm still had the moors in its fierce jaws. Another kind of storm raged inside his head.

Why had he let Jennifer know about his ex-wife? He never

talked about Kimberly if he could help it. Too many bitter memories, he supposed.

Except—

What? What was different?

And then all at once, with a sense of wonder, he knew. He was no longer bitter. He had let the past go, and Kimberly along with it.

When had that gone and happened? Somewhere over the last twenty-four hours, he figured. But why now and not anytime during the months since his divorce? Yeah, *why* was a much more relevant question. He knew the answer, didn't he?

Because twenty-four hours ago you didn't know Jennifer Rowan.

Oh, yes, Jennifer had something to do with it all right. In fact, a lot of *somethings*. And right now one of them had him painfully hard, with a longing to have her body under his. She was so close to him that he could smell her warm, womanly scent. A fragrance that was driving him wild. Hell, it was all he could do to resist the urge to reach out for her.

But resist it he did. He didn't need any more mistakes like Kimberly.

Too late, though. Because on another level, one that wasn't physical but was equally strong, he had already lost the struggle.

Somewhere in those same twenty-four hours his motive had undergone a change. He was less interested now in having her near him to observe her as a suspect in his brother's death than in watching over her to keep her safe.

A man's primal instinct to protect his woman. It was a powerful aphrodisiac.

Don't fool yourself, McKenzie. Whatever Jennifer Rowan has come to mean to you, you've still got that last, little, niggling doubt about her innocence. And until you deal with that...

"CAN YOU EXPLAIN to me just what we're doing?" Jennifer asked.

She watched Leo as he wrapped a napkin around an orange, a boiled egg, and a muffin from the breakfast buffet that the monks had laid out for their guests on the sideboard. His selections were all food that could be eaten on the run.

"I told you last night. I have questions about Geoffrey's activities, and until we get some answers, this investigation is going nowhere. Come on, pick something for yourself. I want to get out of here before any of the others show up and delay us."

They were alone in the dining parlor. The hour was very early, too early for Jennifer to have been roused out of bed by an eager Leo.

"Uh, wouldn't it be simpler to wait here until Geoffrey arrives instead of trying to hunt him down? Not that he's likely to have those answers for us when we do find him."

"I know that. My questions aren't for Geoffrey."

"But who else would have answers?"

"Maybe Father Stephen. I've been wondering if the abbot knows his novice is sleepwalking through the castle every night and why. Don't think he'll mind if we eat in his office. Maybe he'll even have coffee to offer us. Is that all you're taking?"

"It's all I want," she said, wrapping a single buttered scone in one of the napkins.

But Leo's haste was unnecessary. Father Stephen was not in his office. Nor were any of the other monks in evidence. The broad, stone-floored gallery was deserted.

"Wonder where they all got to," Leo said. "Think we dare look for the padre?"

"What I think is that we'd better wait right here. We can't interrupt them at terce, because I imagine that's where they are."

Leo looked at her, puzzled. "What does that mean?"

Jennifer explained it to him. "Terce is one of the canonical periods of devotion. If I'm right, this should be the hour for it. Listen. You can hear them now."

The door to the chapel must have been opened, because from around a corner in the gallery came the muted chants of the brothers in the litany of their regular prayers. It was a soothing sound, even in this place where the peace had been so savagely violated.

"Guess we'd better make ourselves comfortable then," Leo said.

But comfortable wasn't something Jennifer was feeling with Leo this morning, not when her memories of his intimate presence last night were still so potent. Maybe he was experiencing the same uneasiness, because they ate their breakfast in silence after they settled themselves in the abbot's office.

Father Stephen seemed pleased to find them there when his tall, angular figure appeared in the open doorway some minutes later.

"I've been hoping to hear a report from you," he said, shutting the door behind him and seating himself at his desk. "How is the investigation progressing?"

Jennifer let Leo relate what they had learned yesterday and what they hadn't learned. The abbot was disturbed by the presence of the knife in Patrick's room, but none of their other discoveries in the search merited any alarm from him.

"I imagine they can all be explained," he said. "Perhaps even the knife isn't significant, but Patrick must satisfy me about that if he is serious about joining our order."

"I agree," Leo said. "But there's something else that worries me, and that's really why we're here."

"Oh?"

"It's Geoffrey, Father. Did you know your novice has been sleepwalking at night?"

The abbot didn't know and listened attentively to Leo's account of last night's episode, as well as Jennifer's experience the night before.

Father Stephen nodded gravely when they were finished. "I'm sorry to hear of Geoffrey's distress, because I believe that's just what this sleepwalking is all about. It's not uncommon, you know, for a brother to have doubts before he takes his final vows."

"You think his sleepwalking is a symptom of that?" Jennifer asked him.

"I do, and I'm glad you told me about it. It gives me the opportunity to counsel him, and with prayer—"

Not satisfied, Leo interrupted him. "Excuse me, Father, but the kid wasn't just wandering around. Sleepwalking or not, I'd swear he was looking for something."

"Something he is missing emotionally, yes. Something that is entirely spiritual in nature."

"There was nothing spiritual about that generator being turned off," Leo reminded him.

Father Stephen frowned. "Yes, that part is mystifying. But not connected with Geoffrey surely."

Jennifer wasn't convinced of that, and she knew by the way Leo's mouth had tightened that he wasn't convinced either. But neither of them pressed the abbot about it.

"Of course," Father Stephen said thoughtfully, "there is another matter that may very well be related to Geoffrey's sleepwalking. I'd forgotten how worried he's been in that direction. It's his father, you see."

"Trouble?" Leo asked.

The abbot nodded. "The family phoned a few days ago to let us know that Geoffrey's father is in the hospital. He needed surgery for a heart ailment. Geoffrey was so anxious about it that I permitted him to accompany Brother Anthony to London to visit his father."

"Let me get this clear," Leo said, leaning earnestly toward

the abbot. "Are you telling us that Geoffrey was with Brother Anthony when the Warley Madonna was taken down to London to be handed over to my brother, Guy, for evaluation?"

"They traveled together, yes."

Jennifer and Leo traded significant glances, and she knew they were thinking the same thing. It was her turn to lean forward in her chair.

"Father, was Brother Anthony worried about the welfare of the Madonna when he left the monastery to deliver the piece to Guy?"

The abbot thought about it for a few seconds before he shook his head. "To my knowledge, he was not. Of course, he intended to be very careful with it, as anyone would with something of great value."

"Which means that somewhere between here and London he did find a reason to be worried about its safety. Father, do you remember what I told you yesterday after Brother Anthony's death? How he told Guy when he turned the Madonna over to him that he was concerned about it?"

The abbot stared at Jennifer, his lined face registering a series of emotions. Bafflement at first, then understanding followed by shock. "You cannot seriously be suggesting that Geoffrey—No, it is unthinkable, as well as impossible!"

"Father," Leo said severely, "my brother was murdered and the Madonna stolen. And if Geoffrey was there in London when that happened—"

"But he was not. He and Brother Anthony parted when they reached London. Geoffrey went on to Guildford. He was there in the hospital with his family when your brother was killed."

"How can you be certain of that?"

"Because I phoned the hospital that night to ask about the condition of his father. I was able to speak to Geoffrey himself. He assured me his father was improving and that he would be on the first train in the morning back to Yorkshire."

"And Guildford is…"

"Much too far from London for Geoffrey to have reached your brother's shop and returned to the hospital to be there for my call, which I made very close to the time of Guy Spalding's death according to the news report."

Leo sat back in his chair. "And that leaves Geoffrey with a solid alibi."

"I am happy to say that it does."

A rap sounded on the office door. When the abbot responded to it, the monk called Brother Michael poked his head in.

"Sorry to interrupt, Father, but you're wanted in the workshops. Another problem with the illuminations that needs your decision before we can proceed."

The abbot rose to his feet. "This shouldn't take long," he informed his visitors. "If you'd care to wait, we can resume our meeting when I get back."

"That won't be necessary," Leo informed him. "I think we're finished here."

"Then for now…"

The abbot left them sitting there. When he was gone, Jennifer turned to Leo. "Thoughts?"

"We didn't get that coffee I was hoping for."

"I was referring to something a little more profound than that," she said. "Like Geoffrey being in the clear. At least where Guy and the theft of the Madonna are concerned."

"Looks like it. It would have been the perfect explanation for the kid's sleepwalking, too. Guilt over Guy and the Madonna. Still…"

"What?"

"This thing of Brother Anthony warning Guy the Madonna might be in danger. If you're right about that…"

"*If?*"

Was he suggesting that Guy hadn't told her any such thing? That she'd been lying about it? Maybe to provide another reason why she couldn't have killed Guy herself and taken the Madonna? If so, that meant Leo had yet to be entirely convinced of her innocence.

"I didn't mean that," he said hastily. "It's just that you might have misunderstood Guy."

Jennifer wasn't sure she believed him. Wasn't certain he didn't nurse a lingering doubt about her. It was a depressing possibility.

"I didn't misunderstand him," she said emphatically.

"Okay. Then it leaves us with the riddle of Brother Anthony having some cause to be worried about the Madonna on the trip to London."

"Which brings us back to Geoffrey, since he was Brother Anthony's companion on that journey."

"And Guy didn't tell you why the monk cautioned him?"

"He didn't know. I had the impression Brother Anthony was reluctant to explain it to him."

"Figures."

"How?"

"Because if it was Geoffrey who concerned him, he wouldn't want to name a fellow brother."

"He wasn't a fellow brother," Jennifer reminded him. "Not yet. But I suppose the same explanation could apply to a novice about to join his order. Anyway, all of this is only speculation. And none of it is any good with Geoffrey having an alibi. We're back to another dead end."

But Leo was unwilling to settle for that. "Dead ends can be funny things, Jenny," he said when they came away from the abbot's office. "Sometimes they're not dead ends at all."

"Is that private eye talk? If it is, I wish you'd translate it for me."

"I'm just saying that things don't always turn out to be what they seem. Like the padre's explanation for Geoffrey's sleep-walking. He's convinced it was purely emotional, that what the kid was looking for was spiritual in nature."

"And you don't buy that?"

"Don't think I do. I think maybe Geoffrey was subconsciously hunting for something more solid than that."

"Like what?"

"Who knows. But maybe…"

Jennifer watched him as he turned his head to gaze along the gallery in the direction they had been following the novice last night.

"The kid was on his way around the corner down there when we lost him," he said. "Wonder what's around that corner."

"And," she added, "whether the lights went out just because somebody didn't want us to know what's there."

"Yeah, but we don't have to worry about that now. We've got the daylight, and I've got a P.I.'s itch that needs to be scratched."

Chapter Ten

"More passages in this place than an Egyptian tomb," Leo said.

And as cold and dim as one, Jennifer thought, rounding the corner and entering another corridor.

It was not as wide as the gallery they left behind, nor as long. There were no doors along its stretch, only a shallow flight of stairs waiting at its end. Reaching the steps, they mounted the deep, stone treads to a landing where a broad archway framed what seemed like an immense cavern.

"Cozy, huh?" Leo remarked as they passed through the archway.

"It's the great hall," Jennifer said, looking up toward the lofty ceiling where the soaring rafters were all but lost in the heavy shadows.

"Don't think they've had any banquets here lately."

No, she thought, the enormous hall couldn't have been used in decades. A thick coating of dust testified to that.

Panes on some of the lancet windows high on the walls were broken, admitting snow along with a weak, winter daylight that cast the whole place in a gray gloom. The invading dampness had rotted the floorboards in several places, leaving treacherous gaps which they carefully avoided as they moved around the hall.

"Whole place has been stripped," Leo observed. "Not a stick of furniture in sight."

Nor could the yawning fireplace have seen a blaze on its hearth since the day the furnishings had been removed. And Jennifer would have welcomed a fire. The air was frigid with the kind of raw, numbing cold that penetrated to the bone.

"Okay," Leo said, "so I was wrong about that dead end. It is one, because it doesn't look like there's anything here that could have interested Geoffrey."

"Or any reason for the generator being shut down to stop us from following him here."

"Which means if the kid did have some secret destination, this can't be it. Come on, let's get out of here."

But Jennifer hung back. Although the great hall might be hollow and bare, it had one intact glory to recommend it. The usual minstrel's gallery overhung the room above them. She could see that the carving on the oak panels supporting its railing, even dulled as it was beneath a layer of grime, was very fine.

This was the kind of thing her career in antiques was all about, and she wanted a minute to admire those panels. She was doing that when her gaze was captured by a movement on the wall behind the gallery. Even from this distance, and as slight as it was, she was convinced it was there. Or did she *feel* it rather than actually see it?

Grabbing Leo's arm as he was turning away, she issued a low, urgent, "The stone mask up there on the wall!"

"What about it?"

"It must be the other side of the mask in the dining parlor. You know, the squint with the hollow eyes."

"And?"

"The eyes aren't hollow now. Someone is up there in the old solarium watching us!"

"Your vision must be better than mine because I can't tell. But if you're right—"

"I am right!" She *was* feeling it, that flesh-crawling sensation of being spied on from a hidden source.

"There's a door there at the end of the gallery," he said. "It probably leads into the dining parlor. If someone *is* in there watching us, I want to know who and why."

A hanging stairway provided direct access from the floor of the great hall to the minstrel's gallery above them. Leo raced to the flight and up the stairway, with Jennifer directly behind him.

The staircase was a fragile-looking affair, but she knew from experience that such ancient structures could be made to look delicate by their builders without sacrificing their strength. She didn't worry about it. Not until midway on their climb when the stairway began to tremble under their weight. Or did she imagine it?

They were nearing the top, with no hesitation from Leo in front of her, when she knew she *wasn't* imagining it. The stairway was shaking in earnest now.

"Leo, stop! This thing is coming apart!"

He halted, looking back at her. "It's weak from age, but I think it's still sound enough to—"

He got no further. The threat became a reality when, without another warning, the stairway collapsed. There was the alarming sound of wood tearing away from its support, a cry that only afterwards Jennifer realized was her own and immediately following it the rumble and crash of plummeting timbers.

She reached out to save herself, but there was nothing to clutch. Nowhere to go but down. She remembered falling into space but not the lightning impact that punched the wind out of her when she hit the floor. As awareness returned, she found herself lying in the wreckage strewn across the hall.

Only that wasn't altogether accurate. Not after she recovered her senses enough to check her situation. She saw now that large sections of the flooring on both sides of her were gone.

The splintered beams from the stairway had smashed through the decayed floorboards, taking everything with it but the joists.

Jennifer had ended up on one of those wide joists and was sprawled along its length, all but her arms which dangled on either side of her into the black hole where floorboards and stair timbers had vanished. A cellar? If so, it was a deep one because she couldn't see the bottom.

Lifting her head, she peered around the hall, searching for a sign of Leo. Dear God, had he been carried into that awful chasm below her?

"Over here," he called.

She could see him now through the cloud of dust that was beginning to settle. To her relief, he had been thrown several yards away from her, landing where the floor was still solid.

"Are you hurt?" he asked her, picking himself up from the scattered remnants of the stairway.

Breath restored sufficiently enough to answer him, she managed to squeeze out a slow, "I don't—don't know. I don't think so. You?"

Getting to his feet, he tested his limbs. "Nothing broken. Maybe just a few bruises." He glanced up at all that was left of the stairway, a ragged scrap clinging to the underside of the minstrel's gallery. "Damn, that was some explosion! I think I'm going to have to start listening to you from now on."

"Good, because I have something to tell you."

"What?"

"I seem to be stranded out here on this beam."

"Hang on, I'm coming to get you."

"Better not. I don't know how safe it is. I'll come to you."

"Can you manage it?" He had reached the edge of the hole where he was hunkered down, gazing anxiously at her where she hung precariously on the joist.

"Piece of cake."

Hands locked over the top of the beam, she levered herself

into a sitting position so that she was straddling the joist. But when she started to scoot herself along its length, she heard the sound of splitting wood, felt the beam begin to sag under her concentrated weight.

"Well, maybe not," she said.

"Don't move!" Leo warned her. "Not another inch!"

Freezing, she watched him fearfully as he flattened himself on the floor.

"All right," he instructed her, "lower yourself back down. Slowly now."

Jennifer stretched herself along the beam. But as careful as she was to distribute her weight again, the joist creaked, threatening to buckle and spill her into the void below.

"That's enough!" Leo said. "Don't try to crawl over to me. Just hold out your arms toward me as far as they'll go. If I can grab your hands, I can haul you off that thing."

She obeyed him, extending her arms. Leo's own long arms reached out for her from his flattened position. But they weren't long enough. Space still separated them from any connection. When he tried to wriggle forward to gain a few more inches, the flooring on the lip of the gap started to crumble.

"This is no good," he said, backing off.

"Maybe if I—"

"No! Whatever you tried would involve movement, and I don't want you risking it. That joist could give way at any time. I need a line, something I can throw to you."

"You'll have to go back and find one of the brothers. They should be able to provide a line."

"That would take too long."

"But—"

"I'm not leaving you, Jenny," he insisted. "Not unless it becomes absolutely necessary."

Leo scrambled to his feet. She watched him as he swiftly scanned every corner of the hall. But there was nothing that would serve his purpose. Even the broken timbers from the fallen staircase were too short, and not dependable anyway in their decayed condition. The best of them had probably plunged into the hole.

Stretching his head back, he gazed into the shadows above them. "There!"

Jennifer lifted her gaze and saw a rusted iron chandelier whose sockets had once held thick candles. The fixture was suspended by a heavy chain from the rafters overhead.

Her eyes followed the chain. At its highest point it passed through a ring, where it became a stout rope that was stretched over to a side wall. From here the rope descended through several other iron rings embedded in the wall, ending at a cleat around which it was tightly secured. Once unwound from the cleat, the rope would have permitted the chandelier to be lowered to the floor in order to light its long vanished candles.

"Just hold on," Leo encouraged her. "I'll be as fast as I can."

Not daring to stir, muscles tense, her whole body was burning now in her effort to go on clinging to that joist. She didn't trust herself to imagine the consequences if the weakened beam collapsed before Leo could rescue her.

All she permitted herself to do was to watch him as he sped to the wall, rapidly unwound the rope and, once free from the cleat to which it was anchored, allowed the fixture to drop to the floor where it landed with a clatter.

Working with haste, Leo dragged the chain and rope down from its rings until it was coiled at his feet. The rope was long enough that it could remain attached to the chain. She just prayed it wasn't as rotten as everything else in the hall.

Leo already had a large noose prepared in the free end of the line when he strode back to the joist where she was pinned.

"Don't try to reach for it," he said, crouching down on the edge of the gap. "Just stay put and let me get it to you. Ready?"

"Understood. Just get me off this thing."

It took him several tries with the makeshift lasso until one of his tosses finally settled in front of her nose.

"Okay, now ease it over your head and under your arms."

Jennifer felt like a human thread trying to squeeze its way through the eye of a needle without overturning the sewing basket. But somehow she managed to work her way inside the loop. Once it was in place, Leo tugged on his end of the line until the noose closed snugly around her body.

"I've got you now. If that joist goes under, you're not going with it."

The rope tightened as he drew her slowly toward him. The ancient wood groaned with the strain, the joist beginning to cave beneath her. Jennifer felt herself sinking with it. Would the old rope hold or snap in two along with the beam?

The old rope did hold. The beam didn't. It suddenly gave way under her and went crashing to the depths below. But Leo's grasp on the rope that held her enabled him to pull her to safety. Once he had her on solid flooring, he reached for her, gathering her up into his arms.

Jennifer thought that no rescue could have been sweeter. She was clasped fiercely to his chest and held there firmly, as if he'd come within a breath of losing his most precious possession and feared now to let it go. She submitted to his embrace, clinging to him in relief.

It wasn't enough. She wanted more than just his arms around her. Yearned for it. But it didn't happen. Another weakened joist failed in that second with a sharp crack that jolted them back to reality. Leo released her.

"Let's get this thing off you," he said, his fingers working to free her of the rope. "And then we'd better get out of here before the rest of the floor decides to collapse on us."

Jennifer knew he was right, that she couldn't afford to be disappointed. That to linger here was an invitation for further disaster. But she *was* disappointed. She didn't express it, however. Didn't utter a sound until, after casting the rope aside, he scrambled to his feet, lifting her up with him.

It was only then, with her weight on it, that she felt a stinging in her left leg. And reacted to it with a muttered, "Oooh."

"What?" he demanded sharply. "What's wrong?"

She looked down, noticing what she had been oblivious to until now. There was a long tear in the leg of her slacks, exposing her calf and a smear of blood.

"Damn. One of my favorite pairs, too."

"You're worrying about the pants?" Leo was already crouched down and examining her calf.

"They were expensive."

"Right. And that's important. How about the leg? In case you're interested, you've got a gash here with blood seeping out of it."

"Oh. Well, it can't be much. It's just a little sore."

"Jenny, it needs attention. You're going to the infirmary."

He surged to his feet. Before she could stop him, he had scooped her up into his arms and was carrying her swiftly out of the hall.

"Leo, this is crazy. I can walk there. It's not much more than a scratch."

His only reply was to tighten his hold on her.

"THAT'S A RARE TREAT, that is," Brother Timothy observed as he cleaned the blood away from her wound.

"How bad is it?" Leo hovered over Jennifer anxiously.

"I'm thinking amputation," the monk said solemnly.

Leo stared at him.

Brother Timothy chuckled. "Easy, laddie. It's little more than a scrape needing a bit of a plaster. After what happened, lucky not to be something much worse, I'd say."

"Leo, do you have a dog back home?" Jennifer asked him.

"No. What are you talking about?"

"I've got this tough, older brother. He hates people fussing.

But one time the family dog broke a leg, and guess who went all to pieces. I just think that's interesting."

"You're delirious from your injury," he said gruffly.

Brother Timothy had just finished patching up her leg when a worried Father Stephen, summoned by Brother Michael, arrived on the scene.

"Is she all right, Timothy?"

"As right as rain," the monk told him cheerfully.

Reassured, the abbot directed his attention to Jennifer and Leo. His concern turned into a rigid disapproval that bordered on anger. He had obviously been told what had happened in the great hall and wasn't pleased about it.

"Why in the name of all that's holy would the two of you risk going into the hall when the notice pinned on the barriers clearly marked the room as unsafe, not to mention the other notice at the bottom of the gallery stairway."

Jennifer and Leo traded startled looks.

"What barriers would those be, padre?" Leo asked him.

"The trestles, of course, that were placed both at the foot of the stairway and across the entrance to the hall. You call them sawhorses, I believe. With the badly leaking roof in there having caused so much decay, the trestles were a temporary measure until we could afford repairs. But apparently they weren't sufficient since you chose to ignore them."

"Father," Jennifer informed him quietly, "there were no sawhorses or posted warnings anywhere in sight."

The abbot's expression registered his alarm. "You are telling me they were removed? *Deliberately* removed? *All* of them?"

"All of them," Leo said. "Looks like someone didn't want us to know how dangerous the place was."

Father Stephen was silent for a minute as he dealt with the shock of the latest violation in his well-ordered monastery. Then, collecting himself, he said decisively, "This evil can't go on. It must be stopped."

"Believe me, padre, we're doing our best to discover who's responsible for it."

"Yes, before another tragedy occurs. But I implore you to be very careful. You must both promise me this."

The abbot departed after receiving their pledges. A moment later Brother Timothy released Jennifer from the infirmary, telling her there was no reason she couldn't resume normal use of the leg but recommending that she rest it first for a few hours.

To Jennifer's exasperation, Leo insisted on obeying the monk's instruction. Although this time he refrained from carrying her, he escorted her directly back to his room where he ordered her to stretch out on the bed. Touched though she was by his concern, she stubbornly resisted it.

"I'm not climbing onto that bed until I have a bath and change my clothes." She eyed him critically. "And you need to do the same. Look at us. We look like a couple of refugees from a landfill."

Although he grumbled about it, Leo complied with her decree.

After a visit to the bathroom, and wearing fresh outfits, they returned to his room. Jennifer settled on the bed, propping herself up with a mound of pillows while Leo mended the fire before sprawling in a chair facing the bed.

She tried not to be distracted by the sight of those long legs stretched out in front of him, by the way his faded jeans clung to his muscular thighs and narrow hips, how those same tight jeans displayed—

Well, never mind what they so blatantly displayed.

Lifting her gaze, she made an effort to concentrate on his face. But even here she ran into trouble, unable to stop herself from being fascinated by that crescent-shaped scar on his cheek. By the way those whiskey-colored eyes of his gazed at her so intimately, firing a memory of how his arms had wrapped around her in the great hall, of that brief but urgent closeness they had shared.

"I think we should talk," she said with a briskness meant to defuse the moment.

"Talk is good," he agreed, although she wasn't sure she liked the way he said it, his voice slow and thick with what sounded like something other than business.

"It's also necessary." And safer, she figured.

"Okay," he relented, "what did you have in mind?"

"About the accident that wasn't an accident. Someone had to have realized the power outage last night wouldn't stop us from trying to learn where Geoffrey went and why. They removed those barriers and the notices for a reason."

Leo nodded. "Sure. And we both know what that reason was."

"To entice us into the great hall. They wanted us to climb that stairway. They were watching from the squint hoping we would."

"A lure."

"Exactly. And it worked. We went up the stairway because we wanted to know who was on the other side of the squint. They were counting on that, and they got what they wanted. The stairway collapsed. What they didn't get was our broken necks."

"Must have been a big disappointment."

"But who and why?"

"The why is easy, Jenny. We're snooping, and someone doesn't like it."

"Which means there *is* something to find, and they're worried about that. The thing that Geoffrey could have been looking for last night. Only what is it and where is it?"

"Well, not in the great hall, at least not this morning or we wouldn't have been lured there. As for the who—" He shrugged.

"So what comes next?"

"Geoffrey," he said without hesitation. "It's time for the kid to answer some questions."

"Maybe he doesn't know the answers. Not if he has no memory of where he was sleepwalking and why."

"We'll see what he has to say over lunch."

BUT THE NOVICE WASN'T in the dining parlor when all of them gathered for lunch. Patrick explained his absence to Jennifer and Leo.

"I'm on my own today," the young man said. "Geoffrey is with the brothers in the workshops. They're teaching him how to illuminate Psalters."

Leo looked bewildered.

Jennifer, remembering how Brother Michael had earlier called the abbot back to the workshops because of a problem with the illuminations, enlightened him. "It's the ancient art of illustrating books of devotion. The medieval monks were masters of it. But that it's still being practiced today…"

"There's a market for reproductions of the old, holy manuscripts using the original methods," Patrick informed them with an uncharacteristic enthusiasm. "It's how the monastery supports itself, that and woolen products from the local sheep."

"How long has Geoffrey been in the workshops?" Leo wanted to know.

"They called for him right after breakfast," Patrick said. "I imagine he'll be there for the rest of the day. I'd love to learn illuminating myself," he added wistfully.

Which means it wasn't Geoffrey who'd spied on them from the squint, Jennifer thought. Not when he had an alibi that could be easily checked. That left one of the others.

Which one of them? she asked herself, gazing around the table after she and Leo joined the company with their plates from the buffet where they had spoken to Patrick. Who cut the power last night, lured us into the great hall this morning, watched us from the squint in this very room?

Leo had to be thinking the same thing. But instead of just speculating, he made an effort to identify the culprit.

"What have you all been doing to pass the time this

morning?" he asked them amiably. "Wasn't there some mention of getting up a bridge game here in the parlor?"

Roger Harding answered him soberly. "I'm afraid none of us has been in any mood for cards. I believe we all went our separate ways after breakfast."

But someone returned to the dining parlor and that squint, Jennifer thought.

"Don't have to wonder what you and Ms. Rowan were up to, old man," Harry Ireland said. "Bad scene down in the great hall, what?"

Leo fixed a steely gaze on the salesman. "You heard about the accident then?"

"Word gets around."

"It's another bad omen," the superstitious Fiona Brasher mumbled.

"You don't want to go messing around in dangerous places," Harry warned them cheerfully. "Pass me the shaker there, would you, Mrs. Harding? Eggs need a bit of salt."

Jennifer noticed that Sybil's hand trembled when she handed him the salt. She looked unwell. Nor had she contributed any word to the conversation, which was unlike her. It was rather apparent that she was suffering a bad hangover and that her husband was concerned about her. Roger kept glancing at her with expressions of sympathy. Jennifer didn't know who to feel more sorry for, Roger or Sybil.

The others, too, were silent after that. It was no use. She and Leo weren't going to learn anything here. The group had closed ranks against them since hearing about their investigation. They were wary now.

And clearly worried about the evil that had Warley Castle in its grip. Worried also about the confinement forced on them by a storm that made it impossible to escape from that evil. Jennifer could almost smell their tension.

She was feeling the same stress, the same sense of helplessness when she and Leo returned to his room. Depressed by their efforts that had yet to produce any answers, she went to the window and looked out at the blizzard. This was the second day of it, and it showed no sign of slackening.

But it couldn't go on forever. It *would* quit, if not later on today, then perhaps sometime tomorrow. And when the castle was no longer cut off by the weather, there would be nothing to keep its reluctant guests from leaving. She would lose her chance to prove her innocence.

Turning her head, she saw that Leo had seated himself on the chair. He had a pencil in his hand and was bent over a notebook.

"What are you doing?" she asked him.

"What I always do sooner or later on a case. I'm listing the suspects along with the sequence of events. Getting it down on paper helps me to get a clearer picture of the whole thing, even come up with a fresh lead."

"Does it work?"

"Sometimes, if I'm lucky. Shouldn't you be on the bed resting that leg?"

"The leg is fine. Well, actually it isn't. It wants action."

One of his eyebrows lifted. "Such as?"

"I don't know. I just feel we should be doing something." Anything, she thought, but hiding away here in this room waiting for inspiration.

He closed the notebook. "I'm open to suggestions."

"How about looking again for whatever it is our culprit is hiding?"

"That's a plan. Where do you think we should start? Down in the dungeons? Gotta be dungeons in a place like this. Or how about the chapel? Or maybe all those rooms that aren't being used? Couldn't be more than, say, a few dozen of them."

He had made his point. Warley Castle was a huge, sprawling structure. This vital thing could be concealed anywhere within its labyrinth, much of it off limits to them anyway. They could search forever and not find it, particularly when they didn't know what they were searching for. That is, if it existed at all. They were only surmising there was something because the evidence seemed to indicate it.

And anyway, she thought dismally, even if they could locate whatever it was that was being so carefully protected, there was no solid reason to believe it was connected with either Brother Anthony's death or Guy's, in which case all their blind chasing after it wouldn't help her to prove her innocence.

Still…

In the end, it was her desperation, her sense of time running out and the need to save herself before it was too late, that *did* give birth to an inspiration.

"The cars!"

He thought about it for a moment and then nodded. "I think I see where you're headed. But go on and tell me."

"All of them arrived here in cars, just as we did. If you wanted to hide something, and the castle itself turned out to be no good, like we're assuming was the case with the great hall, then why not put it somewhere that's both familiar and at the same time unlikely? Inside your own car, or maybe even one of the others that were garaged in the old stables. Huh?"

Leo leaned forward on the chair. "Good idea. And not just because of what might have been taken out of the great hall and placed elsewhere. People leave all kinds of stuff behind in cars. So, what we didn't find when we searched their rooms yesterday—"

"We might find in their cars!" she said, her excitement beginning to build at the prospect of learning something essential to their investigation. Not to mention the opportunity to get out of this room and away from potential intimacy with a man whose kisses rocked her. And whose sexiness was making her crazy with longing.

What's the matter with you anyway?

Totally exasperated with herself by now, Jennifer thought about that longing when she went into her own room to get her things. The problem, of course, wasn't her frustrated desire for Leo but her perpetual resistance to it. That was the matter.

But for Pete's sake, wasn't she a modern woman with healthy appetites and no attachments? Leo clearly wanted her, and she wanted him. So why didn't she just give in to her strong need?

Only it wasn't that simple, was it? Not when it could never be just a physical thing for her. Not when at this point she knew her emotions were seriously involved. When she feared that, at some level, he might still be her enemy. Or that maybe he hadn't gotten over his ex-wife, which was always a complication in a relationship. Or that—

But she didn't need a whole catalog to explain her reluctance. It was enough to know that she didn't fully trust either his feelings or her own, and until she could—

"What's keeping you?" Leo called out to her through the connecting door.

"Indecision." Afraid he might start questioning that indecision, she added a quick, wry, "Can't settle on what earrings go best with my stilettos."

CLAD IN THEIR BOOTS and coats, they made their way down the broad staircase to the front entrance of the castle. They met no one along the route.

It wasn't until they reached the heavy oak door that Jennifer thought of something. "How are we going to get into the cars without keys? I don't even have mine. It wasn't returned to me after one of the brothers garaged the rental for me."

"Jenny, there isn't a car I can't open."

"Just what kind of a childhood did you have?"

"Childhood had nothing to do with it. Comes with the P.I. territory."

She should have remembered that breaking and entering was included in his repertoire. Hadn't he managed to get into her mews cottage back in London?

"It might not be necessary anyway," he said. "Could be the cars were left unlocked when the brothers put them away."

They let themselves out into the bailey. The wind and the cold made her gasp. Snow blew in over the rooftops, carried by the strong gusts that deposited it in long, white ridges that curved across the yard.

The cars were parked with noses out in the open-ended stalls of what had once been the stables at one side of the bailey. There were six of them in the row. Since the old van farthest from them had a cross in its window, Jennifer guessed it served the monastery. The one nearest to them was her rental. The others presumably belonged to Patrick, the Brashers, Harry Ireland and the Hardings.

Crunching through the snow, they made their way toward the stalls. She noticed that Leo, his face lifted into the driving snow, was scanning the tall walls on all sides.

"What are you doing?" she asked him.

"Checking the windows to make sure no one has spotted us out here."

She watched him as his gaze drifted past the long abandoned gatehouse on the far side of the bailey. A second later his gloved hand dragged her to a sudden halt.

"What is it? Did you see something?"

He didn't answer her immediately. He was staring at one of the high twin towers that flanked the portal on either side.

"We're not alone," he warned her. "There's someone up in that first tower."

Chapter Eleven

Jennifer's eyes lifted to the open battlement on the circular tower's crown.

"Not there," Leo corrected her. "In the window below."

She lowered her gaze, peering through the falling snow that stung her cheeks. "I don't see anything."

"No, not now, but there was a figure up there."

"Did you recognize him?"

He shook his head. "It was too quick. Just a rush of movement past the window."

She could have told him he must be mistaken. That his glimpse had been too brief. That the curtain of snow had tricked him into imagining a figure. She didn't. She trusted his claim.

"The guy gets around," he said. "Maybe this time we can corner him. Let's find out."

Abandoning their intention to search the cars, they changed direction, wading through the snow to a door in the base of the tower. If whoever had preceded them left tracks across the bailey, they were obliterated now by the blowing snow. Unless there was some other entrance into the tower.

There wasn't. That was apparent when, reaching the tower, Leo scraped the door open. It was hard to be absolutely certain since the light was so weak, but there was no sign of any other opening in the curving stone walls.

The tower contained nothing at this level but a spiral stairway winding up into the heavy gloom. Leo didn't need to caution her not to speak. She understood the necessity for silence as they stood there at the foot of the flight, listening for any sound above them.

Not so much as a whisper stirred through the shadows.

Leo motioned for her to look at the lower treads of the stairway. Bits of snow clung to them, evidence that someone had recently climbed the flight. And must still be up there somewhere.

Pressing his mouth to her ear, he murmured, "You want to wait here while I check it out?"

Although this stairway was solid stone and couldn't collapse on them like the wooden stairs in the great hall, she wasn't eager about climbing it. Not with the possibility of someone lurking up there ready to trap them again. On the other hand, it was preferable to waiting down here alone in this sinister twilight.

"I do not," she whispered back.

Leo didn't argue with her about it. "All right, but make sure you stay a few steps behind me in case of any surprises."

Like an unfriendly somebody leaping out at them, she thought. In which case, what did Leo expect her to do? Turn and run like hell and ask questions later, she supposed. Okay, she had no objection to that.

"Got it."

They ascended cautiously up the coiling flight, still listening, still watching. It was a somber place, dank and smelling of age. The light, poor as it was at the bottom of the tower, dwindled to almost nothing as they climbed. Other than that solitary window at the top, which had yet to reveal itself, there were no others along the route.

There wouldn't be, Jennifer realized. She knew the gatehouses in ancient castles were the first lines of defense against any attacking enemies. Other than narrow loopholes, openings in the outer walls of fortresses were rare.

The silence, except for the soft shuffle of their feet on the treads, was absolute. And downright eerie. Whoever was up there, and Jennifer was starting to question her conviction about that, was being awfully quiet. Had he heard them coming? That was an unnerving possibility right there.

Leo must have thought so, because he slowed his steps as they neared the head of the flight. A few yards above them was a landing. He waved her to hang back, but she ignored his command, staying close behind him as he crept up to the landing.

Leo scowled at her when he turned his head to see that she had disobeyed him. But he offered no criticism. They were both too busy recovering their wind as they stood on the landing, examining the situation.

Almost invisible in a corner where the shadows were deepest was another stairway, a miniature of the one they had just climbed. Impossibly steep and narrow, it wrapped itself around an inner stone wall, curving out of sight above them.

Must be the way to the open battlements overhead, Jennifer concluded.

It was far less interesting than the archway directly in front of them, where the door that opened outward was folded back against the inner wall. The arch beckoned like an invitation that promised a worthwhile discovery. If you were willing to risk it. Leo was.

She followed him across the landing as he edged his way toward the doorway. Reached it. Stood to one side. Looked slowly, carefully around the stone frame of the arch.

Pressed against his back, Jennifer peered around him. She found herself gazing into a small, irregularly shaped room that was lit by the tower's single window. The room was bare, nothing in it.

That was her first thought. But then, following on it swiftly, was the realization that the chamber wasn't altogether empty.

As she stretched forward, she could make out in the dimness of one corner a furry mound huddled on the floor.

"An animal!"

She was so alarmed by the sight of it that the words burst from her before she could stop them. Having uttered them, there seemed to be no point now in preserving their wary silence.

"How did it get in?" Dumb question when all that mattered was it was here, it was too big to be cuddly, and it was probably some wild beast that— "Forget I said that. Let's just get out of here before it wakes up and decides it's hungry."

"It isn't an animal," Leo said, already on his way through the archway. "It's a fur coat, and someone is inside it."

He was crouched on the floor and bending over the figure when Jennifer caught up with him. He was right. Now that they were up close and the murky light no longer mattered, Jennifer could see it *was* a fur coat. The woman bundled in it was either unconscious or dead. Her ash-blond hair streaked with blood identified her. Sybil Harding.

"Leo, someone attacked her."

"And whoever it was sure didn't pass us on our way up. Which has got to mean— Damn!"

He leaped to his feet, but his realization came too late. Before either of them could swing around—because Jennifer, too, suddenly understood the danger—the door to the archway crashed shut behind them.

Even as Leo spun around and raced to the door to throw himself against it, Jennifer could hear the sound of a heavy bar dropping in place on the other side. It was followed by the muffled clatter of footsteps swiftly descending the spiral stairway.

Leo slammed his fist against the thick, unyielding planks. She knew the angry curses that accompanied his useless action were as much for himself as whoever had locked them in.

"How could I have been such a dope to come rushing in here without checking first? Why didn't I stop long enough to realize that when a door opens out instead of in there's a reason for it? Look at this thing. Banded with iron from top to bottom. And the window over there—"

He turned his head, directing her attention to what neither of them had paid any attention to until now. The narrow window, located above a seat in the thickness of the wall, was striped vertically with three iron bars. Although one of them was a broken stub, the other two were still intact.

"It's a cell all right," she said, recognizing the room now for what it was. Or what it had been when prisoners must have been kept here in the Middle Ages.

"A solid one. And the bastard who trapped us in here knew that."

"He probably heard us coming and took himself out of sight up around that other stairway." Her gaze shifted to the inert figure on the floor. "Shouldn't we…"

"Yeah."

They went back to Sybil, squatting down on either side of her. Leo turned her on her back and parted the collar of the fur coat, his fingers reaching under her silk scarf to search for a pulse at her throat. Waiting for his verdict and fearing the worst, Jennifer stared at the woman's face, which was white as plaster, at the wound on the side of her head. The injury was bad enough to tell her that Sybil must have been hit very hard. With rage.

"Is she—"

"She's alive," Leo reported, sinking back on his heels. "I'm no medic, but her pulse doesn't feel very good to me."

"This cold in here doesn't help. It's brutal."

Jennifer looked over at the window. It wasn't glazed, had probably never been glazed. There had once been interior shutters. Iron hinges still embedded in the wall were evidence of that, but the shutters themselves were long gone. That left nothing to keep the wind out.

Reaching for Sybil's hands, she stripped off a pair of expensive-looking leather gloves before removing her own gloves. The woman's flesh felt like ice. Jennifer began to briskly massage those lifeless hands.

It was impossible to know whether it was her treatment that roused Sybil or whether she would have drifted back to consciousness anyway. Either way, there was a result.

"She's stirring."

Sybil's eyes opened. She frowned, making an effort to focus on the two faces that leaned over her anxiously.

"Who did this to you, Sybil?" Leo asked her gently. "Can you tell us?"

For a moment Jennifer thought she was unable to speak. Then, in a thready but startlingly savage voice, she told them, "He's not entitled to it! By rights it belongs to me!"

"What belongs to you?" Leo coaxed her.

"You tell him that! You tell him—"

Sybil lost the struggle to continue. Her eyes closed and, with a long sigh, she sank back into unconsciousness. Jennifer and Leo looked up, exchanging mystified glances.

"I don't think she knew where she was," Jennifer said, "or who she was talking to."

"Or what she was talking about. If she could have just told us who attacked her and why…"

"She may never be able to tell us if we don't do something about her." Jennifer looked down again at Sybil's face. It was as frighteningly still and pale as a mask. "Leo, she's going to die on us if we don't get help for her."

She didn't add that both of them would also perish from the cold if they didn't get out of here. It wasn't necessary because she knew that Leo had to be thinking the same thing.

"I wouldn't say no to a good suggestion," he said.

"If we shouted from the window, maybe signaled with something like a scarf—"

"And then what? Someone just happens to stroll outside and hear us? Or maybe they happen to look out a castle window on this side and spot our signal."

He was right. Neither of those could possibly work. Even if they were lucky enough to have someone listening or looking, their shouts would be carried off by the wind, their signal obscured by the falling snow.

"Have to help ourselves, Jenny."

"How?"

"Dunno." He looked around the cell. "Door's too strong to batter down, even if we had something to batter with. That leaves the window."

"And two iron bars. I don't see either one of us squeezing through them."

"No."

He got to his feet and went to the window. Jennifer rose and followed him. Gripping both bars, he tested their strength. When he shook them, they rattled in their anchors.

"Stone is so old it's crumbling away," he said. "Look how loose they are."

"You think you can remove them?"

"I'll have to dig away more of this stone and cement. I'll need a tool."

They began to search the cell for an instrument that Leo could use.

"Nothing," he said. "Not even a manacle was left behind."

"But this was."

Jennifer had noticed that one of the iron hinges from the long vanished shutters was no longer secure. It hung down from the wall, needing only a sharp twist of her hand to tear it away.

"Will it do?" she asked, handing it to him.

He examined the pointed end of the hinge. "Perfect."

"Good. There's just one other little problem."

"What?"

"How do we climb down from this tower once we get through the window?"

"*Me. I* go out the window, make my way to the ground, then come back up the stairs and unbar the door, and you and Sybil are free."

"As simple as that, huh? A monkey might be able to do it, but—"

"You didn't look at what's out there," he said, drawing her attention to the window.

Kneeling on the window seat and pressing her face close to the bars, Jennifer looked down. Seven or eight feet directly below the window was the ridge of the portal's gabled roof. The roof connected the two towers of the gatehouse.

"See?" he said. "Once I'm through the window, I can drop to the roof."

"Which is still awfully high from the ground."

"And no ladder in sight. But that window over there in the other tower is. No bars on it either to stop me from crawling inside once I make my way across the roof. Gotta be another stairway in there."

He made it sound easy, except Jennifer knew with all that wind and snow it would be a dangerous undertaking. But their only choice.

She left him scraping away at the deteriorating stone and cement and went back to tend to Sybil. Not that there was much she could do for the woman other than to sit beside her on the drafty floor and resume chafing her hands. Her action was probably of little help, but at least it was something.

Jennifer thought about Sybil and her assailant as she worked. What had they been doing up here in the tower? And what had Sybil meant about a mysterious *he* not being entitled to something and that by rights it belonged to her?

Her thoughts were interrupted by Leo's triumphant, "Got the first one."

She looked up to see him sliding one of the bars out of its upper socket as he dragged its lower end through the trench he'd gouged in the ledge, then dropping it on the floor where it clattered. He moved on to the second bar.

She continued her own effort with Sybil, pausing when a new thought occurred to her. Perhaps Sybil's illogical assertion could be blamed, not on a dazed state resulting from her attack, but on liquor. If the woman had been drinking again…

Jennifer leaned over her, smelling her shallow breath. She could detect no alcohol fumes. Shock then had to be the explanation for her raving.

Or maybe…maybe there *had* been a sane meaning to her claim.

What if Sybil had been referring to the elusive something she and Leo were chasing themselves? That unknown thing that had brought them out to the bailey to search the cars. That same whatever-it-was that the killer, who presumably was Sybil's attacker, was so determined to keep a secret.

It was a possibility that Jennifer wanted to discuss with Leo, but it would have to wait. He had succeeded in removing the last bar. Except for the short stub, which was all that remained of the third bar, the window was entirely open.

"I'm going out," he said, casting the second bar to the floor. "You know any good prayers, this is the time for them."

Pulling on her gloves, she picked herself up from the floor and went to the window. "Be careful."

"Always," he promised her, swinging a leg over the ledge.

He was a big man, and the opening wasn't all that large. Could he fit himself through it and manage to lower himself onto the roof? He could and did. With all the virtuosity of a contortionist, he twisted his body through the window and, seconds later, disappeared over the side.

Once he was out of the way, Jennifer crowded herself into the window seat and stuck her head through the opening. Leo already stood below her astride the ridge of the roof. Looking up, he saluted her with a confident grin.

"See you at the door," he called above the howl of the wind.

This time, with the skill of a high-wire artist, he turned himself around and began to work his slow way across the roof where in places the wind had cleared away the snow. Jennifer followed his progress, her nerves as taut as that invisible wire.

Arms stretched out on either side of him, swaying only slightly, Leo maintained his balance with seeming ease. An ease that would have carried him to that window in the other tower if he hadn't been robbed of it by a sudden, powerful blast of wind. He was midway along the ridge when it slammed into him.

Gasping, she saw him fighting to keep his balance by reaching for the figure of a leaping stag perched atop a weather vane. The ornament would have steadied him if the mast that supported it, like so many others things at Warley Castle, hadn't suffered the ravages of time and weather.

The rod toppled under Leo's weight, carrying both him and the stag with it.

Jennifer watched in horror as he was pitched over backward. He landed on the slope of the roof where his head must have struck one of the slate tiles. Struck with such force that, after skidding around in a half turn, he lay sprawled there, unable to move, in danger of sliding all the way down and over the edge.

"Leo!" she shouted, hoping her cry would rouse him, enable him to save himself. "Leo, can you hear me?"

Useless. He was obviously more than just stunned. The blow had knocked him out.

He can't help himself. You have to go out there and do it for him. Before it's too late. Before you—

Go ahead, say it. Before you lose him.

Whether it made any sense or not, and maybe it didn't, Jennifer realized now just how important Leo was to her.

Enough to risk her life on that perilous roof in order to save him.

There was no question about her resolve, no hesitation. Except for one thing. How was she to get down onto the roof? Leo had managed it without a problem. But she didn't have his height or his athletic agility.

Too far, she thought, judging the drop. She'd need some means of lowering herself to the ridge. What?

Turning her head, she gazed frantically around the cell, as if she could will a rope to magically materialize. No rope. But there was Sybil's brightly-colored scarf peeking through the fur of her coat. And there was her own woolen scarf. If she knotted the two of them—

Yes, that would give her a line that should be long enough.

She went to Sybil, lifted her head, drew the scarf from around her throat, whipped off her own scarf. Within seconds, she had both twisted scarves lashed together. Jerking at them to test their strength, she was satisfied they would bear her weight.

What she was less certain about was the reliability of the iron stub protruding from the window ledge because she would have to tie her makeshift line to that broken bar. There was nothing else. But if it failed to stay anchored in its socket...

She'd soon know just how dependable it was, she thought, swiftly securing one end of the line to the stub. Then, hanging on to the other end, she lifted a leg through the window, ducked her head, and climbed through the opening.

Booted feet scrabbling against the rough side of the tower in an awkward effort to support herself, she worked her way down the line. Her foot slipped and she lost her purchase on the stone wall, dangling in space, her body turning under the impact of the harsh wind. Mercifully, the line held until she was able to get a fresh foothold.

With a breathless relief, her boots finally touched the roof.

Unlike Leo, she didn't trust herself to remain upright. Not until she was seated facing the other tower, legs straddling the ridge, did she release the line.

Leo. She needed to check on Leo.

Squinting through the swirling snow, she saw that he was still there on the slope just below the ridge. But if she didn't get to him soon, the relentless wind tugging at his body could send him down the incline that had to be slick with snow and ice. And once on his way and out of her reach, he would plummet to the ground. And maybe his death.

Stung by the wind and the slanting snow, Jennifer scooted her way along the ridge. Her progress was slow but steady. Finally abreast of him, she faced a new problem.

He was solid and heavy. Maybe too much of a load for her to move, provided she could even get a grip on him. Legs clinging to the roof, she leaned over carefully, stretching out her arm.

His body had ended up with his head closest to the ridge. Just near enough that Jennifer was able to lock her hand over his coat collar and hang on.

How she ever managed it she would never know. Maybe the urgency of saving someone who mattered, mattered more than she'd been willing to admit until she had watched him go down, fired her with a strength she ordinarily wouldn't have possessed.

Or maybe the ice and snow on the slate tiles, before this an enemy and now an ally, provided a lubrication that helped her to drag him toward her in slow stages. Straining every muscle, she finally succeeded in heaving him onto the ridge.

Now what?

Taking a moment to rest, she considered their dilemma. The window in the other tower was only yards away. Unlike the window behind her, it was low enough to the roof that she could probably scramble through it and go for help. For now Leo was all right on the ridge, his arms and legs dangling over the sides holding him in place. On the other hand, if he should stir in her absence, he could go tumbling down one of the slopes before he was sufficiently alert to save himself.

She couldn't chance it.

That left only one option. She had to make an effort to rouse him. Not by shaking him or rubbing snow on his face either. She had tried both of those at the scene of his car accident that first day, and neither one had produced a result. But a third attempt *had* worked.

His head was turned to one side, cheek exposed. She leaned down over him. "Like they say," she apologized, "this is going to hurt me more than it hurts you, but I don't know what else to do."

Peeling off her glove, she lifted her arm to deliver a stinging slap. Her flattened palm came down, but it never made a connection. It was stopped in its descent by a strong hand that shot up and closed around her wrist.

"You try it," he growled, "and you'll be eating snow."

"You're awake!"

"With all the abuse my body was being subjected to, something had to happen."

"Careful," she warned him as he started to push himself up from the tiles. "I don't want all my work going to waste."

"Uh-huh." He lifted himself into a sitting position, legs straddling the ridge like hers, and looked around. "What is this? You're rescuing me?"

"What other choice did I have? I mean, didn't you save *my* skin back in the great hall?"

"Yeah, but not by risking my own neck. Well, not by much. I'll be damned. How did you ever manage to get yourself out here and me up on this ridge?"

"Don't ask. And if you're going to make a fuss about it, I could always put you back where I found you."

"Bad idea, Jenny. It would mean leaving you, and I wouldn't like that."

They were silent then as they sat there facing each other. Perched on a hazardous rooftop as they were, with a storm raging around them, it was a crazy moment to be sharing something that was suddenly deeply emotional. But that's exactly what happened as Jennifer met his long, intimate gaze.

When she felt herself growing light-headed under the sensual assault of those sinful eyes, in danger of losing her hold on the ridge, she forced herself back to reality with a concerned "Are you going to be all right?"

"I will be as soon as I get us off this roof."

Levering himself around, he played it safe this time by imitating Jennifer's technique of scooting himself along the ridge. She followed, and by the time she reached the tower, he had already clambered through the window and was lowering his hand to help her inside.

Though it was a relief to be off the roof and inside again out of the cold, Jennifer was equally thankful for another winding stairway that took them down through what had once been a guardroom and out into the bailey.

They were on their way back to the other tower when Leo asked tersely, "Sybil?"

"Still unconscious when I left her."

"Let's hope it's not too late for her."

THEY STOOD in the gallery outside the closed door to the infirmary, waiting anxiously for a report on Sybil's condition. Brother Timothy, who had been joined by the abbot, was in the process of examining her. Both men had been told the essentials when Leo carried Sybil into the infirmary.

"Uh, do me a favor?" Leo asked Jennifer now.

"Like?"

"Don't mention my little accident on the roof to Brother Tim. We've already got the reputation of the walking wounded. I don't want to add to it."

"But he should check you out when he's finished with Sybil. I mean, after that lump on your forehead in the car and now another one on the back of your skull—"

"They weren't the only knocks I've had, and probably not the last. The legacy of a P.I. I've survived them, and I'm still here. I've got a hard head."

"I won't give you any arguments about that."

He grinned at her. "You saying I'm stubborn?"

Since she might have gotten herself into trouble with her answer, it was just as well they were interrupted at that moment. The infirmary door opened, and Father Stephen emerged.

"How is Mrs. Harding?" Jennifer asked the abbot.

"In a serious state. She should be in a hospital, but as that's not possible until the storm clears…" He shook his head. "Brother Timothy will do all he can for her. He intends to remain at her side, through the night if necessary."

"I've got a recommendation about that, padre," Leo offered.

"Yes?"

"Get Brother Tim to lock himself inside the infirmary with his patient. If he needs anything, or anyone wants to communicate with him, it can be handled through the hatch there in the door. But no one gets admitted. And I mean absolutely *no one*."

"I think I understand. You're afraid her attacker may try to eliminate her before she can name him."

"Unless she's regained consciousness and already told you something useful."

"She has not."

And may never regain consciousness again, Jennifer thought sadly.

"Your suggestion is a sound one, Mr. McKenzie, though I'm afraid her husband will be unhappy about his inability to be with his wife. But Roger is a good sort. He'll understand the strict need for her protection when it's explained to him."

"Has he been told what's happened?" Leo wanted to know.

"Not yet. I've sent Brother Michael to find him. If you'll excuse me, I'll give Brother Timothy instructions now about the door. Then I must hurry on to the office. I need to be there when Brother Michael arrives with Roger. This is going to be a terrible shock for the poor man."

Turning away, Father Stephen started to go back inside the infirmary. Then, pausing, he faced them again.

"This all grows worse," he said, and Jennifer knew he was referring to the ongoing trouble in his monastery. "If there is anything you can do…"

He left the rest unsaid, but she understood him. He wanted them to put an end to that trouble.

When the abbot was gone, Jennifer looked at Leo and saw that his hands were clenched into tight fists down at his side. The expression on his face also registered his frustration. And so did his voice.

"The man is counting on us, and all we seem to be doing is letting him down."

"If we could learn who Sybil's attacker is…"

"That's easy. We'll just ask everyone. Whoever it is is bound to tell us." He must have regretted his sarcasm the moment it was out of his mouth because he apologized to her with a muttered, "Sorry."

"I know. It's getting to me, too." And why wouldn't it when proving her innocence depended on a solution to this whole thing? "I don't suppose there's any way to establish who was where at the time of the attack. Is there?" she added hopefully.

His silence told her there wasn't. All of the suspects would claim alibis. At least one of them would be lying, of course, but how could they possibly tell which one? They needed evidence.

Jennifer thought about that, and then something occurred to her. Something they had overlooked in their urgency to rescue Sybil and themselves.

"What were they doing there?" she asked Leo.

"Uh, you want to expand a little on that?"

"Sybil and her attacker. Why were they up in the tower?"

Leo must have sensed she was more than just speculating aloud, that she had something definite in mind. "Go on," he encouraged her.

"I mean, why did we investigate the great hall? And why were we on our way to search the cars in the old stables? Because we thought the culprit had something he wanted to hide. Something important. What if we were right about that, only wrong about where he intended to conceal it?"

"The tower," Leo realized.

"It's possible, isn't it? If whoever it is somehow discovered the perfect hiding place somewhere in that cell, and Sybil, for whatever reason, followed him... well, it could explain why they were there. Couldn't it?"

Leo didn't say anything for a minute. Then, hand clamped to his jaw, he asked her brusquely, "What are you trying to do, Jenny? Put me out of business?"

The admiration in his gaze lit a warm glow inside her. Dangerous. She countered it with a sassy "I'm experienced, remember? Have to be a detective when you're tracking down antiques."

"Okay. You ready then?"

"For?"

"Us to go back up into that tower?"

Minutes later, they stood again in the cold, barren cell at the top of the tower.

"It's not very promising, is it?" Jennifer observed, her hope dimmed by the sight of the chamber that long ago had been stripped of everything in it, leaving only the bare floor and the blank stone walls.

Leo didn't answer her. His attention was fixed on the recessed window seat.

"Nearly all of it is stone," he said. "The bottom, the side walls. But not the seat itself. Seat is wood."

"They often were, unless cushions were intended as a barrier against the damp and cold of a stone seat. But in a place like this that kind of comfort wouldn't have been considered."

Leo went to the window seat, hunkering down in front of it. "The seat is a single, wide board. You notice that, and how it's been fitted here at both sides into slots in the stone? Not nailed down or pegged, just slid snugly into the grooves."

Jennifer joined him at the window. "Well, they could afford to be generous with the wood they used. Timber was plentiful in England in those days, and the medieval carpenters and masons were master craftsmen."

"Wonder just *how* snugly it fits. Let's see."

Understanding then why he was so interested in the seat, she watched intently as he grasped both ends of the overhanging lip of the thick board and tugged. It moved toward him a few inches and then jammed in the grooves. Able now to get a better grip on it, he applied more pressure. This time the slab skated the rest of the way out of the slots, coming away in his hands.

Leo dropped the board on the floor. Jennifer squeezed up close beside him. The area under the wood was not the solid stone it might have been, but a deep hollow.

The space had probably never been meant to conceal anything of value, serving only as a form of storage in the absence of a chest. But to someone aware of its existence, it made an ideal hiding place.

Did it contain a secret? The secret she and Leo hoped to find? Jennifer asked herself as she reached into the murky cavity.

Chapter Twelve

"Empty," Jennifer said in disappointment.

Unsatisfied, Leo plunged his hand into the hollow, his fingers searching the bottom and sides.

"Got an opening in the wall on this end. A hole of some kind."

She waited, her excitement renewed, as he strained forward to reach into the pocket, his groping hand exploring its surfaces.

"Nothing," he said, withdrawing his arm and getting to his feet.

Jennifer's hope sank again. "We should have known. He wouldn't have left anything here, not if Sybil caught him in the act. Not when he locked us in the cell where we could have found whatever it is. *If* it even is."

"It wasn't a waste, Jenny. We've learned that a hiding place *does* exist. Gotta mean he intended to use it until Sybil interrupted him. Like you said yourself, why else would he have been up here?"

"If that's true, then he had to have carried this thing away with him. We're no closer now to getting our hands on it than we were when we started."

"Not necessarily. I'm thinking that after Sybil arrived on the scene, then you and I showed up, he would have been nervous about trying to take it back into the castle. Maybe decided to stash it until it was safe for him to come back for it. Somewhere close by. Huh?"

"The cars."

"Right. They're just outside the tower, and if we thought they were a good bet before…"

He spread his hands in a gesture meaning they were a strong possibility again.

"SO, WHERE DO WE BEGIN?" Jennifer asked him as they stood at the edge of the bailey, gazing down the bank of open-ended stalls.

"Might as well take them in order."

The first vehicle in the row, the one closest to them, was a van that had seen better days. Jennifer knew that vans weren't common in England, not as family cars anyway. Where they did occur, they often served as minibuses for establishments like churches and senior centers. That knowledge, along with a cross hanging from the rearview mirror, indicated the van was probably the monastery's transport.

Leo tried the driver's door. It opened without resistance. "Let's hope the good brothers who garaged this fleet were trusting enough to leave all the rest of them unlocked as well. You want to start in the back, and I'll take the front?"

They covered the van from nose to tail. Leo even checked under the hood, but they found nothing that didn't belong there.

The next vehicle in the range was a late-model Volvo, also unlocked. The owner's registration in the glove compartment revealed that it was the property of Sybil and Roger Harding.

"Anything?" Leo asked after he finished looking under the hood and in the trunk.

"Nothing," Jennifer reported, emerging from the interior.

They moved on to an old, battered Jeep. A collection of sporting gear dumped in the back seat, along with a boy's school jersey, suggested the Jeep belonged to Patrick. It, too, disclosed nothing of interest.

The fourth vehicle was another van. Only this one had paneled sides.

"Could use a car wash," Leo observed. "Looks like it might actually be white under all that road grime. What do you bet it belongs to Harry Ireland and that the inside is as messy as his room?"

Leo was right. The interior, when they examined it, was littered with odds and ends. Among them in the back end was an assortment of packages waiting for delivery along the salesman's route. All of the packages were sealed and their contents clearly marked, with no sign of having been opened since they'd been collected from their source. But their presence, along with the rest of the junk, made the van more difficult to search. If there was anything suspicious, however, they were unable to locate it.

In contrast to the van was the conservative, gray compact parked beside it. Judging by the neatness of its interior, it could only belong to Fiona and Alfred Brasher. It was easily and quickly searched. And again it concealed nothing.

"That's it then," Jennifer said, discouraged as they came away from the compact.

"We're not finished," Leo said. He jerked a thumb in the direction of the last stall.

"My car? But it couldn't—"

"Why not, if it was left unlocked like all the others? Think about it, Jenny. If you wanted to stow something, why not use the most unlikely place to hide it? Maybe the last place we'd be expected to look."

"I guess that makes sense." She wasn't convinced, but she was willing to make the effort.

Avoiding a snowdrift, they made their way to the rental sedan. Leo searched the back, Jennifer the front. There was nothing in the interior that hadn't been there when she'd left the car that first night, including under the seats and in the glove compartment.

Leo backed out of the car. "You'd know better than I would what's supposed to be in the trunk. Why don't you take that while I have a look under the hood?"

Jennifer popped the latches for both the lid of the trunk and the hood before sliding out of the car. She went around to the rear of the little Ford at the back of the stall. The light was poor here but sufficient enough for her to investigate the trunk.

Not, she decided after raising the lid, that there was anything for her to see. The trunk was empty except for the spare tire. She checked under its cover to be sure there was nothing there but the spare. There wasn't.

Another dead end, she thought.

Her hand was on the lid, ready to slam it shut, when something stopped her. Tucked over in the farthest corner of the trunk were the tools needed for changing a flat. She'd been aware of them but had thought nothing about them. Until this moment.

What were they doing out in the open like this? Shouldn't they be packed away in— Where?

Yes, down inside the well that had been provided for them. Its cover, equipped with fasteners on either end and flush with the floor of the trunk, was over on one side.

Jennifer's hands trembled in anticipation as she turned the fasteners, lifted the cover and stared down into the well. The tools, she realized, had been removed for a reason.

"Yo," Leo called to her from the front of the car. "You get anything back there?"

She didn't answer him. She was too excited about her discovery, too intent on retrieving what had been squeezed down into the well.

"Hey, Jennifer!"

Her silence must have worried him. She was dimly conscious of the hood banging down, of the tread of his booted feet as he hurried toward her.

By the time he joined her at the open trunk, she had it in her hands. An oblong bundle tightly wrapped in layers of brown paper, bound with string and placed inside a clear, protective plastic sleeve.

Leo whistled at the sight of it. "You got something all right."

Jennifer looked up from the bundle, meeting his gaze. "You know what it is, don't you?" she asked him softly.

From the beginning, when they'd first decided that their culprit had something vital he would go to any lengths to safeguard, she had sensed its identity. She hadn't named it, couldn't bring herself even now to name it, because it seemed too fantastic a possibility. But on some level she had *known*. Felt that Leo, too, must have known. Or at least guessed.

"It doesn't make any sense," he said, "but, yeah, I think I know."

They were silent then for a moment, their eyes focused on the bundle.

"You want to unwrap it here?" Leo asked.

She shook her head. "I think Father Stephen deserves to be present for the unveiling."

FATHER STEPHEN, frowning, handed Jennifer a pair of scissors from his desk drawer. "Hidden in the boot of your car, you say? This is all very baffling, but if somehow…"

He didn't finish what he started to say. Maybe, Jennifer thought, because he, too, guessed what the bundle contained but, like her, was afraid to put it into words.

She and Leo had agreed on the way to the abbot's office not to express their conviction about the bundle's content. They didn't want Father Stephen to be disappointed if they were wrong, and they very well could be.

It was time to find out.

Scissors in hand and with the door locked behind them, Jennifer leaned over the desktop where the bundle, freed of its plastic sleeve, rested.

The two men crowded close to the desk, watching as Jennifer sliced through the string in several places.

Her anticipation had climbed to an almost unbearable level

by the time she had the string removed. She could sense Leo's silent command for her to hurry as she began to part the thick layers of brown paper, could swear she heard the whisper of a prayer on Father Stephen's lips.

When the last wrappings fell away, the three of them looked down in wonder at what lay there in the nest of shredded paper. It wasn't necessary for the abbot to verify their discovery. Jennifer knew she was looking at the Warley Madonna.

Perhaps eighteen inches in length and less than six inches in width, allegedly crafted from a section of the cross on which Christ had been crucified, the carving depicted both the Madonna and Child.

Religious art was not Jennifer's specialty, but she knew enough to realize that the stiff, almost crude quality of the work marked it as a product of the early years of the Christian era. That was evident in the figure of the Child, more like a small adult than an infant, that the Madonna clutched to her breast. Considering its vast age, the relic was in a remarkable state of preservation, its paint chipped and faded but the colors remained vibrant.

It was Father Stephen who ended their long silence with a soft, reverent "You will be in my eternal prayers for its recovery."

"Father," Jennifer asked the abbot, "may I examine it for a moment? I'll be very careful."

"Of course."

She gently lifted the relic from its bed of paper, turning it over in her hands. It was only about three or four inches in depth, which it would be if it had been fashioned from some part of the cross, but surprisingly heavy for its size. She had noticed that when she'd carried it into the castle.

But there was *something*….

"It's beautiful, isn't it?" the abbot said.

"Very," she said, placing it back on the desk.

"Why the thief would bring it back to Warley, of all places,

I cannot begin to imagine. It's altogether mystifying. If there is an answer, I trust you both to learn it."

"In the meantime, padre," Leo advised him, "I think the Madonna needs to be put under lock and key, someplace where our culprit can't get his hands on it again."

"It will go immediately back into the muniment room."

"And that would be?"

"There," the abbot said, indicating an iron banded door in a corner of the office much like the heavy door to the cell in the tower. "In the medieval days, valuable documents and weapons were stored in such strong rooms. We still keep our important documents there, but it was also where the Madonna was locked away except for display in the chapel on feast days. The room is as safe as a vault."

Satisfied, Leo turned to another subject. "Any change with Sybil?"

"None. Her husband is keeping a prayer vigil in the chapel. He looks unwell. I'm concerned about him."

"Let's hope his wife recovers." Leo went to the office door and unlocked it. "Coming?" he asked Jennifer. He seemed eager to get her away from the office.

She looked one last time at the Madonna. Then, before joining Leo, she turned to the abbot. "Father, is there a library in the monastery?"

"There is. Nearly all of the volumes are faith-connected, of course, but we do shelve some secular works."

"Would it be available to me?"

"It would, and you're welcome to use it. We have no formal checkout, but if you wish to take any of the books to your room, there is a clipboard on the counter for you to sign them out. You'll find the library just beyond the chapel."

He seemed not to be curious about her request, but Leo was when he got her alone out in the gallery.

"What was that all about?"

"Research."

"Yeah, I got that much. I'm asking about the other."

"Other?"

"I didn't miss it, Jenny. Something bothered you when you handled the Madonna. I could see it in your face."

He was much too observant where she was concerned. Uncanny. And a little alarming. Or maybe it meant— But it was safer not to go there.

"It's true," she admitted.

"I haven't forgotten what you told me. That you have this talent for sensing when an antique isn't all it should be. That this was why Guy wanted you to come by his shop the night he was killed. So what are you thinking? That there's something wrong about the Madonna?"

"I'm not sure. I just have this feeling that it isn't...well, right somehow."

"You saying it's a fake?"

She shook her head. "Not that exactly. I'm fairly certain it's very early. All the evidence is there."

"But?"

"I don't know. And until I find out what's gnawing at me, *if* I can, I don't want to say anything to Father Stephen. It would be an awful blow to him if the Madonna turns out not to be all it's supposed to be. But if this is connected somehow with two murders..."

"Then it just might tell us who the killer is. Okay, so you need to do some digging."

"On the subject of early Christian relics, yes."

"Worth a shot."

Jennifer had another thought on their way to the library. "Do you remember what Sybil tried to tell us in the tower?"

"I do. Something about his not being entitled to it and that by rights it belonged to her. I guess we have to assume now that she was talking about the Madonna."

"But why she would claim such a thing, and how she knew who had it…"

"Yeah, just adds to the puzzle."

It took some time in the library for Jennifer to locate several books that might provide useful information. By the time she and Leo came away, armed with the volumes she'd selected, the daylight was gone. They could see through one of the gallery windows looking out on the courtyard that it was dark outside. The snow was still falling.

Was it her imagination, she wondered, or was it falling less furiously? Hard to tell without the daylight, but if the storm *was* easing, then the time to get the answers they needed was already slipping away from them.

DUMPING THE BOOKS in Leo's room, they went on to the bathroom to clean up. After showering and changing, they found their way to the dining parlor where dinner was waiting for them. Harry Ireland and the Brashers were already seated at the table with their plates of food.

"Where are the others?" Leo asked as he and Jennifer joined them with their own selections from the buffet.

"This is all of us tonight," Fiona informed him. "Geoffrey is in the refectory with the brothers, and Patrick was invited to dine with them. One assumes," she sniffed, "it's an indication of his acceptance in the order."

And she seems to resent that, Jennifer thought, remembering the argument Fiona and her husband were having with Patrick just before lunch yesterday. It was another mystery among too many mysteries in this place.

"As for Roger," Alfred said, "he refuses to leave the chapel. Plans to spend the night there, I understand. I imagine the poor devil has no appetite."

Yes, they would have all heard about Sybil, Jennifer thought. Nothing seems to remain a secret here for very long.

Except for the secrets that mattered. The ones she and Leo were striving to solve. They would get no closer to unlocking them in this company. The Brashers ate in silence after that, and the habitually talkative Harry Ireland was quiet himself tonight, looking worried.

With good reason, Jennifer decided. Weren't all of them worried? Understandable, when Sybil had been attacked so savagely on the heels of Brother Anthony's murder.

Who would be next? They must all be asking themselves that question. All of them except the culprit himself.

And since no one here was in a mood to talk— talk that might help Leo and her find the key to the murderer's identity—Jennifer could only hope that the books waiting in Leo's room would speak to her.

They settled down with those books minutes after they were back in the room, Jennifer on the bed with her back against the headboard, Leo on the chair with his feet propped on a stool.

"What am I looking for?" he asked her, one of the volumes open in his lap.

"Anything that refers to the materials and craftsmanship of early relics."

They read in silence while the fire hissed softly on the hearth.

"What about this?" Leo asked. He read her a passage about a catacomb painting in Rome celebrating the Virgin.

Jennifer shook her head. "That's wall art. I'm hoping for a reference to something freestanding."

They went back to their books.

"Here's something promising," he said, reading her a description of a Byzantine statue. "Sounds as frozen as the Warley Madonna."

"Sorry. I'm not getting anything from it."

Or from anything else, she realized as they continued with the search. It wasn't the tedious material either. Clues could have leaped out at her in bold print and she wouldn't have grasped them.

She simply wasn't able to concentrate on the pages. All she could seem to be aware of was the man who sat there only a few feet away from the bed. She kept sneaking glances at him, noticing the way the glow from the fire lit his strong features, of how long and muscular his legs were stretched out to that stool. Kept remembering what they had shared throughout the day, the closeness that had resulted from the episode in the great hall, then an even more powerful closeness on the roof of the gatehouse.

All of it had been emotional, sensual, strengthening the bond that had been slowly developing from the moment of their first contact. And now there was this throbbing awareness that demanded—

"It's no good, is it?" he said.

He had looked up from his book, caught her gazing at him.

"We just have to be patient," she said.

"I'm not talking about this stuff." He thumped his knuckles against the book, closed it and dropped it on the floor beside the chair. His whiskey-colored eyes seemed to darken as he leaned toward her, his husky voice deepening to a slow rasp that sent shivers through her. "I'm talking about us. About this thing that's been sizzling between us all day. What are we going to do about it?"

Unbearable. The tension between them was suddenly unbearable. Shoving her own book away from her, she swung her legs over the side of the bed, got to her feet and crossed swiftly to the hearth, where she nervously fed chunks of turf to the fire. In no hurry about it, Leo unfolded his length from the chair, stood and ambled across the room where he inserted himself between her and the hearth.

"What are you afraid of, Jenny?" he challenged her.

She asked herself the same question. Why did she keep resisting Leo when she so clearly wanted him?

"Is it because you think I'm not over Kimberly?" he said, referring to his ex-wife. "You're wrong, if you think so. Kimberly isn't even a bad memory anymore. You took care of that."

"Did I?"

"Oh, yeah."

There was a promise in his voice when he reached for her, sliding his arms around her, drawing her against his hard body. A promise that he wouldn't hurt her, that she could trust him. And she did, suddenly and totally.

His mouth found hers in a kiss that was slow, breath-robbing and thoroughly intoxicating. Overcoming any lingering reservation, Jennifer responded by parting her mouth in an eager invitation as she pressed against him tightly. Her surprising abandon must have pleased Leo, if his tongue very busy with hers was any indication.

As the kiss deepened, his breath mingling with hers, she savored the flavor of him, his masculine scent, his clean taste. Pleasurable though they were, they weren't enough. She wanted more, expressing her longing by clutching at his back where his muscles bunched under her hands, by squirming against his body.

That must have also pleased him, because she felt a ridge of flesh thrusting against her groin. Then, answering her impatient demand, he broke their kiss long enough to scoop her up into his arms and carry her to the bed.

When they were stretched out side by side, he resumed his attentions, placing a series of kisses in all her most sensitive areas. The hollow of her throat, her eyelids, the tender places just below her ears.

How he seemed to know exactly where she was vulnerable was amazing. And so seductive she would have lost all control if she hadn't seized an opportunity to preserve her reason. Momentarily anyway, though it cost her a considerable effort.

"Where—" Struggling to free her arm pinned between their bodies, she raised a hand to touch the scar that had fascinated her ever since she had noticed it high on his cheek. "—did this come from?"

"Hockey puck."

She was dimly conscious of him lifting her sweater, dragging it over her head. When it was out of the way, she continued with her interrogation.

"When you were a kid?"

"Nope, just a few years ago. Hold still."

He began to work on the buttons of her blouse.

"You were a hockey player?"

"Yeah, a forward."

His skillful fingers managed to free her of the blouse. She found it more difficult to breathe when those fingers moved on to the clasp of her bra.

"Um, are we—" Hard to get it out with her speech so ragged now. "—talking about *professional* hockey?"

"Amateur. A city team. Strictly for fun."

"Aren't players supposed to wear protective masks?"

"That's a goalie."

"Oh."

He succeeded in removing the bra. She felt the cool air on her breasts, then the warmth of his mouth. She gasped, losing all interest in the mystery of the scar. For the next few moments she cared about nothing but the marvelous sensation of his tongue on her rigid nipples.

When he lifted his head from her breasts, it was to ask her gruffly, "Are we through with the hockey quiz?"

"Definitely."

"Then let's concentrate on something more important," he said, tugging on her slacks.

She had no memory of what followed, only the result when their clothes had been shed. Her naked body next to his own naked body. His stormy eyes gazing into hers. Their hands exploring each other.

He was all hardness and heat. And much more than that as he began to kiss her again. Blistering kisses that left her raw with need. She wanted him inside her, pleaded for their joining.

But Leo was in no hurry. He caressed her breasts, crooned endearments into her ear. His hand finally slid between her thighs, his fingers gently invading her moist petals. Finding her nub, he teased it until she was lost in a mindless, rapturous haze.

"Enough," she whispered. "Please, no more waiting."

Only then did he answer his own urgency, seized by a longing for her he could no longer resist. Lifting himself over her, he eased his swollen length deep inside her, resting when their melding was so complete that it felt as if they were one being.

Even then it wasn't enough. She wondered if it could ever be enough. But Leo was prepared to achieve the ultimate satisfaction for both of them. When she stirred under him impatiently, he began to rock slowly, building the tempo of his long strokes until she was beyond control, her own rhythms wild and wanton.

The rapture they shared in the moments that followed was indescribable, as awesome as it was wonderful. An age-old force that had them climbing the pinnacle together. With cries of fulfillment, they reached the peak almost simultaneously before sliding over the edge into a blinding oblivion.

Afterwards, cradled in his arms, Jennifer remembered something she had told herself yesterday when they had returned to their rooms after Leo had kissed her in the alcove. How she had acknowledged she was in lust with him. But not in love. Love required so much more. All the things that they didn't share.

She realized now how wrong she had been. Because, although those things were certainly important, in the end they didn't matter. Only one thing really counted. Trust. And she knew now that she could, and did, trust him.

There was something else she knew. She *was* in love with Leo McKenzie. And that scared her, because she longed for him to love her in return. But if he didn't, if what they had just experienced…

No. Her concern about that subject would have to wait. Leo had drifted off to sleep. With his arms still cherishing her, Jennifer also slept.

SHE AWAKENED to an unfamiliar light. For a moment, head lifted from the pillow and squinting against the brilliance, she was puzzled. Then she understood. Early morning sunlight was streaming through the window. Was it possible that the storm had ended?

Managing to free herself from Leo's arms without waking him, she eased herself off the bed, recovered her panties and sweater from where he had cast them on the floor and quickly donned them. Too anxious to bother with her other clothes, she padded on bare feet to the window.

It was true. The storm had ended in the night. She could see the long sweep of the moors under a clear, blue sky. Moors that, though heavily clad in snow, were silent and still, an indication that the wind had died. There was something else. The room didn't feel as cold as it should feel, dressed as she was only in panties and a sweater and with the fire nothing more than cold embers. That had to mean the temperature was on the rise.

"What's happening?"

Turning away from the glass, she found Leo sitting up in bed. The blanket she had drawn over them last night before falling asleep was down around his waist, leaving his chest and biceps with the sexy salamander tattoo exposed. A tempting sight, but under the circumstances…

"No more blizzard," she reported.

He frowned. "That's not going to help our investigation. Without the snow to hold them here, we could lose our suspects as soon as the roads are clear."

"They'll have to make themselves available to the police, won't they?"

"Yeah, with a murder in the castle, the police will want to question everyone."

"Then they can't leave until the police get here. And, anyway," she said, moving toward the bed, "even if we don't know who killed Brother Anthony or why, now that the Madonna has turned up we do know that whoever stole it from Guy had to have murdered him."

Leo didn't say anything.

"Don't we?" She reached the bed and stood there looking down at him, waiting for his answer, feeling suddenly uneasy.

His hesitation was too long, the expression on his face too revealing. Jennifer felt sick at heart, her trust of last night shattered by his silence.

"I guess I have my answer," she said in the slow, measured voice that expressed her anger and deep disappointment. "I guess, even after everything that's happened, you're not completely certain I'm not guilty. You still wonder if I could have killed your brother."

There was something else his silence answered for her. He didn't love her. Not if he questioned her innocence. It was a terrible blow to her.

"Jenny, no." He swung his legs over the side of the bed, came to his feet with the blanket wrapped around him. "All I was doing was wondering whether we had enough to clear you. Not giving you an answer straight off didn't mean anything."

"Oh, I think it meant everything." She began to collect the rest of her discarded clothing. "For instance, that little silence of yours told me what last night meant to you and, more importantly, what it *didn't* mean."

"Okay, I'm not denying it," he admitted, plowing a hand through his sleep-tousled hair, "but if you'll just listen to me, maybe you'll understand—"

"I don't want to hear it. I'm going to change." With the articles of clothing heaped in her arms, she started for the connecting door. "In *my* room," she added, "and I'd appreciate being left alone while I dress."

To his credit, he didn't try to follow her. When she closed the door behind her, she felt as if she was doing more than just shutting the door between them. She felt as if she was shutting him out of her life.

All right, maybe that was an exaggeration. But hadn't he betrayed their bonding with his silence? Gone to bed with her last night, made love to her with a shadow of doubt still lingering in his mind? How could he have deceived and hurt her like that?

Jennifer was still aching when, after rapidly dressing in a fresh change of clothing, she remembered the books. She had left them behind in the other room.

Leo had dragged on a pair of jeans and was just slipping into a shirt when she went back into his room and began to purposefully gather up the books she had borrowed from the monastery's library.

"What are you doing?" he challenged her.

"I'm going to return these, and then I'm going to dig some more in the library. I want to see if one of the other books there will have what none of these gave me."

"Can't that wait until after breakfast?"

"I don't want any breakfast. The question of the Madonna's authenticity is still gnawing at me. Maybe it's not important, but it's all I can think to try at this point."

She needed to occupy herself, not just to seek answers but in an effort to ease her anguish. Hopefully, burying herself in research would put Leo out of her mind, at least for a couple of hours.

"All right, give me a minute to finish dressing."

"You're not going with me."

"The hell I'm not."

"I don't need you playing bodyguard anymore. I can take care of myself."

She had the books, but where did she leave her purse? Right, back in her room. This time he followed her through the connecting door.

"Jenny, you can't go out there on your own. It's not safe."

Before she could argue with him about it, there was a rap on her door. She answered it to find one of the young monks standing there bearing a basket of peat turf.

"Are you down on your supply?" he asked. "I've some fresh fuel for your fire if you are."

He looked a bit embarrassed to see a half-dressed Leo behind her. This was a monastery, after all.

"I think we have enough, Brother—"

"Luke," he supplied.

"But I do have a favor to ask. Are you going anywhere near the library on your rounds?"

"Happens I am."

"Great. Then maybe you'll let me go with you, and if along the way I could stop for a minute in the loo to brush my teeth…"

"'Course."

"Will there be any other brothers in the library, do you think?"

"Brother James is sure to be there. He's a great scholar."

Jennifer turned her head, sending Leo a look to tell him Brother Luke's assurances should satisfy him she would be adequately protected and that he needn't worry about her. She didn't wait to see if he agreed or not. Snatching up her purse, she sailed out into the corridor with the young monk hurrying to catch up with her.

"Jerk."

There were a lot of other names Leo was prepared to call himself. Except none of them would be sufficient to describe the fool he had been, though for good measure he slapped his forehead with the palm of his hand.

How could he have been so stupid to hurt her like that after what they had shared last night? It had been pretty special all right. *She* was special. And he had gone and blown it with that significant silence.

He was tempted to go after her and the monk, but it would only make everything worse. She was in no mood to listen. Anyway, what could he tell her? The truth was that, for a moment there, he *had* suffered a lapse of faith in her innocence, and Jennifer had immediately sensed it.

The best thing he could do now was to let her cool down. She'd be safe enough in the company of the monks. He would check on her in a couple of hours, and maybe by then he could make her understand how wrong he had been. And how sorry. Hell, he'd crawl to her on hands and knees if that's what it took to earn her forgiveness.

And in the meantime…

Yeah, what he needed to do for her was to prove that she *was* innocent of Guy's murder. Because the truth was, however completely ready he was now to believe in her, he knew that the London police would still consider her a strong suspect. Unless he could give them the real killer.

You're supposed to be a P.I., aren't you? Fine, so put your skills back to work.

How? he wondered. But that was obvious. As Jennifer had said, one of the guests here in the castle had to be Guy's killer, as well as Brother Anthony's. Okay, he would question them again one by one. Question them in depth, whether they liked it or not, until he had squeezed out of them every secret they were hiding.

It was time to get tough.

Chapter Thirteen

It took Jennifer almost two hours to find what she was looking for, but in the end...

Yes, here it was tucked away in an obscure little book with a chapter that described the crucifixion in detail. A passage explaining that the Romans of that period fashioned the crosses they used out of cypress.

This was what was wrong about the Warley Madonna. What had bothered her when she had handled it yesterday in the abbot's office. Not its style or craftsmanship but its material.

Although familiar with the oak and elm of English country pieces, Jennifer was no expert on wood. But she did know enough to realize that the Madonna was much too heavy to be cypress. Had Guy suspected there might be a problem in that direction? Was that why he had wanted her to examine it, trusting in that gift of hers to sense when something wasn't right?

The Madonna would have to undergo tests, of course, to determine its material with any certainty, but it looked like it couldn't have been made out of any part of the true cross.

Jennifer thought about going to Father Stephen and telling him what she had learned, but she didn't have the heart to do that. Not just yet, though he would have to know eventually.

The abbot would be deeply disappointed by her discovery. He'd been counting on the enormous value of the Madonna to save his monastery. On the other hand, true cross or not, it *was* an early relic whatever its material. She was confident it would bring a considerable sum when it was sold, probably more than enough to cover the costs of repair to the castle.

Jennifer had her own disappointment to contend with. Her discovery had brought her no closer to an explanation for the two murders or the identity of the killer. All of it was still a mystery, including the theft of the Madonna and its baffling return to Warley.

She'd been so absorbed in the little book that she had paid no attention to her surroundings. But now, aware of a flurry of activity in the library, she looked up from its pages. She was perplexed to see several monks unwrapping sheets of plastic, which they proceeded to drape over the shelves at one end of the room.

"What's happening?" she asked one of the brothers, who was on his way past the table where she sat.

He stopped to explain it to her. "We're protecting the books. The snow is melting on the roofs, and we get leaks on that side of the library."

The snow melting? Was it already that warm? It seemed hard to believe after the length and severity of the storm, but then English weather was famous for shifting from one extreme to the other.

Feeling in the way, she replaced the book on the shelf where she had found it and left the library. In the gallery outside she encountered a team of monks equipped with brooms and snow shovels. Brother Luke was among them.

"We're on our way to clear the bailey," he told her cheerfully.

She watched them march off, thinking that more than just the weather had changed. It was as if the castle had suddenly come to life after a long, dark sleep. A life that threatened her efforts to prove her innocence.

Anxious about the conditions outside, and how they could

bring an abrupt end to her investigation, Jennifer felt a need to check on them herself. There would be no danger to her if she stayed in the area of the bailey where the brothers would be working.

Except she had neither her coat nor her boots with her. And no matter how mild the temperature might be now, the air would still be too cool to venture outside without them. Leo would tell her she was risking herself to go back to her room on her own to fetch them, but Leo wasn't here.

She didn't want to think about Leo. She thought instead about Sybil as she passed the closed door to the infirmary on her route to the stairs. Brother Luke had earlier told her on their way to the library that Mrs. Harding was still unconscious and that her husband had spent the night in the chapel praying for her recovery. Jennifer hoped his prayers would be answered.

She met no one on the stairs or in the upper corridor, but the brothers had been here before her. A series of plastic buckets had been placed at intervals along the passage. Water was already dripping into them from leaks in the ceiling, evidence of just how badly the roofs needed those repairs.

Jennifer was relieved not to find Leo waiting for her when she reached their rooms, and at the same time she was annoyed by her perverse letdown. She had no idea where he could have gone or what he was up to. All she knew was that she felt alone and miserable without him, and that, too, she found irritating.

Putting him out of her mind with a determined effort, she went down to the bailey where the brothers were busy scraping and sweeping. She was shocked by how high the temperature had climbed in just a matter of a few hours. The air felt almost balmy.

There were still drifts through which the brothers were cutting paths, but where the snow had been shallow, the stone flags were already exposed. However, it was hard to tell in the enclosure just how extensive the sudden thaw was. Jennifer needed to know.

Finding her way across the bailey, she went out through the portal of the gatehouse to the open road beyond. Standing there in the gentle breeze, she surveyed the terrain on both sides. The snow was melting so rapidly that in places there were open patches where the bare ground steamed under the March sun.

Jennifer had a dismal feeling that her time may have run out. They could already be clearing the roads across the moors, making it possible for the linemen to restore the power and telephones. The castle would soon no longer be isolated, and if Guy's charwoman back in London had regained consciousness and told her story…

The police. They could even now be looking for her, perhaps had already traced her to Warley. Within a matter of hours, they would be able to reach the monastery. There was nothing to prevent them from arresting her.

Jennifer had never known it was possible to experience such a sense of sick desperation. It was in this state of despair that she turned around and started slowly back to the gatehouse.

Her thoughts diverted by the cry of a rook overhead, she lifted her gaze in search of the bird. That was when her attention was captured by the sight of a badge carved in the stone above the portal. Though worn by centuries of wind and rain, it was still possible to detect its characters. Jennifer assumed the coat of arms belonged to the knight who had built and originally owned Warley Castle.

She could make out a checkered shield supported by a miniver on one side and a ram on the other. The shield, bearing a helmet, was crowned by a pair of crossed swords.

There was something familiar about the emblem. She had seen it before, hadn't she? Where and when? And then suddenly she remembered. Or was fairly certain that she did. It was the same device embossed in the leather on the cover of Sybil Harding's vanity case. A family crest.

If she was right, it meant Sybil could be a Warley descendant. It would explain her strange claim to Leo and Jennifer that, by rights, "it" belonged to her. Sybil had to have been referring to the Warley Madonna.

Jennifer had no idea how her discovery could possibly help her to save herself from being charged with murder. She only knew she was excited by the possibility this was somehow the connection she needed. The thing she and Leo had been looking for.

But before she took it any further, she had to be sure that the crest on Sybil's vanity case did, in fact, match the coat of arms above the portal. She had to have another look at that case.

LEO'S EFFORT to get the truth out of Harry Ireland, the Brashers and the young Patrick turned out to be much harder than he'd figured. All four of them were stubbornly determined to hang on to their secrets.

Hoping they would be less resistant with their appetites satisfied, he waited until they finished breakfast to confront them. Ireland was on his feet and ready to leave the dining parlor when Leo stopped him.

"You don't want to go, Harry."

The salesman was amused. "I don't, old man?"

"No, you don't." Leo looked around the table. "And I think the rest of you will want to stick around with him."

"And just why is that?" Fiona demanded.

"Because I need to question all of you."

Her husband wore a mutinous expression. "We've answered enough questions."

Fiona pushed back from the table. "Alfred is right. You have no authority to interrogate us."

"Oh, yeah, I do. Or are you forgetting that Father Stephen has appointed me to investigate all the nasty little stuff that's been going on here in the castle? Like, for instance, Brother Anthony's murder."

Alfred Brasher threw down his napkin and got to his feet.

"I, for one, have no intention of telling this man anything. I say we all wait for the police to answer any further questions."

He was ready to lead the way out of the room. The others, all of them on their feet now, were prepared to follow him. But they hesitated, looking uncertain when Leo said, "Sure, you can all wait. Except it probably will take some time yet before the cops are able to get here. And until they do…"

"What?" Patrick prompted him.

"I'm still in charge. Which means, wherever you scatter to after you leave here, I intend to hunt you down. One by one, if necessary. I'll hound you until you tell me what I want to know. Or you can make it easy on yourselves and talk to me here and now."

"Are you going to let him intimidate you? You're fools, if you do." Alfred headed for the door.

Realizing it was time for him to use the ammunition he'd been saving, Leo called after him, "And if anyone refuses to talk to me…well, I'm just apt to assume he's the one who's got something really vital to hide. Say, something connected with murder. Why hold out otherwise? Huh?"

Muttering under his breath, Brasher turned and came back to the table.

"That's better," Leo said. "Look, don't worry about it. Just make yourselves comfortable in here. I'll see each one of you separately, or the Brashers together if they prefer, outside on the stair landing. That way, whatever you have to share with me that's confidential will stay confidential."

It was a long and grueling session, taking more time than Leo had anticipated to sort out alibis and possible motives. But, one by one, he got the explanations for everything he and Jennifer had considered suspicious.

He started with Harry Ireland. The salesman, nervous about being confronted with the subject of the compromising letters in his room, suddenly lost his phony speech and reverted to something that Leo thought might be a Midlands dialect.

"Mum always said I'd come to no good if I didn't watch myself with the women. Like 'em too much, y'see. Well, you know how it is out on the road. A bloke gets lonely, and Betty was that eager for company. A real luv, she is."

"Also real married," Leo pointed out. "And wanting to leave her husband to run off with you. Providing, if I remember her letter correctly, one of you could get your hands on enough money. Apparently, what a salesman earns isn't enough for Betty."

"I'll not say I wasn't tempted. Still am. Only, short of winning the pools, it's daft to think there's a way. Anything criminal? Never!"

Leo believed him. Harry was too emphatic about it. And too scared to even consider theft, much less murder.

The Brashers, whom he questioned next, admitted it was no accident they were here at Warley. They had followed Patrick to the monastery.

"The photograph of the cricket team you found in our luggage," Fiona said, "the one with Patrick in it. It was taken in their last year at school. I say *their,* because the young man standing next to him was our son, Gordon. He and Patrick had been close friends since boyhood."

"Was?"

"Gordon died a few months back," Alfred said.

He went on to tell Leo that their son and Patrick had been on a climbing holiday in Scotland. The two of them had scaled far more difficult peaks in the Alps, but something had gone horribly wrong this time. An accident involving a rope. Gordon had strangled to death before Patrick could free him.

The Brashers didn't blame Patrick. An investigation had exonerated him. All they wanted was for Patrick to share with them their son's last hours on that mountain, his final words. But Patrick refused to talk about it.

And that, Leo thought, explained the quarrel he and Jennifer had overheard the other morning here on the landing. Tragic circumstances but otherwise innocent.

Patrick, whom he saw last, corroborated what the Brashers had given him.

"They want me to tell them something about Gordon that will comfort them," Patrick said, his voice thick, "but I can't, because there isn't anything that will help. There just isn't."

Guilt, Leo thought. The kid is suffering guilt because he was unable to save his friend. Which could be the reason why Patrick wanted to join a monastery. If so, it was a bad reason. But that was something for Father Stephen to handle.

"There's still the matter of that wicked-looking knife in your luggage," Leo pressed him.

"Don't you understand? I should have had a knife with me to cut Gordon loose from that rope, and I didn't. I'd left it behind in our hotel. A knife is something a climber should never be without."

And now, Leo decided, Patrick couldn't bear to go anywhere without a sharp knife accompanying him, even if it was in his luggage. Irrational maybe but understandable.

"That's why I kept my door locked," Patrick explained. "I didn't want anyone finding the knife and thinking the wrong thing about it. It was bad enough having Geoffrey resent me because he didn't feel I was serious enough about becoming a monk."

Everything the four of them had confessed was understandable. And none of it had anything to do with the murders or the theft of the Madonna. Unless he was overlooking something, and Leo didn't think he was.

He had eliminated everyone but Geoffrey and Roger Harding. Neither of them was a strong possibility, especially the novice, but he meant to question them anyway. He'd sent all of his four suspects back into the dining parlor after he'd finished with them. They were waiting to be released when he joined them.

To his surprise, two of the brothers arrived just behind him.

They began to set the sideboard and the table for lunch. The time had gotten away from him. He was a little anxious about that, realizing he should have checked on Jennifer long ago.

"Either of you know where I can find Roger and Geoffrey?" he asked the two monks.

One of them said Geoffrey was in the workshops. The other thought Roger was still in the chapel. Thanking the Brashers, Harry Ireland and Patrick for their cooperation, Leo left the dining parlor and made his rapid way to the ground floor.

He spared a quick look into the chapel on his way to the library. Brother Michael was there polishing the altar rail, but there was no sign of Roger. The library, when he moved on to it, was dim and deserted.

Where was Jennifer? he wondered. And why, no matter how emphatically she had refused to let him accompany her, had he been such an idiot to let her go off virtually on her own?

IT WAS ALMOST NOON when Jennifer, still wearing her coat and boots, stole along the silent corridor of the wing where the other guests were quartered. They should be gathered for lunch by now down in the dining parlor. Roger Harding would either be with them or still in the chapel. She was counting on that, though there was always the chance he had remained in his room and would challenge her presence here.

She was willing to risk that, even though she knew she probably shouldn't be doing this on her own. That she ought to find Leo and convince him to accompany her. But that would take time, and she didn't want to spend the precious minutes. She had lost too many of them as it was.

It would be all right, she promised herself. She'd just have a quick look and be out of here.

So far she had encountered no one. Nor, when she reached the first of the four rooms and paused to listen, did she hear anything. The stillness indicated the wing was deserted.

Continuing on her way past the closed doors of the rooms that belonged to Harry Ireland and the Brashers, she came to the third door. This was the Hardings' room, she remembered.

Wanting to make certain no one was inside, she rapped on the door. If the unlikely happened and Roger answered her knock, she was prepared with an excuse. She'd simply ask him if he had any news about his wife, express her sympathy and make a fast retreat.

But there was no response to her knock. She tried the door. It was unlocked, as it had been before. Opening it cautiously, she looked inside. Empty.

Quelling her nerves, she slipped into the room, closing the door behind her before she hurried to the wardrobe. This was where she had found the vanity case on that first visit. But there was no sign of it now. The tall cupboard contained nothing but clothes.

Among the garments was the monk's robe she had noticed earlier, hanging from the same peg in a dim corner, one end of the cord that fastened around its waist dangling to the floor of the wardrobe. Why the sight of the robe should bother her now when she had barely noticed it earlier she couldn't imagine. But it did somehow.

Hastily closing the doors on it, she looked around for some evidence of the vanity case. There were toilet articles strewn across the surface of a small table, a clear indication that the contents of the case had been emptied. But what had happened to the case itself?

It was then that she detected an odor in the room. The smell of something that had been recently burned in the fireplace. Not peat either. This was different.

She went to the fireplace and crouched down on the hearth. There were smoldering embers in the grate, the smoking, blackened remains of—

Yes, the vanity case, which must have been hacked into

pieces and the chunks fed to the flames. She could see a charred piece of its leather down in the still glowing coals.

If the door to the corridor made any sound opening and closing, she never heard it. Maybe because she was too focused on the destruction of the vanity case. Not until she was addressed in a quiet voice behind her did she realize she was no longer alone in the room, and then it was too late.

"Snooping again, are we?"

Jennifer whirled around on the hearth to see Roger Harding standing against the door, his tongue against his teeth making a sound of mocking disapproval.

"I don't have to ask what you were looking for this time," he said. "I can see you already found it. Or what's left of it. Well, I suppose it was only a matter of time before you—what is it you Americans say?—began to figure things out. But your friend, Mr. McKenzie, hasn't arrived at that point yet, has he? No, or you wouldn't be here on your own. I still have time then."

Jennifer came slowly to her feet, afraid to make any sudden move. This was an unfamiliar Roger Harding she was dealing with, the *real* Roger behind the gentle, mild-mannered persona he had created. She knew that now. She also realized he was a very dangerous Roger and that she would have to be extremely careful.

"Leo is a little late," she said, striving to conceal her terror, "but I expect him to show up here at any second."

Roger smiled sadly, as if deeply disappointed in her. "We both know that's not true, Ms. Rowan. Or may I call you Jennifer? It does seem to me that we've reached a stage in our relationship where we ought to be comfortable with Christian names."

How could she have been such a stubborn fool? Jennifer asked herself. Coming here all alone had been a huge mistake, one that could very well cost her her life.

"No, your friend isn't going to turn up," Roger insisted. "He's busy elsewhere interviewing suspects. I made certain of that before I came back to the room after realizing that burning the vanity case was only a precaution of no real consequence. That there's something much more important I need to destroy, reluctant though I am to sacrifice it."

Jennifer watched him cross the room to the wardrobe. She waited until he had his back to her as he occupied himself with opening its doors, removing something from inside. This was her opportunity. She began to edge her way toward the door.

He must have sensed her intention to flee. With his back still turned to her, he cautioned her softly, "Running would be a serious mistake, Jennifer."

She saw him slide his free hand into an inside pocket of his tweed jacket. When he swung around to face her, he was holding a small but very lethal-looking pistol.

"Let's do hope it won't be necessary for me to use this."

She froze in obedient terror. Nodding in satisfaction, he returned the pistol to his pocket. But she knew he would whip it out again if she tried to get away.

Draped over his other arm was the article he had taken from the peg in the wardrobe. The monk's robe. He stroked its folds with an affection amounting to reverence.

"I wore this when I was a brother here. That was many years ago. There was a different abbot then. One not nearly so kind and understanding as Father Stephen."

When Roger's gaze lifted from the robe and met hers, she saw that his face had tightened in anger.

"He felt I didn't belong, that I was a misfit. I was persuaded to leave the order. And do you know why? It was all because of my veneration for the Madonna. Ignorant. They were all ignorant. None of them approached the adoration the Madonna deserves. They don't now, even though very few of the brothers I knew then are still here at Warley."

There was the hot glow of a zealot in his eyes. Jennifer could see it on his face as well, hear it in his voice. The fever of a fanatic who had worshipped the Madonna for itself and not for what it symbolized. His deranged mind still worshipped it.

"I married Sybil after I left the order because she's a Warley descendant. But you know that now, don't you? Sybil was a connection to the Madonna, you see. That was a mistake. There was no solace for me in the marriage. I found that only in my regular retreats to Warley where the Madonna never failed to restore my faith."

Until you learned it was to be sold.

Jennifer thought the words were something she said to herself. But she must have nervously expressed them aloud, because Roger looked at her as if he was pleased that she could relate to his absolute devotion to the Madonna.

"That's right. You understand why I was outraged, don't you?"

"What I understand is that you murdered Guy," she said, finding the courage to accuse him.

Unwise though her reckless charge might be, she needed to know. All she cared about was Roger's admission of guilt.

"Spalding refused my appeals to let me return the Madonna to Warley where she belongs," he said plaintively.

"And so you killed him, didn't you?"

"He was angry that I'd misrepresented myself as a wealthy collector interested in buying the Madonna. I knew it was the only way he would let me come to his shop that night. He laughed at my proposal when I got there. I had every reason to kill him for that, but I didn't. Not then. Not until he committed the unpardonable."

"By?"

"Telling me that the Madonna would be tested for authenticity. Daring to suggest that she might not be a product of the true cross."

"And you couldn't allow that."

"I was livid, and the loaded dueling pistols were right there on his desk." He lifted his shoulders in a little shrug. "I had no choice. It was the only way I could save the Madonna from that sort of humiliation. The only way I could take her and bring her home."

He had continued to unconsciously stroke the robe throughout his confession. Now, aware of his action, he left the cupboard and moved toward the fireplace with the garment still over his arm. Jennifer shrank back as he approached her.

"I was wearing this under my coat when I met Brother Anthony in the courtyard. It seemed appropriate somehow. And, as it turned out, also useful."

Jennifer shuddered as he slowly fingered the cord at the waist of the robe. She understood now why the sight of it in the wardrobe had made her so uncomfortable. The cord must have served as a garrote when he had strangled Brother Anthony.

The fire was still burning in Roger's eyes as he leaned toward her with a kind of sickening intimacy.

"Brother Anthony was here in the old days," he said. "We were monks together. He knew of my deep devotion to the Madonna, which is perhaps why it occurred to him when he learned of Spalding's death that I… Well, he slipped a note to me in the chapel during laud asking me to meet him in the courtyard when he took his exercise there. It was the one place where we could speak privately. He was willing to break his vow of silence for me. Touching, isn't it?"

"Because he suspected you murdered Guy," Jennifer said rashly.

Roger smiled that sad smile again. "Brother Anthony was naive, I'm afraid. Unwilling to expose someone who had once been a fellow brother in his order until he could be certain. There seemed to be no use in denying it when he asked me if I'd killed Spalding and taken the Madonna. I promised him I would confess if he would pray with me before we went to Father Stephen. There's a little shrine there in the courtyard. Possibly you noticed it. Saint Joseph, a favorite of Brother

Anthony's. I like to think he died seeking spiritual guidance from Joseph."

As though lost in some insane dream, he stared down into the fireplace at the smoke that continued to rise from the remnants of the vanity case.

"He died because you executed him with that cord," Jennifer said, unable to prevent her anger. "It *was* the weapon you used, wasn't it?"

"What?" Roused from his reverie, he glanced at the cord he was still fondling. "Oh, you mean this. Yes, you're right, and that's why I have to burn it together with the robe. I was convinced they could never be connected with Brother Anthony's death, and so I kept them. But then it struck me that with today's police technology… Well, it's best to dispose of them, don't you agree?"

With a sigh of regret, he cast the robe and the cord into the fireplace. They lay there on the grate for a moment over the bed of hot coals. Tiny flames began to lick at them, slowly at first and then building rapidly into a blaze.

Roger watched them until he was certain they were being entirely consumed along with any lingering evidence of the vanity case. Then he went back to the wardrobe, withdrawing a winter coat and putting it on. When he joined her again at the fireplace, where he transferred the pistol into an outside pocket, there was a decisive expression on his face and in his voice that sent her heart plummeting.

"And now, my dear Jennifer, it's time for you to make yourself useful to me. You're going to help me get the Madonna—oh, yes, the whole monastery knows she's been recovered and locked away in the strong room—and then you and I are going to put her where she will never be found again."

RETRACING HIS ROUTE, Leo stopped in the chapel to speak to Brother Michael. "Have you seen Ms. Rowan?"

Brother Michael had not seen Jennifer.

Maybe she found what she was looking for in the library and went to tell Father Stephen about it, Leo thought.

He hurried off to the abbot's office, wanting to believe that's where he would find Jennifer. But he was worried in earnest now. He had a bad feeling about this whole thing.

The door was closed when he reached the office. He rapped on it. Not waiting for an answer, he opened the door and stuck his head inside. There was no one there.

He started to retreat when he heard a muffled thumping in the direction of the strong room. Swiftly crossing the office, he laid his ear against the iron banded door. The low pounding continued from the other side, accompanied by shouts that the thickness of the door made incomprehensible.

He tried the door. Locked, of course, and no key in sight. Nor would he waste his time in searching for it, because he wouldn't find it anywhere in the office. Whoever had locked the door would have taken the key with him.

Leo knew this with the same desperate certainty that he knew Jennifer needed him as he sped back to the chapel where Brother Michael was still working on the rail.

"Is there another key to the strong room?" he demanded, not bothering to lose time with an explanation that could wait.

The startled monk gaped at him.

"Man, don't just stand there looking at me. It's urgent. Someone has been locked inside the strong room, and the key is gone."

"Father Stephen has all the keys, but the prior keeps a duplicate set for everything in the monastery."

"Find him. Tell him to hurry with those keys!"

Leo raced back to the office and tried to communicate with whoever was trapped inside the strong room, wanting to assure them help was on the way. He got a muted response, but it was nothing he was able to understand.

Waiting and worrying about Jennifer had him ready to tear

the door down with his bare hands by the time the prior arrived with the spare keys. Several excited monks followed him, crowding through the doorway.

Finding the right key, the prior unlocked the door and flung it open. Father Stephen stumbled out into the office. The monks started forward with the intention of supporting him, but he waved them back.

"It's Roger!" he said, steadying himself after drawing a deep breath. "He has a gun and is holding Ms. Rowan hostage! He threatened to shoot her if I didn't give him the Madonna! He's gone mad!"

"Where are they?" Leo demanded. "Where did he take her?"

The abbot shook his head. "That I can't tell you."

One of the monks was the young Brother Luke. He spoke up with a swift, "They left the castle by the postern. I had a glimpse of them from the refectory window headed down the footpath to the valley. But I had no idea—"

Leo sharply cut him off. "Show me the way to the postern."

Brother Luke led him out of the office and along the gallery in the direction of the great hall. Leo damned himself as they negotiated a series of passages leading to the castle's back door.

How could he have let himself be fooled by Roger Harding's innocent devoutness? He had messed up by overlooking the obvious, because only someone thoroughly familiar with Warley Castle would have discovered the existence of that hiding place in the gatehouse tower. Someone like Harding.

Jennifer. The bastard had Jennifer, and if he hurt her—

Leo was out of his mind with fear and rage long before they reached the postern. He had to find them wherever they had gone, had to get Jennifer away from that lunatic before it was too late. Because there was something else he knew. Something he hadn't fully acknowledged to himself until this minute. Jennifer meant everything to him.

He couldn't lose her and live with himself, he thought fiercely. *He couldn't.*

Chapter Fourteen

Jennifer was disheartened to see that the thaw was so far advanced not a trace of snow remained on the steep path that wound its way to the valley below.

There would be no footprints for anyone to follow. Nor was there the possibility that she and the man at her side would leave any traces of their passage on the rough trail. It was all rock and gravel.

The Madonna was inside a canvas bag the shocked abbot had provided for its protection. Roger had ordered her to carry the relic so that he could make quick use of his pistol if it became necessary. The bag had grown heavy by now.

Pausing to shift the weight to her other hand, she used the opportunity to look quickly over her shoulder. But there was no hope there. The castle on its craggy height was already out of sight behind them.

Leo, she thought. Where was he? She missed him desperately, reproached herself for having pushed him away in anger. *Oh, Leo, Leo, I'm so sorry.* Now she was on her own because no one had seen Roger and her leave the castle. No one would know where they had gone. The man she loved so deeply wouldn't be able to follow or help her. She was alone out here with a madman.

Jennifer had no illusions about her survival after Roger

finished using her as his hostage. He couldn't afford to let her live once she learned the final destination for the Madonna. That she had managed to save Father Stephen's life was her only consolation. She'd made it clear to Roger that, if he harmed the abbot, she would refuse to help him, no matter what he did to her.

"Go on," Roger ordered, prodding her impatiently in the ribs with the gun. She caught a glimpse of a band of wild moor ponies off in the distance, but otherwise there was no sign of life.

She had no choice but to continue their descent. A chill mist had developed, rising from the deep hollows of the moors where great brown patches on the upper slopes had emerged from the melting snow. The mist thickened as they neared the valley. Another disappointment for Jennifer, but it suited Roger.

"No one can find us in this," he said. "We're safe now."

Safe? She was anything but safe, but she wasn't ready to surrender. If she could somehow manage to get away from him…

How? She didn't know, but it might be useful to learn where they were going.

"Where are you taking me?"

Roger didn't immediately answer her, but then he must have decided it wouldn't matter if she knew. Not if he planned for her to never leave their destination, but she wasn't going to let herself be defeated by that realization.

"To an ancient place suitable for the Madonna. The Romans once mined lead there, but the diggings were abandoned and forgotten centuries ago. There is no entrance now. It was buried long ago. All but a very narrow opening hidden behind gorse and rocks and just wide enough to squeeze through."

They reached the bottom of the valley where the trail divided into several paths.

"There are peat bogs out there," he said. "Dangerous places. Sheep sometimes wander into them and are sucked down. But I know how to avoid them. I walked these moors when I was a monk here, but we'll need to be careful in this mist. We go this way."

He led the way along one of the footpaths.

"I know now," he went on with a chilling rapture in his voice, "the divine hand that guided me to the opening in the mine all those years ago did so for a purpose. I was meant to place the Madonna deep in one of its tunnels until some far day, when it's safe, another true believer will be led to her, and he will return her to the castle where she will be honored as she deserves."

Jennifer knew it was useless to argue with him. He was beyond all reason. All she could do was silently hope that he did know where he was going. She had lost all sense of direction in this confusing maze where the paths themselves seemed firm enough, but the ground on either side of them was so soggy that one false step could land them in a bottomless mire.

Finally, when the fog became so dense it was impossible to proceed, Roger halted them on the edge of a solid slope. "We'll wait here a minute until it clears a bit."

There was a dark pool a few feet away from them, swollen from the melting snow that fed it. Jennifer could hear a slow trickle of water. Otherwise, the silence was absolute. They didn't talk as they waited, but she was aware of her captor watching her with an exultant half smile on his face.

She didn't know what was more terrifying, the clammy fog that hid the lethal marshes all around them or being trapped here with Roger Harding and his taunting smile. In the end, unable to endure the eerie silence, she began to ask him questions whose answers she no longer cared about. Anything to relieve the tension. Anything to preserve hope. Because there was the chance, unlikely though it was, that if someone should be out there and heard their voices...

"You had to have discovered the Madonna was to be sold," she said. "How was that possible?"

"Why, Geoffrey, of course. We became friends on my last

two retreats. Geoffrey feels the same about the Madonna as I do. I suppose being a novice is the reason why he wasn't told about its sale until he learned of it from Brother Anthony on their trip down to London."

And if Geoffrey had registered any alarm about that news, Jennifer thought, it would explain why Brother Anthony had been troubled. Why he'd cautioned Guy in London that the sale of the Madonna might be opposed.

"Geoffrey phoned me in London between trains to let me know what was happening. That was when I contacted Guy Spalding."

Like a flow that, once started, couldn't be stopped, Roger talked on, telling her everything. How he'd managed to smuggle the Madonna back to Warley inside his luggage without his wife's knowledge. How, when they'd reached the castle, he'd been unable to place the Madonna in the mine until the storm cleared.

With Geoffrey's help, Roger had hidden her temporarily inside the flue of the unused fireplace in the great hall. But Geoffrey had failed him. His conscience had resulted in those episodes of sleepwalking that would have led Jennifer and Leo to the great hall, if Roger hadn't arrived on the scene at the last moment and managed to cut the generator.

So it wasn't concern for his father, or any misgiving about taking his final vows, that accounted for Geoffrey's sleepwalking, Jennifer thought. It had been guilt.

"You and McKenzie were a considerable nuisance to me with your eternal prying," Roger said.

He went on to tell Jennifer how, after he'd transferred the Madonna to a chest inside one of the empty guest rooms, he'd tried to sabotage their investigation by luring them onto the dangerous stairway in the great hall. When that, too, failed, he'd realized the Madonna needed to be moved again. This time it would have to be a place far more secure than anything inside the castle with all its risks.

That was when Roger had remembered the hollow under the window seat in the gatehouse tower. But on this occasion it was Sybil who had interfered with his plan.

"I'm sorry to say that my dear wife and I have been a disappointment to each other," Roger said unhappily. "What with our marriage having deteriorated through the years, and her inheritance dwindled…

"Really, I should have known from the way she kept looking at me and how she was drinking more than usual that she was suspicious. Unfortunate she should have followed me out to the gatehouse, and that I had to deal with her when she found me with the Madonna. I suppose she thought that, if she could get her hands on the Madonna, prove that as a Warley descendant she was entitled to a share of her sale… Ah, well."

Roger had continued to watch her throughout his explanation with that intense, burning gaze. He stared at her now, as if eager for her approval.

"You can understand now why everything I did was necessary in order to keep the Madonna where she belongs. That only here at Warley can she work her miracles of healing and soothing." He leaned in close to her, his voice dropping to a whisper. "Can't you, Jennifer?"

What she understood was that everything he had done was despicable. And all because of his blind, maniacal dedication to a piece of wood.

He sighed in regret when she had no response for him, stood back and looked around. "I think it's beginning to thin a little," he said, his voice flat now. "We can move on."

He started to lead them away from the pool when there was a thunderous noise off to their right. Jennifer had no idea what she was hearing. Nor from the alarmed expression on his face did Roger. The two of them stood there in dismay.

Then, before they could get away or the animals become

aware of their presence, a half dozen of the wild moor ponies burst out of the fog and came racing toward them.

The band had probably come down to the pool to drink. Whatever the explanation for their arrival, Jennifer realized this was the opportunity she had been praying for. The ponies were suddenly on them, pushing toward the water, their shaggy bodies dividing her from Roger.

Jennifer didn't hesitate. She turned and ran, plunging through the wall of fog, counting on its thickness to hide her from her captor. If she could avoid him long enough to reach the path back to the castle…

Within seconds, she realized she was lost in the fog, unable to get her bearings. Higher ground. She needed to get to the higher ground, away from the deadly bogs. But in which direction was the higher ground?

Puffing from her flight, she knew she'd be better off ridding herself of the heavy canvas bag. But abandoning it was unthinkable. She wasn't about to let Roger Harding get his hands on the Madonna again. Clinging stubbornly to her burden, she went on.

Her lungs were burning by now, forcing her to stop long enough to recover her wind. The fog hadn't lightened at all. It was thicker than ever. Buried in the stuff, she could feel its rawness licking at her, was able to both taste and smell it in her nostrils.

Where was he? Striving not to panic, her senses on full alert, she listened for any sound that would betray his presence. There was only the stillness, so hushed that she could hear nothing at all. Unless they were no longer in the area, even the ponies were silent.

But Jennifer knew that Roger was out there somewhere. She could *feel* him stalking her.

It wasn't safe for her to remain here. Fear clawing at her, she moved on through the sinister shroud. She'd gone less than three yards when she became aware that she was no longer on firm turf. The ground was squishy under her boots, evidence that she'd chosen the wrong direction. She hadn't gone up, he'd gone down and was in the peat bogs again!

This was no good. One wrong step could have her sinking in the mire. Afraid to go on, and equally afraid to try going back, she stood there in helpless indecision.

It was then that she heard it. The soft, cautious tread of approaching footsteps behind her. Gasping, she whirled around to confront her enemy, prepared to slam the bag into him if he attempted to grab her.

Tense seconds passed. Then, with every nerve in her body screaming, she watched as a tall figure emerged like a phantom from the fog. Disbelief seized her, followed by pure joy.

Leo!

Not caring how he had gotten here, only that he had managed to find her, Jennifer rushed toward him with relief. His waiting arms folded her tightly against his solid, blessed length. Oblivious to the bulky bag that got in the way, he lowered his head and kissed her with a ferocity that needed no translation. His mouth on hers plainly said that she was safe in his arms where she belonged.

When he finally held her away from him, there was a fierceness in the whiskey-colored eyes that searched her face. "Are you all right?" he asked, his voice like a rasp. "Did he hurt you? If the bastard touched you, I swear I'll—"

"I'm not hurt."

It was then she noticed he wasn't wearing a coat. It was an absurd thing to worry about at a time like this, but she couldn't help herself from caring. He mattered that much to her.

"Where is he?" Leo asked her gruffly.

"He's right here, Mr. McKenzie."

The menacing voice spoke from somewhere behind her. Jennifer wheeled around. She and Leo had been so busy with each other they had failed to notice that the fog had started to melt away. It had lifted enough to reveal Roger Harding standing only yards away, the pistol in his hand leveled at them.

"Put the bag down, Jennifer," he ordered her calmly. "Yes, that's right. Now both of you back away from it."

Having placed the bag on the ground as he'd instructed, she put her hand on Leo's arm, feeling his angry resistance as she drew him into a quick retreat. His steely gaze remained fixed on Roger when they stopped several feet away from the bag.

Nodding his approval, Roger approached the bag. He was bending over, reaching eagerly for the prize, when a rook somewhere out in the lingering shreds of mist uttered his shrill call. Startled by the sound, Roger made the mistake of turning his head in the direction of the cry.

Leo didn't hesitate. He launched himself at Harding, catching him off guard in a state of vulnerability. The two men went down under the fury of Leo's impact, struggling for possession of the pistol.

Though Leo delivered several powerful blows, his opponent hung on tightly to the gun, refusing to release it. For a moment Jennifer watched the battle in stunned surprise. Then, collecting herself, she started forward to help Leo.

Her effort proved unnecessary. Before she could act, Leo, gripping Roger by the wrist, succeeded in banging his arm down on the wet earth with such force that the pistol leaped out of his hand. Arcing through the air, the weapon landed amid tufts of grass several yards away.

With a heaving body and curses of rage, Roger managed to shove himself free. Leo made a grab for his legs, but before he could capture his adversary again, Roger had sprung to his feet and was on his way to retrieve the gun.

He had traveled only a few yards toward the tufts when the deceptive surface began to quake, sagging under his weight. Only then, with an expression of horror on his face, did he re alize that in his rush to get the gun, he had plunged into one of the treacherous quagmires.

By the time he turned and tried to go back, it was too late. He was already floundering in mud up to his calves and sinking with an astonishing rapidity. Held fast, he was unable to lift a foot out of the ooze.

"We've got to help him!" Jennifer cried. "We can't let him die like that!"

Her appeal had already been answered by Leo, who was crawling on hands and knees toward the edge of the path.

"Stay back," he ordered her.

Flattening himself where the earth was still solid, he stretched out a hand toward Harding. Useless. Though he strained to reach him, the gap between the two men was too wide.

Jennifer looked around wildly, searching for a limb. But there were no trees out here in the marshes. Nothing they could extend to Roger, no line they could throw to him.

When she looked back, he was up to his waist in mire and whimpering in terror.

"What can we do?" she implored Leo. "There must be something."

Getting to his feet, Leo came to her. "There's nothing," he said quietly.

Roger was praying now, a series of garbled supplications as the mud continued to suck him down. Jennifer couldn't bear to watch the gruesome scene, to hear the prayers that turned into the terrible howls of a trapped animal. Leo held her tightly while she buried her head against his chest.

"It's over," he said a moment later.

When she lifted her head and looked, Roger was gone, a victim of his own frenzy. Nothing remained on the surface of the bog that had claimed him but his last bubbles of air.

Except for the croak of the rook, there was silence again in the valley.

JENNIFER AND LEO SAT side by side on a bench situated in a corner of the bailey where they warmed themselves in the late afternoon sun.

"You okay?" he asked her, reaching for her hand.

She nodded, her fingers curling gratefully around his. "I will be as soon as the police tell me I'm no longer a suspect in Guy's death."

"With all we've got to give them, there won't be any question of it," he promised her.

She was lying. She wasn't worried about that. Nor could she be all right when she and Leo's future remained unresolved. Perhaps what she longed for so passionately, she and Leo making a life together, would never be possible. Not if he didn't feel what she felt for him. It was a subject that had yet to be addressed. And it scared her.

She wondered if Leo sensed her anxiety, if he was avoiding the issue with something safe and unemotional because he didn't want to hurt her. Maybe that's why he asked, "What did Father Stephen say when you told him the Madonna was probably not made out of any part of the cross?"

"He accepted it, especially when I told him that, cross or not, the Madonna was sure to realize a big sum when it was sold. At this point, I think he's more concerned about Geoffrey."

"He has reason to be. Even though Harding committed all of the crimes, there's every likelihood Geoffrey will be charged as an accessory."

"Father Stephen knows that, but it doesn't matter to him."

Jennifer remembered what the abbot had told her after he had locked the Madonna back in the strong room. "Whatever happens," he'd said, "Geoffrey is still one of us. We won't abandon him."

While she'd been in the office with Father Stephen, Leo had gone to the infirmary to check on Sybil. And since he seemed to want to stick to safe subjects, Jennifer asked him about that.

"You already mentioned Brother Timothy told you Sybil was conscious for a brief time and that he was encouraged by that. Did he say anything else about her condition?"

"Just that he thought she had a good chance of recovering, providing the ambulance got her to the Heathside hospital in time. And since the paramedics are already on the way…"

Yes, Jennifer thought, the road was open now. They were no longer isolated. This, together with the repair of the power and phone lines, had enabled Father Stephen to contact both the hospital and the police. The police were also on their way to the monastery, which was why she and Leo were waiting in the bailey for their arrival.

"Poor Sybil," Jennifer said. "We thought Roger was spending all that time in the chapel praying for her survival. And all along it was just an excuse to be near the infirmary so that, if he got the chance, he could make certain she didn't talk before he was able to put the Madonna away in the mine."

"He actually tell you that?"

"On the way from his room to the abbot's office."

"Nice guy," Leo said dryly.

Yes, she thought, but even though Roger Harding had been an atrocious human being, no one deserved to die like that. She shuddered over the memory of it.

"He tell you anything else?" Leo wanted to know. "Like how he planned to get away once he'd accomplished his wacky scheme?"

She shook her head. "He was so completely obsessed with making sure the Madonna never left Warley that I don't think he thought about or cared what happened to him afterwards."

Explanations exchanged, they sat in silence on the bench with Jennifer still wondering when, and if, they would ever get around to talking about them.

A moment later a restless Leo, who was still holding her hand, drew her to her feet. "Let's go see if there's any sign of the cops."

They strolled across the bailey, through the portal of the gatehouse and out into the open beyond. Standing there side by side on the lane, they scanned the ribbon of road that wound across the moors where the last of the snow under the strong March sun would soon be nothing but a memory. As yet, there were no vehicles in sight.

Leo had released her hand. She glanced up at him. He wasn't looking at her. His attention was on the road, leaving her still wondering. Would he ever express his feelings one way or another? She couldn't take any more of this. She had to know.

"What happens after we've all been questioned and released?"

He turned his head then to gaze at her. "How do you mean?"

"Us," she said impatiently. "You and me."

"Right. We take your car and go and get my car out of that ditch. I'll need it."

"To go back to London?"

"No. To follow you back to that cozy little inn in Heathside. I plan for us to take up where we left off last night."

"You do?"

"Yeah. I figure on one room with one wide bed. That's all we'll need."

"Uh-huh. What else do you intend on doing in that cozy room?"

"Telling you what a fool I was to ever question your innocence. Well, that and just how much I love you."

"And that's it?" she asked, wondering how she could sound so casual when she was glowing with relief and joy.

"Not quite. I've got to convince you, whatever it takes and whatever I have to promise…"

"What?"

"That, lout or not, you just gotta love me. I'm thinking, Jenny, I'm not going to make it if you don't."

"Then you can relax, because I do. Love you, that is."

"Yeah?" His eyes shone with an eager happiness.

"Yeah. So, you see, you don't have to wait until Heathside for that."

"Or to waste any more words on it either," he growled softly. "Not when action can say it a whole lot better."

He demonstrated that by sliding his arms around her, squeezing her against him and angling his mouth across her in a deep, rapturous kiss. A kiss that, just as he'd indicated, was far more convincing than any verbal declaration.

"Of course," he said when his mouth finally lifted from hers, "we do have a few other things to settle."

"Like?"

"Where we're going to live."

"You know, Boston is a good place."

"So is Philly."

"And your work is there, while mine is basically in Boston. We've got a problem then."

"Don't worry about it. We'll work it out," he said, holding her close. "There isn't anything that we can't work out. You and me. Together. Way I see it, we've got a whole, beautiful lifetime for it."

* * * * *

New York Times *bestselling author Linda Lael Miller is
back with a new romance featuring the heartwarming
McKettrick family from Silhouette Special Edition.*

SIERRA'S HOMECOMING
by Linda Lael Miller

*On sale December 2006,
wherever books are sold.*

Turn the page for a sneak preview!

Soft, smoky music poured into the room.

The next thing she knew, Sierra was in Travis's arms, close against that chest she'd admired earlier, and they were slow dancing.

Why didn't she pull away?

"Relax," he said. His breath was warm in her hair.

She giggled, more nervous than amused. What was the matter with her? She was attracted to Travis, had been from the first, and he was clearly attracted to her. They were both adults. Why not enjoy a little slow dancing in a ranch-house kitchen?

Because slow dancing led to other things. She took a step back and felt the counter flush against her lower back. Travis naturally came with her, since they were holding hands and he had one arm around her waist.

Simple physics.

Then he kissed her.

Physics again—this time, not so simple.

"Yikes," she said, when their mouths parted.

He grinned. "Nobody's ever said that after I kissed them."

She felt the heat and substance of his body pressed against hers. "It's going to happen, isn't it?" she heard herself whisper.

"Yep," Travis answered.

"But not tonight," Sierra said on a sigh.

"Probably not," Travis agreed.

"When, then?"

He chuckled, gave her a slow, nibbling kiss. "Tomorrow morning," he said. "After you drop Liam off at school."

"Isn't that…a little…soon?"

"Not soon enough," Travis answered, his voice husky. "Not nearly soon enough."

nocturne™

**Explore the dark and sensual
new realm of paranormal romance.**

HAUNTED

BY LISA CHILDS

**The first book in the riveting
new 3-book miniseries, Witch Hunt.**

DEATH CALLS

BY CARIDAD PIÑEIRO

**Darkness calls to humans,
as well as vampires…**

*On sale December 2006,
wherever books are sold.*

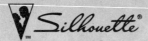

HARLEQUIN® *Romance*®

**From the Heart.
For the Heart.**

Get swept away into the Outback
with two of Harlequin Romance's
top authors.

Coming in December...

Claiming the
Cattleman's Heart
BY BARBARA HANNAY

And in January don't miss...

Outback Man Seeks Wife
BY MARGARET WAY

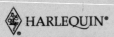

HARLEQUIN®

American **ROMANCE®**

IS PROUD TO PRESENT

COWBOY VET
by **Pamela Britton**

Jessie Monroe is the last person on earth
Rand Sheppard wants to rely on, but he needs
a veterinary technician—yesterday—and she's the
only one for hire. It turns out the woman who
destroyed his cousin's life isn't who Rand thought
she was. And now she's all he can think about!

"Pamela Britton writes the kind of
wonderfully romantic, sexy, witty romance
that readers dream of discovering
when they go into a bookstore."

—*New York Times* bestselling author
Jayne Ann Krentz

Cowboy Vet *is available from*
Harlequin American Romance in December 2006.

Loyalty...or love?

LORD GREVILLE'S CAPTIVE
Nicola Cornick

He had previously come to Grafton
Manor to be betrothed to the beautiful
Lady Anne—but that promise was broken
with the onset of the English Civil War.
Now Lord Greville has returned as an
enemy, besieging the manor and holding
its lady prisoner.

His devotion to his cause is swayed by
his desire for Anne—he will have the
lady, and her heart.

Yet Anne has a secret that must be kept
from him at all costs....

On sale December 2006.
Available wherever Harlequin books are sold.

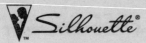

REQUEST YOUR FREE BOOKS!

2 FREE NOVELS PLUS 2 FREE GIFTS!

HARLEQUIN®

INTRIGUE®

Breathtaking Romantic Suspense

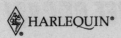
HARLEQUIN®

INTRIGUE

COMING NEXT MONTH

#957 FORCE OF THE FALCON by Rita Herron
Eclipse
After a string of bizarre animal attacks near Falcon Ridge,
Brack Falcon finds a woman left for dead. But protecting
Sonya Silverstein means opening his long-dormant heart.

#958 TRIGGERED RESPONSE by Patricia Rosemoor
Security Breach
Brayden Sloane is a wanted man. He remembers an accident, an
explosion. Was he responsible? Only Claire Fanshaw knows for sure,
but how will she react to his touch?

#959 RELUCTANT WITNESS by Kathleen Long
Fate brings Kerri Nelson and Wade Sorenson back together to save
the life of her son, the only witness to a heinous crime.

#960 PULL OF THE MOON by Sylvie Kurtz
He's a Mystery
She's at Moongate Mansion for a story. He thinks she's an impostor.
But before history repeats Valerie Zea and Nicholas Galloway will
have to put their doubts aside to solve the mystery behind an
heiress's kidnapping.

#961 LAKOTA BABY by Elle James
Returning soldier Joe Lonewolf must enter the ugly underbelly of his
tribe if he's to rescue the baby boy he's never seen.

#962 UNDERCOVER SHEIK by Dana Marton
When Dr. Sadie Kauffman is kidnapped by desert bandits In Beharrain,
her only salvation lies in Sheik Nasir, the king's brother, who's trying
to stop a tyrant from plunging the country into civil war.

www.eHarlequin.com